Into the Tides

REBEKKAH NILES

ISBN-13: 978-0-9914028-2-3
ISBN-10:   0-9914028-2-0

It crossed my mind to wonder if I'd get to find out first-hand what happened to Elizabeth.

Barely a block into the suburban streets I found the Hunter. A pair of wiry-haired ears perked forward, and a few too many teeth grinned at me from a long, narrow snout. Large, dark eyes watched me through long eyelashes that would form a perfect shield from splattering blood, with no indication of mercy or emotion. It could rip me apart in a breath.

"I think you were looking for me." Holding out a trembling hand, I waited.

The jaw gaped into a grin, opening wider than I thought possible, wide enough it could fit my whole head if it so chose. My feet got in my own way and I bumped into a lamp post behind me, unable to see anything but those teeth. I couldn't do this. I couldn't—The whimper that came out of my throat choked all the thoughts out of my head, and I couldn't bear to look anymore, had to close my eyes.

Then a cold nose pressed into one of my palms. *Yes. We'd prepared to fetch you. This makes it easier, though. Follow*, it ordered.

The beast, as tall as a mastiff, a murdering machine with tiger stripes down its back, stood watching me without ripping me to shreds. I raised my hand to my chest and took a deep breath, feeling humiliation burn through me.

It impaled me with a sharp glance before turning and sauntering down the street. I considered running, or screaming. Then I thought about it again, thought of everyone in camp, listened to the steady *sa-sa, sa-sa, sa-sa* of its unlabored heartbeat.

I could do this. I had to do this. Everyone in camp would be safe because I did. So I began to jog after it, through a dead and empty city.

Acknowledgements

To all my friends and family who have supported me and helped make this book possible, up to and including those 3 a.m. phone calls asking about physics and violations thereof. You guys rock, and I'd have never made it without you. Thanks for all the beta reads, sanity checks, and survival tips!

To the members of the HCRW, who showed me how.

To the members of the Durham Science Fiction and Fantasy Meetup Group, for invaluable feedback and fantastic suggestions.

And to my teachers, who gave me the tools in the first place.

Chapter One

The first two things every student should know about magic:
1. *Either you have a Power, or you don't. You cannot change or
   remove yours.*
2. *Power is as much body as it is mind, but also as much mind as
   body.*

I slammed the cover closed on the battered textbook. "Don't
know why I bothered keeping it so long." The class had been over
for ten years. Heck, I'd been out of *college* for three.

Cramming it back into my cornflower-patterned, oversized
purse, I watched the low sun glint off the water of Lake Mendota.
The surface mirrored the sky, looking so opaque it seemed solid. I
threw a stone to break the illusion; the rock skipped three times,
and then sank with a final *plorp*, making the clouds shimmer with
tiny ripples.

Wishing I'd remembered the fuzzy turquoise gloves abandoned on the table at home, I blew on my hands, and tried to convince myself to go into the lakeside used bookstore. "Someone else might actually need it," I said to the air. I'd read the thing cover to cover more times than I could count. It was time to give it up.

I had no reason to cling to the old book. None. And if I didn't hurry, the shop would close before I could push the useless thing out of my life.

The splash caught my ear mid-step. There, in the blade of blue between two grey clouds, a shadow on the surface of the water moved, and a pair of eyes caught the light. My breath stuck in my throat.

Plorp.

It was gone, swallowed back up by a cloud — a cloud that was beginning to bleed pink.

I checked my watch, swore, and ran. Slipping into the shop a minute before it should close, I charged the counter and slid the textbook onto the badger-themed display case by the register. "Selling."

The woman at the shop picked it up, her lips pursed. "Two bucks." She held her key in her other hand, her eyes on the door.

Even online it was worth twenty. "Fine."

Her eyebrow raised. "Really? Sales are final."

"I know."

She stared me down as the clock ticked past her hour of freedom. The tactic had worked before.

This time, I crossed my arms.

The keys slammed down onto the counter, and she yanked out an old ledger. Five minutes later, I was on my way home, finally rid of *Remedial Powers: Your Basic Guide to Using Your Magic.*

Useless piece of junk.

#

My landlady stopped me on my way through the lobby of my apartment building, curly gray hair bobbing with her shuffling steps. "I'm putting a new neighbor in beside you," she said. "This one won't be a problem. I checked his references and he's a sweet fella. Quiet and polite, too."

"That's nice," I murmured, pulling away. "I'll be sure to say hi later."

She leaned to the side to call at a pony-sized pile of boxes entering the doorway. "I don't want you bothering Kelly, you hear? Or her brother."

"Yes, ma'am," a deep voice called up from the boxes edging down the hall, bobbing up to avoid knocking over a lamp on a side table. When they turned toward the elevator, I got a glimpse of blond hair and a sweatshirt with the logo of a gym that had opened last year not far from where I worked. Oh joy, muscles and grunting.

"He's Powered," she said. "Strength power. Brought a sofa in all by himself last trip." Quiet glee undercut her voice. "You just let him know if you need anything moved around. He's such a nice boy, I'm sure he'll help."

I spared a pitying glance at the elevator and wormed my way past. "Thanks. I'll keep that in mind."

I only lived on the third floor, but by the time I got there the sounds of rummaging were already coming from inside the propped-open door beside mine. At least the stairs were good exercise.

"'M gonna be gone three weeks," Trax, my twin, called from his bedroom at the sound of the door slamming closed behind me.

After kicking off my comfy canvas flats onto the shoe rack, the blue tang fish on the heels facing out, I poked my head around the corner. "Just three?" He was packing, of course, some ridiculous ensemble of jeans and blue sweaters and ripped blue tees. He'd moved into my Wisconsin apartment three years ago, as soon as the road restrictions had been lifted. The rent had gone up shortly thereafter, until it rivaled that of his once-trendy New York cubicle.

Nobody wanted to live on the coast anymore, not after the Tides, not after the disaster that had drowned the South in raw magic. The Tides, called that because of the way they advanced and receded in a steady three-month long cycle—such a peaceful name for something that had ripped our lives apart.

Aged guitars and signed photos dotted the steel-gray walls, evidence of my brother's world. There may have been a couple of books shoved under the bed—he'd always liked reading—but the should-be-white carpet was littered with more than enough junk to hide his dirty little secret. The tangle of cords and boxes and blinking bits that were his video games usually distracted anyone from searching too hard for the hobby we'd both picked up from Mom. Most of the video games were classics remade—they'd become popular in the past three years. Dad would have loved it.

"Annie just wants us to hit the major East Coast cities. Apparently, New York's throwing another bash, and Boston and Philadelphia are getting in on the gig." He straightened, his blond-dyed forelock dropping into his too-blue eyes. He ignored it; considering it was more or less the last of his hair, he wasn't keen on chopping it off. The short, dark fuzz that masqueraded as hair around the base of his pseudo-mohawk would soon be put to rest, courtesy of his make-up artist. He was too pretty, she'd said, to sport anything nicer. His fans had to know he was a guy.

"Someday, they're gonna realize that it's a futile effort," I said, leaning against the doorway. Sometimes it just hit me, how much we looked alike. Make him a girl, and we'd be identical. Well, that and the fact that I was a music Power, and he wasn't Powered. But sixth classes were so weak in magic, that barely counted, anyway. I didn't even have to work in a job using my type of magic.

"Maybe not, Kel. New York's supposedly growing again. And Boston didn't shrink last year."

"Hm. You gonna move back?"

A wry laugh followed a complicated-looking set of fashionable belt chains into the suitcase. "Not a chance." He paused to let his fingers brush along Dad's old working-guitar before returning to folding the faded blue jacket in his hands. "Want to hear the intro to the new song I'm working on?"

"Of course."

He put aside the jacket to take down the instrument, fingers caressing the strings and tickling the knobs until he'd hit a point that resonated with him. Unlike me he hadn't inherited mom's genes for tone deafness. I just had to trust that the notes eked out from the guitar sounded better now than they had before he tuned it. The twenty or so seconds he played had a nice rhythm, though.

"That's as far as I've gotten." He twisted the knobs again and hung the guitar back in its spot of honor. Dad had given it to him as a good-luck gift when Trax had gone on his first tour at 18. These days my brother used it for devising his newest melodies and for solving problems, strumming it until solutions composed themselves in his head.

"Like it," I said, once again thankful Trax had missed Dad's genes for magic. Had he been Powered, he would never have been downgraded from a fourth to a sixth, never been able to build a career as a rock star. For anyone stronger than a fifth, something as frivolous as fame was a dead-end road.

He picked up the jacket again, refolding it and stuffing it into the case, and then started throwing clothes around, in search of something. "Where are my striped socks?"

I snorted. "If you did your own laundry, you'd know." His glare brought a smirk to my face. "In your sock drawer, doofus." Next to the unused scuba mask I'd given him six years ago, and on top of a year-old empty bottle of antidepressants he hadn't quite managed to throw out. These days it was harder to get a refill without an empty bottle.

Grumbling, followed by a flurry of more seemingly haphazard stuffing of his case. Strangely enough, there was an order to his madness. Trax miraculously never forgot anything. The dishevelment in his room was like that, too. Clean it up, and he was like a little kid in a maze, but leave it as it was, and he never lost a thing.

I left him to it. I had a dinner — for one — to plan, and a job to attend in the morning.

#

He was gone by the time I woke up. His agent had collected him before sunrise for the plane trip, as usual, leaving me in the company of a silence that stretched cat-like across the apartment.

By the next evening I couldn't take it anymore. I clicked on the news.

Of course, it was New York splashed across the screen, anchors dodging crowds and interviewing happy strangers. The cities liked to advertise the parties, the good times. If Trax was right, it was working.

I saw him as revelers flicked across the screen in a party montage. A thirty-second clip showed him throwing a big concert in Times Square, him and his band thrashing their music in front of thousands of fans. Since the Tides, the band had really hit it big—people wanted distraction, so every music group with even a modicum of talent was big news. And Trax really was good. He even looked kind of happy on the screen, screaming his anger at the world out, living off the energy of his fans in his bedazzled blue suit.

He'd worn blue ever since the Tides poured over the Southern, engulfing almost everything East of Texas to just south of Virginia. Trax and I had been Carolina kids.

Rockers always wore black or white or both, Trax had said, so those wouldn't mean anything. Blue, on the other hand, had been Mom's favorite color. He hadn't even cared when his agent had told him it was career suicide. It was his tribute, and he'd do it if the fans hated him for it. Of course, it had doubled his audience.

I left the screen playing in the background as I chopped up carrots for tomorrow's crockpot stew. "The receding Tide," the anchorman was saying as I scraped the carrot slices into a bag, "has bared Cleveland, Mississippi; Fayetteville, North Carolina; and Atlanta, Georgia, as well as numerous other communities. Scientists expect that it will drop as far as Montgomery, Alabama and Savannah, Georgia."

Of course he mispronounced Fayetteville. Only city that ever sounded more Southern when said by a Northerner than a Southerner. He'd said it like "Lafayette," of course, not the proper "Fay-it-ville."

"Recovery operations will be active during this season's low Tide, emptying banks, warehouses, and factories for supplies. Former residents may put in a request for home searches at tidal.us.gov. Please remember that searches are completed on opportunity and availability only." *For a fee, of course,* he didn't say. But then, the recovery teams worked a risky business.

6

Recovery, not rescue. There was no one left to rescue. Not living, anyway.

Someone knocked on my door. I looked up from the celery I had planned on assaulting.

Another knock.

It couldn't be one of Trax's friends. They always knew when he was out of town. Maybe one of the neighbors?

"Just a sec!" I put the knife down before leaving the kitchen. Most people didn't take too well to a woman opening the door with a three-inch-wide, foot-long blade in her hand.

They knocked again right as I was reaching the faded blue door.

"Hold your horses," I called out, checking the peephole. All I saw was a lot of blond hair and a shadowed green eye. The color brought to mind pictures my old diving instructor had shown me of a kelp forest, sunlight filtering through foggy blue water and yellow kelp to produce an ethereal sea green. I'd always wanted to go diving in a kelp forest. Sighing with irritation, I opened the door.

I was sort of expecting the new neighbor, Mr. Giant Box Pile of the blond hair and gym sweatshirt.

I was *not* expecting him to be clad in pajama bottoms and nothing else, every line of his well-cut chest and broad shoulders highlighted by the wall-mounted hall lights. Gym rat, indeed. I almost shut the door again, except for the pained expression on his face.

"Bathroom? *Please?*" he begged, wiggling and dancing and hopping.

I opened the door all the way and pointed. Then I went back to the kitchen and picked up the knife again, a blond blur already slamming the bathroom door.

Flssssh. First the toilet, then the sink. *Thank goodness,* I thought, *a man who washes his hands.*

"Better?" *Chop--chop--chop.*

"Yes, thank you." His voice had suddenly dropped two octaves. "Sorry. I locked myself out, and the landlord was going to come, but she hasn't shown yet."

"I'm Kelly."

"Derik."

He nodded with a wan smile and slouched toward the door, cheeks red and eyes not quite meeting mine. I felt sorry for him. "You wanna wait here? I was going to start dinner after I finished making tomorrow's."

"You're making tomorrow's dinner before tonight's?" He padded—barefoot—to the kitchen, a glimmer of light coming back to his lost-looking expression. His gaze flicked over the kitchen and danced across my giant knife like it didn't even exist, landing on the pile of cut veggies I'd dumped into a bag on the counter, and coming back to me.

"Crockpot." I waved the knife around for effect. Nope, still no reaction. Darn.

"Oh. Thanks for letting me stay."

I shrugged, glancing over his shoulder at the TV. It was an excuse not to meet his green eyes, at least at first.

He shifted slightly. "So, what do you do?"

I waved him quiet, putting down the knife. Derik followed my gaze. Lake Mendota was on the screen. Edging around the coffee table, taking care not to disturb my nearly complete 500-piece puzzle, I grabbed the remote off the sofa and turned the volume up.

"It's the fifth confirmed sighting this week," the announcer was saying. "Lake biologists are reassuring everyone that there's no need to be alarmed. There have been no reports of the otters hurting anyone. By all accounts, they're very shy, although they will chase runners and high level Powered."

In the footage, a dark shadow on the surface of the water, just a little longer than it was wide, ducked beneath in a sudden splash. By the grainy quality of the shot, it was probably the corner of someone's phone-captured video expanded well beyond its ideal resolution.

The last frame froze and shrunk to the corner of the screen. "There's no need for concern over the lake's newest denizens. Like all wild animals, they may be dangerous if threatened, but otherwise seem benign. If you have any footage, please contact the number on the bottom of the screen. Biologists are eager to study the otters, which they believe may be a new species with an unusually high affinity for magic. In other news, Lorren's Oil has begun a drilling in upper Lake Mendota..."

"I saw one of those," I said.

Derik looked at me.

"The other day." Dropping the remote back onto the sofa, I turned around and almost ran nose-first into his bare, broad shoulders. He was waiting for more. I avoided those deep green eyes; my diving instructor's voice echoed in my head, telling me how dangerous kelp forests could be. "It just dove right back into the water. You like pasta?"

"Huh?" He followed me back into the kitchen. "Yeah."

I pointed to the fridge. "There's some ground beef. Why don't you start browning it?" Assuming he could operate a pan. I wasn't sure guys with that much muscle came equipped with basic cooking skills.

A smile lit across his face, sea green eyes sparkling. He pointed to the chopping board. "Shirtlessness and grease don't mix. Why don't you brown the beef, and I'll chop the tomatoes. We can switch when the beef is done."

As it turned out, he made the best pasta sauce I'd ever tasted.

#

Tck-tck-tck-tck. Sandra's keyboard rattled under the assault of her rapid-fire fingertips. Apparently, she'd gotten a new column this week. Good. She pretty much single-handedly ensured my job security as a copyeditor.

"Your brother's gone again?" She loved him, poor thing. She was twice his age and wore fake nails, two sins Trax would never forgive in the war of romance.

"Yep. Just me and the empty apartment." I opened another article in my in-box. Whoops. "Golden Ran of Fortune" indeed. *Click-tck-click.* It was some drivel about Rogers' Research Institute on another funding spree. Of course Rogers' was on a funding spree. Mechany's, their major investment before the Tides, had been in the South.

The group had funded the barrage of tutor-researchers we'd had at Mechany's School for the Magically Disabled. Dad had tried to tutor me, at first, but not even he could fix the fact that I'd inherited Mom's complete tone deafness. So while Trax had been taking full advantage of his lack of Powers to do what Dad never could, selling his first record at 17, I had been getting shuttled off to Mechany's, a super-intensive school for "fixing" magical learning disabilities in students of all ages. I wasn't powerful enough to be dangerous, but I was powerful enough that I *could* have been useful — if I could use my magic.

Rogers' had lost most of their research to the Tides, of course; had to find a new pool of subjects eager to be exploited — I mean helped — if they ever wanted to understand the mechanics of Power.

"Empty apartment, hm. Sounds like an opportunity to me," Sandra hinted.

I sighed, and didn't answer, hoping she'd drop the issue *just this once...*

"There's a guy in my church group who's close to your age." A flurry of clicking heralded a check of about seven resources. Sandra was good, at least, about checking her facts.

I deleted a few words, rewrote a sentence, signed off on the article, and passed it along to the other editors for a second review. Three-fourths of the way through the next article, I was hoping she'd forgotten.

She stood up and stretched, her trendy, vintage made-in-America cotton blouse completely wrinkle-free despite half a day of work. "He's really nice. I think you'd like him."

"You thought I'd like the last three," I shot back. "Sandra, one of them was bald and collected molds. Oh, and *he had grandkids.*"

"He was rich. He had a boat." she defended, sitting back down. "Besides, this one is better. He likes to read."

I glared. "Read what?"

"Books, of course. I learned my lesson with the magazine guy."

That was it. I stood up. "No, Sandra. I'm going to lunch. See you in thirty."

She sighed dramatically as I left.

I walked down the block, hands in my pockets to ward off the chill, to the spot on the corner. It was right beside the lake — our building had a great view from the upper stories — and catered to business people like me, searching for a quick bite of relatively healthy food. The outdoor seating was abandoned, of course, with winter breathing down our necks; most of the city's heat Powers were too busy working in utility companies to waste time heating a couple of benches. I grabbed my hot pita and snagged a table near the window.

Most people don't know that Lake Mendota has tides. Well, technically, all large bodies of water do—the tides are just so insignificant that most people can't notice them.

Not me. I could *hear* them, the slow and steady rush of water, the twenty-four-hour long *shaa-saa, shaa-saa* rhythm. The song wasn't as impressive as the Carolina coast where we'd spent our summer weekends, but I still liked to watch the water. Something about it just... called to me. I guess it was the memories. Back in high school, I'd traded on Trax's burgeoning music career for summer scuba camps of my own. Mom and Dad had been so worried I'd be jealous of him or something, they'd been more than willing to throw in for a decent wetsuit and summer diving classes.

I missed it. I'd left the wetsuit, and the drysuit for ocean diving I'd bought after transferring to UNC Wilmington, at their place. Madison was too cold for scuba, I'd figured, so I'd planned to do my diving when vacationing with them.

The first summer after the Tides had hit, I took a week off. Trax and I had thought about doing a funeral for Mom and Dad. No bodies, though.

I hadn't taken a vacation since.

I put my pita back onto my plate and tried to wash the lump in my throat down with a sip of soda.

A fish thrashed in the water, sending a spray up and bringing me out of my own head. Or was it a fish? I squinted, trying to see it better.

"Hey. Kelly?"

I jumped. A rounded, brown-eyed brunet stared down at me, his hands full of a cheese-steak pita that dripped a little line of diced bell pepper onto a pudgy finger. He wasn't one of my coworkers. "Yeah?"

"I'm Owen. Sandra said you were expecting me."

I could've killed her.

I sighed. "Sort of. She didn't quite get far enough to say you'd be meeting me." I waved at the other chair. "Want to sit?"

His face became a study in pathetic gratitude as he plopped down. Within fifteen minutes, I discovered that he'd come to meet me because he hadn't been on a successful date in seven years, was born in Atlanta and moved here from Boston, was applying for a job with the oil drilling company that had just settled in the area, and was a low-grade earth Power with a mild Amazon warrior obsession.

He didn't know anything but my name. I'd given him nothing but polite grunts as I ate.

"Sandra was right. You're such a charm to talk to," he interrupted his own spiel about the European exaggerations of the Amazons.

"Thanks." My voice was dry enough to make raisins from grapes. I pointedly looked past him at a billboard in the distance. *Lorren's Oil*, it read, *lighting your world*.

"No, really. I mean, Sandra said that you were just amazing, and interesting to talk to, and usually that means that a girl is ugly, but you're beautiful. *And* interesting." He smiled hopefully.

My finger tapped. I stilled it. He wasn't *that* bad.

His smile flagged just a little.

"My lunch break is almost over," I said. "Sorry, I've got to go."

"Sandra's got my number," he said quickly. "We could get together later this week, if you'd like."

I smiled politely. "Maybe," I didn't promise. "See ya," I called over a shoulder, and started back.

When I got to the office, Sandra's shoulders were tight and hunched. *Tcktcktcktcktcktcktck.* "'Maybe'? Owen said he thought it went *pretty well*." The growl in her voice and the twitch to her eye didn't invite an answer, so I said nothing.

An hour later, I was starting to be afraid for her keyboard's life. I freed a finger from my mouse and touched it to my desk, pulling in the familiar warm and fizzy buzz that permeated everything, always just out of sight but within easy reach. It was more effort than the passive version of my magic, listening, but at my meager level of Power I hardly noticed. *Taptaptaptap-tap-tap-tap-tap-tap.*

Tcktcktcktck-tck-tck-tck-tck.

Having a Power—even sixth class—wasn't entirely useless.

12

Chapter Two

I didn't want to go home to an empty apartment, so I swung by the walking trail that ran along the lake edge. *Flump-flump--flump-flump--flump-flump...* my footsteps beat into the ground as I walked leisurely along. Runners passed me without breaking pace. It was on the dark side of sunset, but Madison was big on the health kick, so even in late fall the well-lit trail was busy. A young flight-Powered electrician worked on the only unlit pole; she hovered six feet in the air with her hand on the pole to steady herself, while a park employee waited below to catch the burnt-out bulb she was unscrewing.

I let my mind drift into the fizz of magic without pulling any of it into myself, enjoying the relative peace of the evening. The tide was on its exhale, the six-hour *saaaaaaaa* — a note in the background behind the *blmp-blmp* of the boat propellers and the -*spsh-spsh* of the birds floating on the surface.

Most music Powers could have listened to the hum of the boats' engines, a single sour note enough for them to know the engine needing tuning up. Or they'd have thrown themselves into the songs of the ducks, discerning nuances that would indicate illness or health.

There was a pond not far from our old home where Dad would take us to watch the ducks and get chased by geese. Occasionally he'd used his magic to eavesdrop on the kids jousting under the branches of the trees lining the path and tell us which ones were lying. A useful skill, he'd said to Trax and me after overhearing some kid bragging about shoplifting, but not reliable; that was why he'd gone into helping out at the medical clinics instead of becoming an investigator. Even first classes couldn't always tell truth from not, especially when there was too much other noise around; and besides which, privacy laws meant most of what you learned couldn't be used anyway, except with certain warrants. But music—music changed the way people felt. Taking away pain always worked; that was reliable. It just took a little music, and for Dad there was always music. To him, the physical world had been a living symphony.

Bmp. Bmp. Bmp. A child's ball bounced against the paved trail around the corner. It just sounded like a bouncing ball to me.

I stepped off the trail to stand on a mound of grass. The water was clear here, shallow enough for me to see a McDonald's cup half-buried in the silt. An old instinct nagged at me to pick it up.

I quelled the urge. The water was icy cold.

A ripple poured over the surface, making the cup dance. I glanced up. Something—a turtle?—floated a few dozen feet away, mostly submerged. Big for a turtle. One of those otters, maybe? I squinted.

Splash. Droplets sprayed as it ducked down so quickly as to send water flying. Huh. Guess it thought I looked hungry.

Come to think of it, I was. Time to head home.

#

The next morning I ran into Derik on the way to work. He was dressed this time, jeans and a button-up shirt. Business casual, if I didn't miss my guess.

"'Morning," he said.

"Hey," I answered, unlocking my car. "Work."

"Me too. Where do you work?"

14

I slung my purse into the little Volkswagon. "Editor at the Daily Grind."

"Really?" He grinned. It made Trax's grins look like amateur work, and Trax had practiced them. "I'm just across the street."

"That's great," I called, slipping into the car. "I'll see you there."

"Hey, wait!" He jogged up, and my instinct for Southern manners made me catch my door before it slammed closed in his face. Stopping just outside arm's reach, he stood with both feet pointed at me, fingers in his pockets with his thumbs sticking out. "We should work out a carpool."

Terrific. Carpool. "Sure. Later, though. I've got to get going." If I'd been born a travel Power, I wouldn't have to deal with this.

"You want to start today? I'll drive." He took a hand out of his pocket and offered it to me, brandishing a boy-in-a-cape smile. Was he saving the world one gas-fume at a time?

Mom had liked to recycle. She'd always scolded me for throwing out bottles.

"Great," I ground out, because I couldn't take that grin off his face without landing in Guilt Trip City. "Might as well get this started now, then." *It's too damn early to be the villain, anyway.*

He worked in the gym across the street. Probably a personal trainer, I decided as he dropped me off; with the real American cotton undershirt he was wearing, I'd bet on a morning interview for something better. He'd promised to pick me up this afternoon, and he would let me drive on Mondays and Wednesdays. Oh, joy.

Sandra, of course, had seen me crawling out of his dust-blue Toyota. My scarf had gotten caught on the cracked handle of the matte black passenger-side door, and I leaned back in to free it before heading up the stairs.

"No wonder you weren't into Owen!" she all but pounced when I tossed the stupid scarf over the hook near my desk. "Why didn't you tell me you were seeing someone? Oh, and he was good-looking, too!"

"He's my neighbor, Sandra."

Her face pursed. "That could be awkward, if you guys break up. Are you sure that's a good idea?"

It occurred to me that I could try again to set the record straight, and she might even believe me. But then, she'd keep trying to set me up. "I'll try not to," I said instead. "Besides, we're just friends right now."

"Ooooh, good plan!" She nodded with sage approval. "Hard-to-get works every time. There's nothing like a girl they can't have."

"Right," I agreed. And then crossed my fingers that it wouldn't prove true.

#

"Can we stop by the lake?" I asked on the way home.

"What?" Derik wove around a slow-moving bike drifting out of the bike lane, the fancy morning attire swinging against the back seat. It'd been replaced by more typical gym-wear: faded red sweatpants and sneakers.

"The lake. There's some good walking trails. You like to walk, right?"

He shrugged. "Sure. But I'm going to steal a bowl of that crockpot stew."

I raised an eyebrow.

"Joking, joking!" Holding a hand up in the air, he spared a glance from the road to grin at me. "Just tell me where it is. I'm still figuring things out from this direction."

I pointed out the way. I wasn't sure why I'd asked him to take me to the lake. I hadn't managed to go during lunch, but that was no big deal. I should have just skipped today.

Instead, we ended up walking a mile along the trail in the fading daylight, with me watching the water most of the way. I didn't see the thing in the water again, but I couldn't help but get the feeling that we were being watched.

"What is it?" he asked when I knelt down by the water, listening. Just the normal sounds, but I wouldn't hear anything more than about twenty feet out, anyway. The tides were just too loud to hear much under the surface.

"I don't know," I said, staring at the same cup I'd seen three days ago. "I just… have a weird feeling about the water."

His sneakers stuck over the lip of the lake as he knelt down to peer into the water, saying nothing. Maybe I was getting to him. I did that to some people.

I thought I heard a splash as I turned away from the water. I looked, but saw nothing.

Our drive back was one continuous traffic jam. The man had patience; while I cursed every road hog who cut us off, he hummed along to the music twiddling out of his dusty speakers. Finally pulling into our parking lot, he snagged a spot in the front row. I hadn't managed to get one of those in nearly a month. Lucky bastard.

"Tomorrow, same time?"

I nodded. The engine rumbled quietly beneath our feet. "My car." I slid the belt off my shoulder, grabbed my purse off the floor, and waited for him to turn the Toyota off.

His hands stayed on the fraying fabric cover of the steering wheel, despite the rather pathetic growl of his stomach.

"Not coming in?"

He shrugged. "Gotta go grocery shopping."

I rolled my eyes. "Really? Can't you go after you eat?"

The redness of his cheeks was answer enough. "Moving, and all. Haven't had much time to shop around the unpacking."

I sighed. "Just come up. I've got enough leftover stew to share."

"You don't have to—"

Raising an eyebrow at him, I reached over and turned off the ignition. "You can't waste a parking spot like this. It's against the rules of the universe."

"I'll cook tomorrow. Steaks," he said, and beat me out of the car. He was grinning all the way up the stairs.

He had me pull over the next afternoon on the way home. "I need to get those steaks."

"This is a butcher's, Derik, not a grocery store," I said.

"Yeah. Steak."

"But—"

He was out the car before I could finish.

They were steaks, all right. A pound and a half of red, bloody, two-inch-thick, don't-look-at-that-receipt steak with perfect marble of the kind that you *had* to go to a butcher's to get, that he slammed down on my counter with the love of a man and his meat. He disappeared just long enough to bring back large frying pan and a pair of tongs, and then stuck his head in my fridge and began rummaging around.

"Something wrong with your stove?" I asked, leaning against the wall at the entrance to the kitchen.

He glanced over his shoulder, his hands full of my spinach and a bulb of my garlic. "Hm? Nah. I just need more pots and pans for the other stuff. Can't eat just steak, you know."

I looked at the monstrosity of a pan. It was over a foot across, the inside tarnished black and dun-gold from use. Mentally I hefted it, and decided it would do some serious damage if he ever tried to use it as a weapon. "You say that like the frying pan is all you have."

He shrugged, adding a lemon to his haul. "Saving up for a good set." He pointed an elbow toward the pan on the stove. "That's my first. Carbon steel, De Buyer, fourteen inches. Isn't she gorgeous?"

That was more love than he'd given his car. Far as I could tell, it was a frying pan. "So what about the set you used before moving?"

"Oh, left it with the roommates. They needed it more. Kind of a communal kitchen, you know."

I would have never guessed.

Shaking my head, I grabbed the garlic and the lemon and a cutting board and stole the other counter. "How many of you were there?"

"Zest and juice that; mince that." He pointed at the spoils in my hands before attacking the bag of potatoes on the floor. "Four. Plus the four guys next door and a couple of ladies upstairs, all of who work at my gym. Ex-army; pretty much everyone at the gym except me was in the service." Waggling his eyebrows over his shoulder, he waved a fork around. "You ever seen a recon girl start to flirt? There wasn't a sacred lock in the building. Poor Travis had his heart stolen before he realized she was picking it. Deadbolts, by the way. Handy things can't be picked from the outside."

My eyes went to the deadbolt on my door. Coming in to use the bathroom, being so eager to carpool, virtually inviting himself over for dinner... each alone wasn't a big deal, but all together, and now this? Hands on my hips, I glared at him. "You know that's kinda a creepy thing to say to a girl, right?"

His neck had been craning around as if he'd been looking for something, but now it froze in a meerkat-like position. "Shit." Scratching at the back of his head, he bent his head down and looked at his feet, cheeks growing pink. "Sorry. I really didn't—I wasn't trying to be pushy or make you uncomfortable."

"Well, you did."

His face grew redder, and his shoulders slumped. "Sorry. I've never really lived alone, so I kind of fail on the concept of personal space. My whole family does. If I do something dumb, let me know, okay? I really need to learn, now that I'm on my own."

I could feel my lips purse. He glanced up, and the way his hands clenched as he crossed his arms in a semi-huddle reminded me of how Trax had curled inward when crying, those months right after moving in. The guilt, the self-hate... "It's fine," I muttered, and put the lemon on the counter. "What are you looking for?"

His eyes flicked up, down again, and back up, the final time with a tentative twitch of his lips that could almost be a smile. "Herbs? Oregano?"

The herbs were in the cabinet right behind him. I poked him out of the way, and he stepped back swiftly, hands going behind his back like a promise to give me as much space as I needed. "Here," I said, holding out the plastic bottle.

He took it in two fingers, not even brushing my hand, and I grabbed the cheese grater from above the stove before returning to the other counter. When I was safely on the other side of the small kitchen, he slowly turned to rummage through my random assortment of herbs and spices.

The way he reached for the rarely-used pepper grinder on the top shelf gave me a very nice view of his broad shoulders, which hunched just a little when he lined up his selection.

I'd seen scolded dogs, with their tails between their legs and ears drooping, look less ashamed. Shaking my head, I grinned and pulled out a small bowl. "This is the first time you've lived on your own? Ever?"

"Yeah. Family, roommates, family and friends of family and then roommates again. Spent the last year and a half with guys from my gym before I was… before I decided to move out and try making it on my own. Weird, you know, going home to quiet."

"Uh-huh." I pushed out of my way Trax's dumb-looking coffee mug, with its music-note handle and embossed guitars, the one he claimed was his favorite but never actually seemed to use. "So your last roommates, they put you in charge of the kitchen?"

"They gave me command." Derik dug a cutting board out from beside the microwave. "This group, they all joined the military so young, none of them knows basting from barding. They were so used to mess food that they'd live off Cheetos and Mountain Dew for a month if I'd let them, just 'cause they could, and I wasn't about to let 'em junk out and then kill themselves exercising. But I managed to teach them how to cook at least a *little* real food before I left."

I began applying the lemon to the grater. "I take it you were in charge of the shopping, too, then."

He shrugged, testing the edge on my favorite cooking knife. Apparently he wasn't too impressed, by the pensive frown on his face. "Someone had to be. You might want to sharpen this sometime soon; dull knives are dangerous. By the way, I was thinking chicken tomorrow, maybe some asparagus and brown rice. We'll need to stop by the store on the way home to pick up some more tomatoes." A pause, and he looked up, eyes large. "Um. If that's okay with you?"

I snorted. "Sounds delicious." I needed to start budgeting more toward groceries, if he was going to insist on frequent fresh produce. Assuming, of course, that he didn't disappear when he figured out I had no idea of what 'barding' was.

#

The next Tuesday, the lake's rhythm changed.

I was eating lunch, watching a few flakes of snow drift down to settle on the semi-frozen ground, wondering if I should pick up salmon for Derik to cook, or if he even liked it. *Shaaaaaaaaaaaa*, the water was saying. Then—

Shhhhhhhhhhhaa.

I looked up. It was the barest change, almost nothing. But the feel of it was just a little off.

20

Nobody else noticed.

"Does something feel different to you?" I asked Derik that evening. "About the lake."

He looked out over the water. "No," he said after a moment. "Just a little more ice on the edges."

The weather had taken an abrupt turn for the cooler, not unexpectedly. The weatherwoman had promised a full-out snowstorm for Friday.

"Huh."

"Why? *Is* something different?" He was looking at me strangely, his lips quirking up in a half-smile. For all those looks that he gave me, though, he still hadn't stopped the carpool. Or dropping by in the evenings to share my dinner, although that was my fault for inviting him.

Having him—*another person*, I corrected myself—having another person in the apartment was nice. Too quiet alone.

I shrugged. "It's just... the lake sounds different."

"Sounds?"

"I'm Powered," I explained. Then, before he could get excited again, "Sixth class, that's all. But I can hear the—the rhythms of things. It's my passive ability." Meaning, the one I didn't have to expend energy to use.

"And the lake's rhythm changed?"

I nodded.

"You never said you were Powered." He grinned at me. "We've got something in common."

I started walking faster.

"Ah, come on!" He caught up. "You know, you are the most stubborn woman I've ever lived next to."

I smirked. "Hope so."

"Tell me more about this rhythm thing."

I slowed enough to talk. Why not? Not all Powers worked in rational ways, and mine was pretty simple. "I can hear rhythms. Like, the lake's tides, or the beat of the boat propellers in the water, or your heartbeat. When I listen for it, that is. If I'm not paying attention, I don't hear anything." I smiled wryly. "I was supposed to be a music Power."

"So that means you can change emotions?" He assumed that if I had a passive ability, of course I'd have an active one. Technically true, anyway, even if mine was faulty.

I shrugged. "I can change small rhythms, calm people down a little, if they're close by."

"That's cool."

Nice way to not call it useless. I just shrugged again, staring at my shoes and the path in front of them until I thought he would be looking away again.

With a profile like that, he had to have girls hitting on him all the time. I'd be setting myself up for a broken heart to ask for more. Better to push him away instead. Even if it did leave a lump in my throat.

We walked in quiet for a little while. He kept drifting just a little too close. He'd been doing that, lately.

He leaned into me, and started talking again. "Do you want to—"

"No."

He scrunched his nose up. "You didn't let me finish."

I smiled up at him. "Nope, I didn't."

He growled and muttered something under his breath. Then, "Go to the Tide Zone with me."

"What?"

He put his hands on his hips. "That's what I was trying to ask. Do you want to go to the Tide Zone?"

I looked him up and down. "You're a civilian. How can you get into the Tide Zone?"

He let his hands fall and started walking again. "I told you, I'm Powered—a strength Power. There's this guy, a sergeant from Texas, who moved to the area after retiring from regular duty and joining the Reserves... anyway, when I volunteered for the Recovery teams, he took me. I help the team members build their strength up." He shrugged. "And I can recommend people. Hearing rhythms sounds pretty helpful. And I know the guys could use some calming."

"I'm only a sixth class, Derik. I can't really help." I followed after him, stretching my legs to match his long stride.

"Me too. They can't take anyone much higher than that, actually. Some fifths, one or two fourths who are really important.

Powers start to go weird in the Zone." He gave me a sidelong grin, wiggling his fingers like creepy, crawly things. "They say that fourths hear the voices of the Lost. And thirds *see* things—*bad* things." His eyebrows danced playfully.

My first temptation was to roll my eyes and say no, because a few weeks by his side and that little burn in my chest could turn into flames. But then again…

I did want to see what was left behind the Tides. What was left of the people, of Mom and Dad.

"I'll think about it. Can I let you know tomorrow?"

The way his smile lit up his face and made his eyes shine gave me the answer before he said yes. God, he had a beautiful smile. I walked away before I found myself agreeing for that alone.

The silence of the apartment greeted me when I got home. I flicked on the TV to see the real news had segued into fluff, an interview going on with a clean-cut man in a sharp suit. "…loss, we're recovering nicely. Of course nothing can bring back those who were lost, but the company is devoted to hiring as many of the displaced as we can." Smug green eyes belied the sympathetic frown on his face. Something about him looked familiar.

"With all the research your division has gathered, have you made any advances toward dropping the Tides?" The anchor's bright pink bottom lip stuck out just a hair, her nose up as if sniffing for a story.

This time the frown really did touch his eyes, and he shifted forward. "Unfortunately, our research branches were based in the South. Even the backups—the servers, you know. Like the science and tech industries, magic research has been set back decades."

I coulda told you that, I thought at the anchor. The tech industry of the South had been booming at the time, and even when corporate security hadn't required private information storage, the loss of the servers built in the area proved how ephemeral electronic knowledge was.

But it was easy to forget such inconvenient facts. Nobody liked thinking about the holes left behind.

"Tragic," the anchor said, smoothing a wrinkle from her sleeve. "Are you planning to start a new school?"

It struck me, where I knew that face. It'd been on the wall in the office at Mechany's—Thomas J. Rogers, affiliate director and major moneybags of the school.

I flicked the TV to another station and reached for an oddly shaped puzzle piece, trying to decipher where it went. The show was an old monster movie, some bad science fiction about werewolves. New Powers had evolved over the course of history by branching off other Powers, but shapeshifting? A stretch of the imagination, like zombies and faeries. I glanced up just as some overly dramatic pop song began to play, a beautiful actress transforming into a snarling beast. *Trax's song "Overwritten" would have worked better*, I thought. *Less whiny, more tragic.*

Sitting on the sofa, holding the last piece of the picture of an underwater shipwreck, I listened to rampaging werewolves, the ticking of the clock in my brother's room, the thumps of people upstairs moving around, and the honks and bustle of traffic passing outside.

"Dad always hated the quiet," I said to the puzzle.

It didn't answer. I set the last piece aside for Trax to put in when he got home.

My world had grown the wrong kind of loud the day the Tides took Mom and Dad away. I wondered if the fish posters in my old room were still on the walls of our empty house.

I probably wouldn't be able to visit home. But whatever was left of Mom and Dad was down there. Maybe seeing that would make it stop hurting to think of them.

Derik answered the door on my third knock.

"Yes," I said. "Let's go to the Tide Zone."

Chapter Three

The form to take a short sabbatical from work to volunteer with the Recovery Teams was back on my desk with a stamp of approval by the end of the day I'd submitted it; it would look good on the company's write-offs, even if a couple of the other editors whined about the extra workload. My boss even offered to fill out some of the official paperwork for me, which is how I also ended up with permission to write a few articles on what I saw down there.

"Just in case you feel like writing anything," he said when the Press Pass arrived, and shoved a handful of forms at me decorated with colorful highlighting in the all the places I had to sign before I could put it on. The seven or so confidentiality agreements promised to let the government review anything I wrote before publication. I would get my camera back after they developed the pictures I was allowed to use.

There had been a week three years ago I'd done nothing but stare at a hibernating computer screen, papers piling up on the corner of my desk. My boss had pushed them onto someone else's, brought me a cup of Starbucks every morning, stayed until I left each night, and made sure no one fired me. So maybe he was also an opportunist. I signed the forms and put the press pass on.

Derik and I flew down to join the convoy starting in Memphis. Memphis was almost a ghost town now. Right on the edge of the Tides, the outskirts were close enough that the Lost occasionally wandered in when the Tides were full. The Lost weren't usually dangerous, and they couldn't go far past the Tide Zone, where the magic was dense enough in the ground to sustain them—maybe a mile, at most. But there was something about them that just... well... Nobody lived in the outskirts anymore.

I admit, I'd gotten so used to being sixth class, it never occurred to me to worry that I qualified as fourth by power alone. By the time I thought of that, we were already packed into the Recovery convoy and headed south, sunlight not yet cracking the sky.

"Do fourth level Powers really hear voices?" I asked the leader in our truck, identified on the roster as "Sergeant M. Valdez." He was one of the few dressed in army fatigues; the civilian volunteers had all gotten a few changes of sturdy gray canvas pants and practical light gray shirts and sweatshirts. Wasn't sure why we needed uniforms; wasn't like there was anyone down there to identify us as being on a Recovery Team.

He looked over at me, his sharply cut cheekbones intensifying his dark gaze. An evil smile passed over his lips. "Yeah," he grunted. "But they don't go crazy. Not like thirds."

"Oh. Well, that's good. Thirds go crazy?"

He leaned closer, the arches of his widow's peak sharp in the pre-dawn light despite his buzzcut. "They tried to send one down with us last year. The guy was a regenerative Power, and a psychiatrist to boot. We figured, he'd fix his own head if something started going wrong with it."

One of the other members of the team snorted, a pretty African American woman with a pixie nose and large, dark brown eyes fringed with amazing eyelashes, her only jewelry a pair of small clock-face earrings. "The guy was always trying to fix us, that's for sure." She crossed her eyes and made a face, and I thought she must be close to my age, maybe a little younger.

"Elizabeth, babe, there ain't no fixin' you." The sergeant tossed the insult like a mark of shame at the woman. She caught it like it was a medal of honor, with a nod and a smirk. He continued. "Within a few minutes he was talkin' about the voices. 'I know they're not real,' he said, 'but it's like they're talkin' to me.' And then, he started *seeing* things."

"What were they saying?" I interrupted, fingers of cold tickling the back of my neck.

Valdez grinned for his audience. "That's the thing, little lady. The Doc could hear 'em, he just couldn't hear what they was sayin'. Like listening to a room full of two-year-olds, he called it."

"What does *that* mean?"

"Babbles." He waggled his fingers by his ear. "A thousand voices babbling at him nonstop, and not one had a story to tell."

Derik leaned forward. "So what did he see?"

Here, the sergeant sat back and shrugged. "He wouldn't say much about *that*. But sometimes, he'd just stop and stare. Took a lot of notes."

Elizabeth broke in. "Until he started to fall apart. It was the sixth day, not even that far in. His hands started to shake all the time, especially when one of the Lost came around. And the more he ran, well, they chase people who run—soon, he was pretty much covered in them."

"Who's tellin' this story, Elizabeth?" He scowled at her until she settled back. "Like she said. Covered in 'em. It was the butterflies that broke 'im, though. The guy just started *screaming* when they landed on him. 'She's dying,' he said, over an' over."

"It's always the butterflies," Elizabeth muttered under her breath.

He sat back, shaking his head. "We took 'im back. Lost two weeks for it, but we couldn't keep him there anymore—it was breaking the rest of us up, all that screaming, all night long. Last I heard, he was still in the hospital, crazy as the kooks he used to fix."

Derik whistled. "But a sixth class is okay, right?"

Elizabeth set her elbows on her knees and gave him an exaggerated wink. "Got you beat. Fifth, heat Power. Still fine." She blew him a kiss and chuckled when he held both hands up to deflect it.

I shivered despite sweat-damp hands. "I'm more powerful than I'm licensed," I admitted, and my voice sounded higher than usual even to me. Would I go crazy? I couldn't be there for Trax if I went crazy. "I got downgraded for a handicap."

Valdez sat up. "What?" The word lost his thick Texan accent.

"I'd be a fourth, if I could use it all," I said. "Should we—?"

He sat back with a sigh. "Don't you worry your pretty little head, sweetheart. Fourths don't get it so bad. Jus' tell us if you need a rest. We can give you some earplugs."

"That works?"

He nodded. "Just voices, sweetheart. And you ain't the only one who hears them, even if you're the only with us who will. Ain't nothin' worth turnin' back for."

I tried to smile like I was reassured, but ended up biting my lip instead.

Derik put his arm around my shoulders, and I realized that I'd leaned into him. Crap. But he *was* nice and warm... "Don't worry, Kel. I'll keep an eye on you."

I sat up. "Thanks."

The *bump-bump-rattle* of the trip wasn't terrible, despite most of the driving being on the shoulder of the road. We took a break every hour and a half, rest stops and such, as the landscape slowly changed around us. The green grass became brown, then purple-streaked as we went farther and farther south.

At one stop Valdez caught me before I could climb out of the transport. "We're about to cross the official Tide Zone line, which during a receding Tide is places that were covered within the past two weeks. You might start hearin' things after this."

I looked around the old rest stop as he reached into a compartment near the back of the truck, the one real soldiers were allowed to touch but verboten to the civilian volunteers. The rest stop was mostly abandoned, since only the Recovery Teams used it these days. Even the birds were quiet—or maybe just missing. I hadn't seen any animals on the side of the road recently, come to think of it, the perfect set for a horror movie. "Do the Lost often come this far out?"

The guns, each as long as a man's arm, stood firing-end up in the compartment, two already missing. With a quick yank he snapped one out of its holder, checking the straps and clicking a piece of metal in and out before slinging it across his back. The black butt of it jutted above his shoulder. "Sometimes they'll leave the Tide Zone, but usually they stay in the areas recently uncovered. I guess 'cause nobody can hear the voices outside that region, there's no point in crossin'. Ain't no fun if ya can't drive someone mad."

We were going moderately "deep"—close to the wall of magic that was the boundary of the actual Tides, where the magic was thick enough to coagulate into a visible barrier between the stuff you could move through and the magic dense enough to rip you apart—because so much of the land around here had already been salvaged. And of course, the more of the year that the land spent under, the more raw Power sank into it, and the stranger it became.

At lunch, Derik and I were sprawled in a meadow that swarmed with blue-black ants. I heard the first voices then, with my hands full of macaroni and cheese. "Did you say something?" I asked Derik.

He shook his head, tapping a small green capsule out of a bottle and washing it down with the sports drink he'd stuffed into his bag before leaving. Same as Trax's bottle: the lowest level step-downs of an antidepressant.

Trax's agent had fought to get them for him and the other band members, as the government had passed emergency rationing on the drugs. Even long-term dependents had been forced into step-down programs and group therapy instead of renewing prescriptions, the shortage had been so bad. But his agent had all but shoved the pills down his throat, and every single Southern-born performing artist in the country thereafter had likewise been issued prescriptions—because if they could go on, everyone else could, too. She'd been pushing him onto stages six weeks after the Tides had hit.

Needless to say, I wasn't too fond of the cold-blooded reptile.

Despite the government force-purchasing the patent to mass-produce the drugs (in the name of eminent domain, an emergency measure lawyers and Congress were *still* debating the constitutionality of), getting a prescription was hard even now. For non-celebrities, it took more than a diagnosis of PTSD to achieve—'non-suicidal survivor's guilt' was almost a synonym for 'group therapy only.' Taking another bite of cheese, I studied the ground and ignored the rattle of Derik slipping the bottle back into the pack.

There were some things you just didn't judge people for.

Chabble-rabble-blather, I heard in the distance. It wasn't the Recovery team—they were around us, and while many of them were chatting, it wasn't their voices I was hearing. Relief made my fake cheese taste like Havarti in my mouth. "Huh. I guess that's what they were talking about."

"What?" Derik capped his precious sports drink and set it aside on a rock, warily checking the rock for ants.

"The voices." I took another bite and stretched my arms, the ache between my shoulder blades already less. "Not as bad as I'd feared. Glad I'm not imagining them."

He looked curious. "Are they saying anything?"

I stood up, brushing some ants off my pants. "Nope. They're fading now, anyway. You about done?"

He nodded, gobbling a few last bites and flicking a final ant off his jeans.

#

"Watch out for the butterflies," Elizabeth said, passing me a tent pole. I ducked to tuck it in.

I had to scoff. "Butterflies?" Not exactly a terror-inducing critter.

She circled to tuck in another pole. "You're hearing the voices, right? I saw you looking around at nothing today." I nodded reluctantly. Between us, the tent began taking shape. "The butterflies are always the worst. That doctor might have been okay, if it weren't for them."

"I'll keep an eye out," I said, looking for the stakes. If it was like lunch, I could handle it.

Something in the corner of my eye fluttered. I glanced over. *Chatter-chi*, the babble whispered in my ear.

"A fox." Elizabeth paused to watch it. "They always make me sad."

I knelt. It crept up, its large red-brown ears slightly back. "These ones aren't dangerous, are they?"

"No." She moved slowly to join me, holding her hand out. Sharp little teeth bared as it sniffed her fingers, but it didn't bite. "They're mostly just lonely." It nudged her hand, and she shuddered. Her fingers stroked the short fur anyway. *Chi-chi-chatter-cha*, the babble whispered.

"I didn't realize they'd let us touch them. Not the nice ones, anyway."

Elizabeth scratched behind the small fox's ears. "They don't mind. You've never pet one?"

I shook my head.

"Try it," she suggested. "Only, it's going to feel cold. Only time I ever feel cold, real cold and not the mental kind, is when I touch them."

I reached out, careful not to move too fast, and let the fox sniff me. *Chi-chi-chi!* His—her?—pelt was soft and cold. So cold. Fingers of ice ran up my arm, tickling, itching, not quite burning. *Chi-hi-hi-please—*

I snatched my hand away. "Oh, that's weird."

Elizabeth nodded without stopping her attentions. "Makes me feel like we're in a video game of some kind, or a fantasy book. Not like normal magic." She shifted her weight, moving out of a squat to kneel in the dirt. "How many did you lose?"

My hands were normal, I noted, looking at my fingers. Focusing on them pulled my heart out of my words, let me talk without my throat closing up. "We were from the South. My parents. All the extendeds. It's just me and my brother, now."

Sympathy touched her eyes as she stopped petting the Lost. "I was at school, in Seattle. Scholarship; my junior year." A wry smile. "Left behind most of my corsets, and a lot of the decor. There was only so much room in the dorms, and the roommate wasn't into steampunk." She stood, and the fox scampered off, startled by her movements. "Here, give me your hand."

I set my hand between hers, as she indicated. Her eyes weren't focused on me, or anything around us; she wore the faraway look I sometimes caught on Trax, or in my own mirror, and not the one that had to do with magic.

Warmth emanated from her palms, bathing my fingers and rolling up to my elbow, banishing the chill while she spoke. "Grandma raised me while Dad worked at the factory. Grandma was the one who got me to take martial arts, made me promise to keep it up when I got accepted to Washington State. She was totally into the corsets, too. Could really rock a fascinator. I think it was church, you know—all that fancy hat practice. She was always about saving people, you know. Mississippi, though."

"I'm sorry to hear that."

She just nodded, and together, we finished staking the tent.

Chapter Four

The highways were in pretty bad shape, clogged with rusty car corpses and cracked by weather, so travel was slow the next morning. We reached the edge of the Tide around ten, glaring sun highlighting every steel-gray pine tree and navy-blue blade of grass.

The subtle haze that had once consumed an entire region of the country in less than an hour now sat tamely in the sunlight, a wall of slightly oily iridescence in the air betraying the difference between primal chaos and magic thin enough for our bodies to handle. Valdez made sure we all knew exactly where the border was — he called it the Edge — before we were allowed to begin.

Brrrn-brrrn-brrrn, called the saw as it bit through the side of the bank. Recovery? Just a fancy name for government-approved looting. Non-organics were affected differently by the Tides, holding their structure; some metals decayed, but not like people and plants and animals, and not gold or silver or lead.

Derik stood amid the brawns of the team, leading them in a few warm-up exercises. I, being a wimpy music Power of editorial origins, got relegated to the sorting group. My camera sat heavy in my hands, so I snapped a couple of pictures. First I got a few shots of the work, but it wasn't moving quickly. I turned to the empty buildings staring at us. A car, red streaks of rust vibrant against the chipped green paint, had hurled itself through the bushes into the side of an old dollar store. Now the shattered windows were filled with blue-black shrubbery, a bright streak of yellow-orange ivy working its way into the vinyl seats. That was an image my boss would love.

The sounds of the saw drove off most of the Lost, but I did notice three or four birds flapping overhead. The Lost were attracted to the living, except that they were terribly shy. It was a love-fear relationship. Or maybe a stalkerish one.

The sorting team hung back while the brawns went through the still-steaming hole in the wall. "You'd think there'd be a bigger problem with looting," I mentioned to Elizabeth.

A wry grin stretched across her face. "The crooks are mostly too creeped out to come down here. And..." She scratched the back of her head.

"What?"

Elizabeth grabbed a box from the hands of a brawn. "The Lost don't seem to like looters. I don't know why they let us down—guess it's the fancy convoy, or maybe they just like the big flag painted on the side of the truck. Either way, they don't bother the real teams."

I handed her a crowbar, which she crammed into the locked box. The lid popped neatly off. She shuffled through the documents, looking for any kind of identification indicating a possible owner. "Name!"

I grabbed one of the bags labeled "claimed" and copied the name onto it, then held it for her to dump the box's contents in.

There were twenty trucks with us, but ten of them were just for holding crap—one team per giant treasure chest, each team assigned to hit a different building in the town. About a third of the space in each storage truck was reserved for private goods, including anything in the safety deposit boxes that had some sort of identification as to the owners.

Of course, if the owners were among the Lost and had no heirs, the government got to keep the spoils. That happened a lot.

"Have you ever met one of the violent ones?"

Elizabeth shook her head. "Nah. I know the Hunters and the Mad are out there, but like I said, the Lost don't usually bother the official teams."

I held the bag for her to dump the next box. Gold, a necklace and a ring, some cufflinks, a couple of keys, a watch, and some papers. Another named set. "The doctor was part of the group."

She shrugged. "He was a high-level Power. Besides, they weren't hurting him. His mind just broke itself."

I glanced up at the Lost circling overhead. *Thirds are more sensitive. Nothing I can't handle yet.*

We hit three banks in the town and packed up to drive to the next one. Our flock of fliers had grown.

The voices were back, too.

Nancha-bibble-ancha-abble whispered in my ears. I rubbed my temples.

"Still hearing them?" Derik asked.

I nodded. "It was quiet for a while. They're back, though."

He frowned, all sweet concern. I leaned away from the hand he raised in my direction, and he backed up, taking the hint to give me a little breathing room. "Still nonsense?"

"Yeah." I hesitated.

"What?"

"It's just..." I glanced up. "Nothing."

He had a wrinkle across his forehead, eyes an intense green. "Do you need —?"

"No." I ran a hand through my hair, taking a deep breath, craving his arms around me and reminding myself that I could handle it. I could chase away my own fears. "I'm fine."

But I remembered the fox fur under my fingers, and wished I dared ask him to watch me. If only I wasn't so certain he would... and so certain I didn't want him to look too close, close enough to see me as I saw myself.

#

It was dark by the time we reached the next city, our truck splitting off from the main caravan with three other teams. We set up camp in a public park. Making graves for Mom and Dad

35

crossed my mind, something to take a picture of to give Trax closure, but then again... My fingers were cold. I tucked them under my arms and tried not to think about the fox.

I'll be less sore in a few days, after I get used to the work.

The chatter kept me up most of the night, until I opened the tent to see a trio of squirrels sitting right outside. "Shoo," I scolded. "I'm trying to sleep, and you're keeping me up."

They scattered.

"Kel?" Elizabeth sleepily rubbed her eyes.

I mumbled something incoherent in a soothing tone, lying back down.

The threesome followed us to the first bank the next morning. As the brawns were cutting their way in, I knelt down. The bravest slunk up to me. *Bahti-mahti-sashi-mashi,* it babbled. I wiggled my fingers, and it crawled a little closer.

"Careful, they're cold."

It squeaked and ran. I glanced up at Derik, mildly irritated. "Yeah, I know."

He shrugged. "Sorry. Didn't know you were making friends."

"I just wanted to try something." Too late now. All three of them had scampered up a tree into hiding.

He knelt down beside me. "What?"

"The other night… I know it sounds weird, but when I pet the fox, I thought he said something."

Derik's eyes were very green, but his face stayed blank. "Thought Valdez said they babbled. Probably just coincidence."

"Yeah." I stood up. "Maybe I was just imagining things."

He regained his feet, wrapping an arm around my waist. "I won't scare it away, next time."

I didn't push him away.

#

I woke up to chattering again. Tucking my toes into my sneakers, I slid out of the tent.

Gnochi-mochi-mole-mollie, the squirrels whispered, scampering in enthusiastic circles at my appearance. I knelt in the dirt, and the icy damp turned my knees into lumps of lead.

The leader, the same brave one from the afternoon, stopped. His little nose popped into the air and twitched. The other two slammed into him, and the trio toppled in a sprawl of fur and tails.

Giggling, I held out a hand. "Grace is not your strong suit, is it?"

Kimchee-mimchi-leesee-loree. It almost sounded bashful.

A little nipping and wrestling left the brave one free. Emboldened perhaps by the empty night, he wiggled his way almost to my knee before hesitating. *Ninnie-pinni-penne-penny*, the chipper chatter went on.

I slowly let my finger come within nipping distance. He didn't nip, so I planted the finger directly on his forehead. *Dinnae-dinner-diner-hey-hey-hey. Listen, listen. Wish you could hear.*

I took the finger away. "Hear what?"

Shiny-piny-rhiney-rhimey. Beady dark eyes met mine and stared pleadingly. He took a little step closer, and nudged my knee with his nose. I stroked him again, letting the numbness seep up my arm once more.

So lonely, so alone, so lonely. They can't hear. I miss her. Miss my baby girl. Hear me, please. So lonely.

"Do the voices bother you?" Elizabeth's voice sent me two inches into the air.

I twisted to look at her, aware of the Lost scampering away. "You scared me."

She nodded without guilt. Kneeling, she held out a hand of her own.

"No," I answered her question. "I want to know what they're saying."

She shook her head. "They don't talk, you know. Just babble. The doctor kept trying to hear things in them, to find patterns, but there was nothing."

I watched a tail twitch by the tree. "They can't understand us, can they?"

She shrugged. "I don't know."

"Please come out," I called softly.

They didn't. A final twitch of fur, and the Lost disappeared entirely. Elizabeth offered her hand to me, and I placed my own in it. The warmth of her magic banished the mild ache in my wrists.

A footstep gave me warning. I looked up and saw Derik coming through the trees, lit by the vibrant moon.

Elizabeth waved. "Watching?"

He nodded, joining us on the ground. "Did they say anything?"

My fingers had stroked fur, and I'd heard it talk. "He seemed lonely." Were Mom or Dad among them? Cold or not, the Lost were very much alive. "I wish they could understand us."

Elizabeth shivered. "I don't," she muttered.

"Why not?" Derik asked.

She rubbed her arms briskly. "They're smart enough. The Hunters... they don't need to know what we're doing before we do it."

"I thought you said the Lost don't bother official convoys," I said.

"Not usually. The normal ones don't. But some... some don't care." Her eyes met mine. They were wide and dark. "The Mad aren't picky."

Derik helped me to stand before I realized he was standing— and before I realized I was getting up. "You should sleep," he muttered when I raised an eyebrow at him. "Long day tomorrow."

I looked back at Elizabeth with Derik's hand on my lower back pushing me gently forward. She had a hand over her mouth, but her eyes were smiling.

I rolled mine.

We both changed before going back to sleep. The ground had been damp with frost.

#

The first breakdown came the next day. "Hey, music girl," Valdez interrupted my bagging, "need you over here."

I finished labeling the bag and handed it off. Valdez wrapped an arm around my shoulders and drew me off to the side.

The guy Valdez pointed me to was sitting by himself. He was trying to cover it up by eating a bag of chips, like he wasn't rattled or anything. The *crink-crink-crink* of the bag told another story, now that I was listening for it. I grabbed a bottle of water and made my way beside him.

"I need a break," I said, stealing the other side of the stone bench he had taken. "Water?"

He shook his head. I listened carefully. *Sasa-sasa-sasa,* his heart whispered. Fast. Too fast. I started tapping a finger against the bench, pulling on my Power gently. *Tcktck-tcktck-tcktck.*

"Did you see the squirrels last night?" I asked, but he answered with another headshake. "They were cute. Cold."

"You touched them?" His voice was tight. He cleared his throat, and it came out better. "You let them touch you?"

I nodded. *Tcktck-tcktck--tcktck--tcktck--tcktck...* "Pet one."

"Thought you heard voices." *Sasa--sasa--sasa...*

"Yeah, I do." *Tcktck--tcktck--tcktck--tck-tck--tck-tck...* I glanced at him out of the corner of my eye. "It's not so bad. They don't say bad things."

Sa-sa--sa-sa--sa-sa. His eyelids sagged. Any more, and I'd put him to sleep. Not what I was going for.

I tossed my head back to look up at the sky. "Have you ever touched one?"

He shook his head, the movement slow, almost drugged.

"It makes your arm go numb." I stared at my palm, and then curled my fingers into a fist, tucking the hand against my sternum. "But you know, besides that, it wasn't so bad. He was soft. And... he had these big eyes. They were lonely."

My patient hugged himself, a shiver running down his arms. "The houses are so empty. It's a ghost town. There used to be so many people here..."

I took off a shoe and sock and buried my toes in the red dirt. The ground was hard, numbingly cold. A pebble wedged under my toenail. I bent to pick it out. "I grew up in the South. My parents were down here."

He looked at me. "Mine, too. And my sister."

I held out a hand, and he took it. Both of our hands were cold, but somehow, it felt a little warmer. "It bothers me, seeing the Edge," I said.

"I won't let you fall in," he promised.

I nodded, and got up.

A couple of hours later, I pulled Valdez aside. "How about some music?" I asked. "'S awfully quiet around here."

He nodded. At the next stop, he pulled out a pair of speakers to hook up to a laptop.

Derik offered me the sledgehammer. "First swing?"

The front windows of the jewelry store we'd been paid to 'salvage' were reinforced glass. Easier to break them than to widen the crack running from the foundation to the roof, but I could see the wires between the thick panes. "Uh, no."

Derik snorted and hefted his instrument of destruction. I took a generous step back, and watched as the hammer turned inch-thick reinforced glass into shards. Grinning, he turned to me and saluted.

"Stop showing off, Holskerski." Valdez pushed past him and stepped into the jewelry store, bag in hand. A ring of keys jingled on his belt.

Elizabeth laughed as she followed him. "C'mon, Kel. Only time in your life you'll be legally allowed to rob a jewelry store."

The music blared in the background as we packed and labeled our small bags, tossing them into a larger bag. Someone got the clever idea to pull up a holiday record. Then I went around the corner to the diamond section, and the music faded behind the walls.

"It's beginning to feel a lot like Christ-mas," I sang out, continuing the song and dropping six diamond rings into a snack-bag sized piece of plastic.

Elizabeth winced. "Geez, girl, you sing like a drunken cat."

Winking, I grabbed the necklaces on display and held one up to my neck. "A cat in diamonds."

She snorted. "Too bad they inventory all these before sending us down. Wouldn't that be a nice souvenir?"

I laughed back. "Too tacky. Where would I wear it?" I tossed the jewels into another bag. "You've got fancy corsets and tiny hats back home. All I've got are pumps and slacks. Besides, I'd hate to give the Lost the wrong idea."

"You'd be eaten by butterflies," she joked. "Okay, I'm done. Let's get our butts back to the group."

Holding up the last bag, I faked a gasp. "Not the butterflies. I'll bribe them with bracelets, how about that?"

Laughing, we stepped out the—now properly unlocked— front door. I thought I heard something pounding behind the beat of the music, a deeper rhythm, like heavy footfalls. I glanced up, toward the trucks.

"Look out!"

Derik was right in its way, loading the heavy bags into the truck with the driver. Valdez heard my shout and swung around, the pump of a shotgun cutting through the havoc, but the angle was wrong—he'd hit one of the team.

The driver screamed as the bear swiped.

Derik shouted and lashed out.

The bear roared, its arm broken. It snapped, and Derik didn't move quite fast enough. Blood sprayed from his forearm.

Derik howled, and punched.

Its eye caved in. Derik staggered back. Two gunshots exploded through the air, and gore sprayed into the air, the bear's skull becoming a ruined mass of pure horror that seared itself into my nightmares. Bile burned the back of my throat, choking me.

And then it was down, and Derik was holding his arm and gasping, and the driver was lying on the ground. The team medic went to the driver first. Valdez tackled Derik, making him sit and waving me over when he tried to pull away. As soon as my shaking hands pressed against the wound, Derik clenched his teeth and stopped struggling, and sat watching my hands turn red with his blood.

The music blared on in the background over the ringing in my ears. *Santa Claus is coming to town,* it lied, and we all ignored it.

Chapter Five

Crossing his eyes did not make Derik look any smarter, I decided. "Valdez put me in charge of feeding you, so you're getting fed. Eat."

He decided to improve his look by sticking his tongue out.

"You are such an ass when you're doped up," I grumbled. "Come on."

The bandage around his arm hid seventeen stitches. The driver didn't look too hot, either—he was sporting a trio of gashes across his shoulder, a mild concussion, and a broken arm. Both of them would recover, though, so it could have been worse. Much worse.

Derik finally opened his mouth to let me spoon him more soup. "Tastes icky," he burbled, spilling most of it.

I sighed and wiped his face. "You were the one who said you wanted chicken noodle soup."

"'S supposed to make me feel better," he pouted.

I shoved another spoonful in his face. Maybe the canned stuff wasn't the greatest, but we didn't exactly have the gear for a restaurant-style homemade meal. Well, all right, we probably did, but no amount of wishful thinking was going to turn the electricity back on in the stoves.

For once, we were sleeping inside. Valdez had kicked down a door to an abandoned mall and claimed a department store's bedding section for the wounded. The rest of us curled up on the ground. No one really wanted to touch anything.

It was worse in here than outside. Much worse. Not in a way we could see, but rather a thickness to the air, a sense of being watched, the constant feeling of pressure on the skin. The smallest rooms, those that had been closed without circulation, seemed to seethe with unseen presences, like the darkest corner in a child's bedroom at midnight. The animals in the mall, on the other hand, were bolder; cats, dogs, mice, rabbits, and geese migrated from store to store. They kept clear of the camp itself, but sauntered up to stragglers, perching almost on the toes of a targeted human until a hand obligingly offered petting.

Valdez poked me when I finished feeding Derik. "You want to work some of your magic?"

I shrugged. "I'll try." So I slid off the bed and into the circle formed in the aisle beside the beds, a fortified knot of human contact. Just the eighteen of us, knee-to-knee, sweating in the cold and trying not to think about how much we didn't want to eat our dinners. "Tell a story," I told him. "I'll work with that."

"Don't know no stories," he grunted.

"I've got one," Elizabeth said. "Hey, guys!" She hit the floor with the flat of her palm. Everyone looked at her. "We've got a campfire, right? So I'll tell a ghost story. Somebody break out the marshmallows."

A couple of members gave a half-hearted titter and the few wanderers settled into place in the circle. Elizabeth cleared her throat and sat up straighter. The cloying aftertaste of contained magic was like the lingering bitter-sweetness of cough syrup, and the yellow dots of the campfire reflecting in small eyes all around us was the exaggerated nightmare of camping-haters everywhere. I had to admit, it really *was* perfect for a ghost story. Pulling in the almost-too-strong fizz around us, I brought Power to my fingers. Quietly, I began to tap, a quick little beat to get their hearts racing.

"Most of the Lost are just cute and cuddly little midgets," Elizabeth started. "Today, we saw one of the Mad. But we're here on official business We don't see the Hunters. They go after looters. They're the reason there's stuff left for us to salvage.

"I knew a guy, back in my freshman year of college. He was sweet on me, bigshot football player, thought he could impress me with fancy dinners and expensive gifts." Her fingers touched an empty spot on her neck, and fondness crossed her face. She shook her head. "Except he didn't think steampunk was something a football player's girlfriend should go for, started acting like he had the right to tell me what to wear, what to like. He wasn't too graceful about it when I left him for someone else. But then the Tides came through.

"His whole family lived in Baltimore. When the Tides started to recede, and they hadn't lost anybody—all they thought about was the *stuff* still lying in the streets. So he took a crew of three down there to get as much as they could.

"The first day was great. They had a ball, tossing crap into the back of their trucks, picking up jewelry and watches and fine silver from people's houses. Of course none of the electronics still worked, but who cared? Copper was still copper, silver was still silver, gold was still gold. And there wasn't anyone around to argue with them about it. Just a bunch of animals. Shy animals.

"They crashed in the first mansion they found that night. It was empty, of course, except for a couple of dogs, a rat, and a parakeet. Weird animals—shy, but always trying to stay near them. It creeped them out. One of the men stepped on the rat. Broke its back. His foot went numb."

She raised her own boot into the air. "He was freaking, flailing, screaming." Her hands waved wildly; her eyes grew wide. "They finally knocked him out." The boot hit the ground hard, a *thud* that echoed like a gunshot in the old mall. "Left him in a bed."

Her eyes scanned the rest of us. "The other two had some tinned soup that night. Some of the old stuff left behind in the house. The pair spent most of the night being sick—you know how it is. Don't touch the local stuff, and all. They forgot about their friend, just completely forgot to check on him until noon the next day." She leaned forward conspiratorially.

"He wasn't there anymore."

A dramatic sweep of her hand cast any questions away. "Not in the bed. Not under it. Not in the bathroom. Just a rusty stain on the sheets.

"The others, they searched. Eventually, they decided their friend had wandered out in the middle of the night. They left to look for him.

"The birds lined the streets, two and three deep. Cats and dogs stared down at them, squirrels within eating distance but completely unmolested. He shot a gun into the air. The animals scattered. And then it was dead quiet.

"Silent as the grave. They split up, one to go around back and the other to go up and down the street. He was checking another house two doors down when he heard the scream. He came racing back.

"He called, but got no answer. Of course he had his gun out as he went into the yard. He was prepared to go down fighting— but there was nothing to fight, no body, no murderer. Just a pair of red handprints streaked across the back patio.

"He's no idiot. Not very brave, but no idiot. He ran for the truck to get out of there while he still could. Tossed the bag out of the back of the truck—'cursed,' he said, and shoved everything out. I think that's what saved him, in the end.

"Soon as he unloaded, he dodged for the cab, got in, turned the key. The engine revved."

She paused.

"*It* was in the back seat."

Her hands clawed the air and her back hunched as she stood, hovering over us. "Claws like talons, fangs like knives, halfway between a tiger and a greyhound, but the size of a mastiff. It *watched* him, grinning, gloating.

"He tried to go for the door, to jump out. But it was faster, and grabbed his shoulder in a bloody grip, impaling right through the bone. Slammed his face into the steering wheel.

"He elbowed back with his other arm, aiming for the face, but getting only fur. Screaming, he threw himself at the passenger seat. With a wet *schlurp*, he was free. He rolled, but it was over him, teeth snapping at his throat.

"'I'm sorry,' he sobbed.

"It stopped. And, he swears to god, it *laughed*. First sound it had made—no growling, no roars, just a laugh." She shook her head. "He woke up a few hours later, alone in the car, weak and still bleeding. Drove back on fright alone—they found him unconscious on the side of the highway, just this side of the Tides. He swears to this day that he only lives to be a warning to would-be looters."

"Of course, we're all looters here, technically. We're just government-approved looters who don't get to keep the stuff we find. But who'd miss a ring or two? Maybe a nice new wallet, or a pretty dress that's just lying around, or a cash register that's sitting open?" A wide, wide grin slid up her face. "If you're tempted… watch your backs," she warned, and laughed.

We all laughed with her, nervous giggles and too-loud snorts, but the tension was less than before. I stopped the tapping, which I'd tapered to the rate of a calm heartbeat by the end of her story.

The circle loosened. I somehow ended up back on the foot of Derik's bed, Elizabeth beside me crowding poor Derik to the top of the mattress. Not that he noticed. He'd turned around so that his head was behind me, and was occupying himself by petting the hem of my frumpy gray shirt. I tried not to be distracted by the finger that kept poking at my hip as he played peek-a-boo with my skin.

"The Hunters are different from the rest of the Lost," Elizabeth was saying. "They don't look like animals."

"Leastways, not real ones," Valdez interjected.

She nodded. "Changelings," she supplied. "Freaks of nature bred to kill. But they *don't* come around official Recovery Teams. Not unless the team does something horrible."

"Like what?" one of the others asked.

"Like keeping stuff that they should turn over," Valdez supplied. "Robbing any place that's not on the list and hidin' the stuff, so it won't have to be handed over."

I batted Derik's finger away from the waistband of my pants. "How do they know the difference? It's not like they know what's on the list in the first place."

Valdez shrugged. "We don't know. But every time a group has gone astray or started getting greedy, the Hunters show up and start killing people off until the team gets rid of the extra loot."

"Maybe they do understand us," I muttered.

Elizabeth uncrossed her legs. "The Lost don't." Another shift of weight had her leaning forward on the edge of the bed. "The Hunters don't respond to messages or pleas or demands. I'd say they can't."

Derik lay his hand over the hem of my shirt and held it down. "Stop that!" I ordered him.

He grinned drunkenly up at me, green eyes hooded and blond hair curling messily around his face. "I'm making sure your heart doesn't escape," he said. "You wouldn't have a heartbeat anymore."

"I won't let it escape. Now go to sleep," I ordered. He rolled over and sulked, the bandaged hand sticking off the edge of the bed. Valdez snickered.

I curled up next to Derik after the medic slipped him a couple more pills to keep him under for the night.

"You sure you want to sleep up there?" Elizabeth asked, dropping my sleeping bag by hers on the floor beside the bed. "He's kind of touchy."

"He's too drugged to be left alone. Besides, if he gets gropey, you can help me tie him up." I waggled my eyebrows at her, because it felt like the sort of thing that should be made into a joke.

"Oooh, kinky." Her chuckle limped a little at the end, though.

Nobody slept much that night. At some point, a few members of the team slipped under the beds, as if they'd be safer there. I could hear Elizabeth's soft breathing directly under me.

It was the pain that woke him, when the pills wore off. The changing rhythm of his heart woke me. Opening my eyes, I found Derik tense and motionless, his teeth gritted.

"More blue pills?" My words slurred with sleep as I lifted my head off his shoulder.

He grunted. "I can deal with it." His uninjured arm was wrapped around my waist.

I rolled over and away, fishing for the bottle the medic had put me in charge of. As soon as I placed the painkillers in his hand, he popped them and swallowed, not even waiting for the bottle of water to wash them down. His arm reached up for me, but I shook my head, slipping off the bed.

Valdez was already up, talking quietly with one of the guys on watch. He stood when he saw me. "Derik any better?"

I shook my head. "Just gave him another dose. He's not going anywhere."

The sergeant sighed. "We'll have to camp here for another couple of days until the pick-up comes. Stone's pretty bad. Good thing we came well-stocked."

"So we're still heading forward?" I looked over at the beds. I'd assumed we'd be aborting the rest of the run.

He nodded. "Being two down's no reason not to go on. As long as nothin' gets infected, we'll press on. We're switchin' to go deep, and letting another team take our route."

We'd started at the edge of the Tide, but we'd been meandering along eastward while it had receded to a different latitude. That meant we were pretty far out. Going deep, on the other hand, would keep us right at the Edge for the entire trip, dogging its heels and hoping desperately it didn't change its mind about the semi-predictable patterns we knew. From there we'd map the damage of the region as it was uncovered. The satellite images were too distorted by static to give a clear picture, and planes had a tendency to lose electrical signals mid-flight, so our maps were iffy at best. When the Tides had hit, planes had crashed and cars stopped mid-highway; while the landscape hadn't changed features besides in color, weather hadn't stopped, either. And without people to fix them, roads went to ruin pretty quickly.

"What if we have to roll out quick? We can't leave them behind."

Valdez shot me a dirty look. *Duh*, it said. "Injured stay in the trucks. But it's not our decision, anyway. We're droppin' Stone off when we pass the other team. Derik doesn't get off so easy. He'll be up to speed in a week, so he's stuck with us; he can do light work soon as he's mobile enough to scramble."

I looked at a rack of pale, threadbare curtains dancing idly in the cross-currents of the old, abandoned mall. Flickering yellow lights from the lanterns mixed with the eerie green of the glowsticks we'd stuck in a dusty plastic Christmas tree. Shadows darted like ghostly mice across the floor whenever anyone moved, and somewhere nearby, small claws skittered across a marble floor. "Two more days," I muttered.

Valdez nodded. "On the bright side, things get weirder the further south you go."

"Joy."

Chapter Six

We were all twitchy by the time we left, despite my best efforts. I was only a fourth class in Power, and a sixth class in skill.

A second class probably could have them all laughing. Dad would have had them at least fighting off the gloom by randomly bursting into song. But me, I just took off the edge. Nobody went crazy.

That's all Valdez asked from me, anyway.

Derik, after two days of oblivion, had healed enough to switch him to something that didn't make him incoherent. He was still in pain, but it wasn't excruciating. The driver had to be dosed for the ride, one of the others taking over for him. We all got moved around to better accommodate the injured, with me stuck between Derik and the ex-driver. I put the latter to sleep before we started.

Tck-tck... tck-tck... tck-tck... His eyes closed as his heart slowed down, and he drifted off, padded greatly by painkillers and pillows.

Derik leaned over me to look, then sat back. "That's pretty impressive," he whispered.

I shrugged, speaking in a normal voice. "Not so much. He wanted to sleep, which helps. Couldn't do it if he was fighting."

One of the other team members was watching avidly. "Can you kill someone like that? I mean, if they're already asleep, and nobody warns them or anything?"

I shook my head. "No. The body fights that by itself." I nodded to the unconscious man. "He went to sleep wanting to stay that way, so he won't wake up for a few hours, which is about as good as it gets."

Elizabeth, sitting by his head, held a palm over his shoulder, and even from where I sat the air became a touch warmer. "Like I can warm him up, but he won't overheat. Third class could make a spark on a piece of lint and burn a person with that, but not burn skin directly; and second could definitely get a good-sized fire within a minute or so from seasoned wood, but even green wood has too much life in it to burn for less than a first class."

I noticed a bunch of the others were discreetly watching us. "Magic that can kill always takes a first class," I reassured them. "And those are all watched by the government. Except the ones the Feds employ directly, that is, which is most of them anyway." I poked Derik's impressive bicep. "How about yours? How can a strength Power kill someone?" If there were first-class strength Powers, it was possible.

He snorted. "Punching them in the face."

I rolled my eyes. "*Without* touching them. You know, just by Power."

Scratching at the edge of his bandage, he explained. "Strength is all about increasing physical ability. A high Power could improve muscle ability past the body's ability to handle it, and give someone a heart attack. I make one or two people gain muscle just a little faster when I exercise with them, which makes things like weight training and endurance building easier. Until you reach third class, it's just variations on how much more quickly your work-out partner develops versus how much effort you put in yourself, and how many people you can affect at a time. A third class can make a muscle develop on its own, without exercise. With a second class strength Power, you can create lingering effects that last a few hours after you stop focusing, and by the time you get to first, you're able to create muscle so fast it can outpace the body's ability to compensate. There's actually a bunch of cases of first-class strength Powers accidentally killing people, when they don't get proper training."

"Wow," Elizabeth said. "Didn't realize that. How come I've never heard of it on the news?"

He stared at the rear exit of the transport. "Most of us get tossed straight into government training, these days," he said. "First-class strength Powers are pretty popular. Heck, anything above fifth class usually ends up in the army, at least. That's why we're known for being the jarheads of the world. Not a ton of choice in the matter, if you've got any considerable ability."

"You sound like you're glad to be a sixth," I noted.

He grunted. It sounded like a *yeah*-grunt.

"Don't Powers usually run in families?" one of the others asked suddenly.

I nodded, as Derik's expression didn't waver, or his gaze leave the door.

"Sometimes," I noted, "Powers get stronger or weaker over generations."

"Oh."

We dropped the subject.

#

The other team picked Stone up mid-morning during one of our rest stops. We waved them off and kept heading down.

We reached the edge of the Tide by noon, taking a back road that the powers-that-be thought might be less blocked than the highway. A stretch of US-82 just past the Mississippi-Alabama border had been jammed when the Tides had hit. The driverless traffic sat stopped both ways. Most caravans drove on the side of the road for the two miles southeast, but we hoped our route would provide a smoother trip.

The small town where we stopped had a bank, so of course we were salvaging it. There were three registered houses in the town, too, that we'd hit after the bank. We'd seen one on the way that we were going to go back to. The garden had been overflowing with plants, winter-dead vines spilling out into the road and window boxes sagging on weakened sills, threatening to drop blue rosemary bushes into the bare golden branches of a hydrangea. I couldn't look at it for very long, but that was okay, because we'd passed by quickly.

Derik's good hand slid around my waist to rest on my lower back. I shot him a warning look. He withdrew it. "Small towns are the worst," he said.

A dog was watching us from under a row of overgrown pink hedges, a light dusting of snow perched on the branches. *Hatter-patter-potter*, the floating voices muttered. The restaurant behind him stared at us through empty, dark windows, tables with long-decayed food still waiting for customers who would never return to finish. *Andi's Diner*, the sign read, all faded paint and dead neon lights.

"Yeah," I agreed, leaning into his warmth, and this time ignoring it when his arm crept back up over my shoulders. "Didn't think it was supposed to get cold enough to snow, this far down. I mean, Carolina, sure. But Alabama?"

His chest rumbled with a low chuckle. "It *is* winter."

"In the *South*." I heard his damn smile. "Shut up."

"What? Need a calendar?"

He made a very satisfying *umph* when I elbowed him in the stomach.

"Okay, lovebirds!" Valdez called from the drill. "Get your butts in gear. Derik, you're on vault duty for money-packing. Music lady—"

"Safety deposit boxes. I know, I know."

I was toting another orphan bag to the loading crew when I heard them. *Nimble-ninny, no-no-lollipop, so-long-cherrytop,* they sang, in a tone unlike any other I'd heard before.

"That's the face I make when diarrhea hits," Elizabeth remarked. "What's up?"

Flittering, fluttering, singing and diving, the butterflies dodged into the street from around a corner.

We all froze. Valdez waved the team members back. Kaufermann, closest to the rabble, backed up slowly.

A hand touched my elbow. I looked up. Elizabeth was watching the butterflies carefully. "Don't run," she whispered, her fingers edging me away.

We steered ourselves into the bushes. A *rustle* spoke of the dog's retreat.

Chinkle-winkle-love-and-song, blog-and-fog-and-lovely-log. The song chased us as the butterflies spun our way, drawn by the running of the Lost.

"Go inside," she whispered when the door hit our backs.

I nodded. The door chimed as I slid inside. I turned, expecting her to follow. Instead, the door closed under the weight of her back, her fingers waving me further in as she guarded the entrance.

The bright blues and pretty golds of fluttering wings swirled around her. I saw her shoulder blades press against the glass. *Swallowsong, love so long, drive us dreaming with a whip, dovetail waters not so swift.* I expected to hear a scream, or a horrified gasp, or something. But she stood and bore it, and moments later, the rabble danced on.

Elizabeth's shoulders slumped in relief.

"You okay?" I asked through the door.

She nodded. "Fine. Dandy."

Her weight was keeping me from coming out. I tapped gently, not wanting to attract the butterflies back as they circled across the street. "They're over there now," I noted.

"You're fine. Just explore the place until they're well and truly gone." She sounded weary.

I worried my lip, not wanting to leave. But she was right—she was fine, and Doc was sitting in the Team's eyes as they glanced our way. I waved and gave a thumb's up.

The marble floor of the diner gave my footsteps back to me, no patrons to cover the noise and only plastic seats and chrome stools to soften it. A cracked bowl lay half under the abandoned bar, pale ceramic glowing softly in the light from the windows, and a plastic-coated menu sat on the counter. I scanned it and swallowed hard. They'd served gumbo and bacon-cooked collards. Oh, and hushpuppies. Damn, when was the last time I'd had a good hushpuppy?

One of the curtains fluttered softly, and I shivered. It was cold in here. Really cold.

I went into the kitchen. I'd never been on this side of a commercial kitchen before. The stoves were on my right, mammoth machines made to serve hundreds. Knives and bowls and pans lay scattered about, dropped mid-motion. An apron on a hook swayed gently as the air stirred, and bones wrapped in leathery muscle sat on one of the counters. Even without wildlife to carry off the meat, three years were more than enough to decay the food into nothingness.

Scolding-water, mommy-potter, dropped-my-knees-in-the-fodder, voices sang. Suddenly, I was glad to be inside. Elizabeth was right—better wait until they were well and truly gone.

Clang. I jumped and spun. The Lost from earlier, the dog, sniffed at the pan he'd knocked over. "You scared me," I said, kneeling and offering my hand. "How'd you get in here?"

Solid-pollid-polsky, he whispered, hesitantly approaching. His cold nose nudged my fingers, and the numbness spread up my arm as I scratched his ear. *Powered woman*, he said. *Butterflies like Powered. Wish you could hear. Butterflies talk so much. Nice hands. Miss hands. Back door open. They come in. So annoying.*

His ear fell away from my hand. I was slowly standing, my eyes tracing past him, my feet taking me morbidly around the corner to a wash basin. The room grew dark as the rectangle of light—not a window after all—filled with tiny, winged bodies.

Then they were there, in my hair, on my face, clinging to my clothes. *Die, want to die, want to die,* the voices sang, thousands of them, all at once, deeper in my head than any others. *My children – momma – my babies – MY FAMILY –*

THE DRILLS. THE DRILLS. STOP THEM. STOP THE DRILLS!

The scream burned behind my eyes, a man's scream from a shattered voice, clawing through my temples and scraping at the inside of my skull. I crammed my fingers into my ears and squeezed my eyes and lips shut, and a face flashed through my mind, wide ice-blue eyes pleading in a skin-covered skull. Chains glared silver in a dark room, blue-black water surrounding me on all sides, and Power flooded into my skull, more than I had ever imagined, fizziness turning into a frothing, raging waterfall inside my head.

STOP THEM!

Pain. Searing and burning, the fizz of high-voltage magic like acid separating my skin from my bones, pushing against the backs of my eyes. Blue lights shaped like butterflies danced in the oily water, and a woman's high-pitched scream ripped through my head, one I vaguely recognized.

Then the water wavered into transparency, and a silver lunch counter and bowls strewn over the floor appeared through the flickering light of retreating blue wings, and that loudest voice faded into a din of pleas and begging. *Help! My babies – Where are – Help!*

Lovely-coconuts-wild-river, solid-armoire-and-silver-mail. I gasped through a burning throat and felt the sting of cold marble burning my knees through my jeans, once again alone in my head.

A cold nose nudged my side. I looked down to see the dog beside me. His eyes were deep, but his voice – thankfully silent.

I tried to say something. My mouth flapped. "The drills," I whispered. And then I started shivering.

The Lost nudged me once more, and wandered off.

Elizabeth ran in seconds later to find me still kneeling on the floor, shaking with cold. "Kelly!"

"The back door is open," I murmured, still putting my brain back together, leaning into the warmth radiating from her hands. "Stop the drills, okay?"

"Oh, god." Quick, heavy footsteps. "Valdez, in here!"

There was a torn wing stuck to my hand. I flexed my fingers. The wing dropped free of the butterfly goo and fell to the ground. "I think I killed one," I said distantly as heavier feet echoed over the kitchen tiles. It must have happened when I'd covered my ears. I looked up.

"Still with us, music lady?" His features were harsh, guarded, shadowed in the lightless kitchen, the golden skin at the edge of his eyes striped with tiny wrinkles.

I nodded, clutching my ringing head. "They were really loud," I told him.

"Shit!" I saw Valdez suddenly lunge at me, felt Elizabeth pulling hard on my arm. I wondered what was wrong with them. Was gravity not working for them, either?

Chapter Seven

I woke up a couple of hours later, a vague ache rolling in the back of my head. Wedging my eyes open was tolerable, though, so I left them that way. The gray sky above me was dark with the onset of night.

Blond hair usurped my field of vision. "Gah!" I gasped.

"You're up," Derik stated. His hand touched my cheek. He looked tired. "You okay, Kel?"

My heart tried to leap out of my ribs, so I pressed it back down with a hand to my chest. "If you don't terrify me like that," I grumbled.

Immediately, his shoulders loosened and lines disappeared from his face. "From now on, you're staying by the truck." A large hand stroked a strand of hair out of my eyes.

I glared up at him from my sleeping bag. "Not your decision."

"No, Valdez's. Orders, Kel." The way he said it, *follow orders* might be the Eleventh Commandment.

"Derik, I mean it. I'm not just sitting out."

He smiled, his teeth white and shiny. "Of course not. We've got truck duty."

I levered myself into a sitting position on the park bench, glaring at the hovering man at my side and pressing my temple in hopes it would make the dull throb in my head go away. Despite that, my stomach felt hollow and empty. "Food?"

Derik produced one of our MREs. "How about some nice cheese tortellini? Camp special. It's about as close as you'll get to good grits these days." He laughed at my raised eyebrow. "Never let it be said that I don't feed you right."

"You *don't* feed me," I grumbled, accepting the pack and ripping it open. I firmly ignored his smug grin.

"Hey, look who's up." Elizabeth leaned over the back of the bench to watch me stab a cheesy noodle from the bag.

I raised the spork in salute as I chewed.

"Funny," Elizabeth said, glancing from Derik to me. "I seem to remember this going the other way." She ripped another MRE she'd brought with her and held it out to him.

He wiggled the fingers on his injured hand. "I'll be back to new in no time. Strength Power, remember?" Taking the bag, he balanced it between his knees and used his teeth to unwrap a spork.

The roll of her eyes told me she'd forgotten that. "Yeah, yeah, muscle generation and regeneration and all that. Get her back on her feet, since you're so resilient yourself."

He made a face. "Trying."

I waved my spork at them both. "This girl can take care of herself."

She watched me closely for a moment through her long lashes, dark eyes serious and steady. Surreptitiously, I probed my teeth with my tongue, trying to figure out what she was looking at. With a sigh that sounded vaguely relieved, she rubbed the side of her face, and turned her gaze on Derik. "Glad you're okay, Kel."

She must have figured I'd gone nuts. Although, considering her last encounter with butterflies, maybe she did have a reason.

Derik raised a noodle-on-a-spork to defend against her staring. "Eating," he said. "You don't have to watch." Sticking it in his mouth and then pulling it out empty, he waved the utensil at her.

With a mock salute, she sauntered off, raising a hand to Valdez in passing.

The rest of the group welcomed me with similar expressions of veiled relief. I was settled by the fire when Louis, the guy I'd talked down a few days ago, joined me.

"Hey, Kel," he said, sprawling on the log beside me, opposite Derik and Elizabeth. Most of the Team had been taking turns in the spot. "Got a trophy for you."

"A trophy?"

He nodded, fishing around his breast pocket. "You survived the butterflies, right? Makes you smarter than Doc, so I figured you get a trophy for it."

I snorted. "You mean, less powerful? Sure." I saw something glitter, a thin wafer on a silver chain. He pooled it into my hand.

Elizabeth cursed and knocked it away.

A silver-blue wing gleamed in the fire pit before disappearing in a *puff* of flame.

"You idiot!" she scolded Louis. "Didn't you listen to my story *at all*? You want the Hunters coming after Kelly-girl here?"

I looked at the hand that had squashed the butterfly. In the firelight, I couldn't tell what it had done. Could they?

"I'm s-sorry," Louis stammered. "I didn't think—"

"No! You didn't!"

I turned, smiling. "It's okay," I said to Elizabeth. "It was an accident. I'm going to bed now."

Nothing bothered me that night.

#

Valdez ordered me to stay with Derik in the truck during his shift. I was fine, but I figured it would give the others peace of mind, so I did. Derik locked us in the cab, about as relaxed as a gym-jock used to eight hours of powerlifting a day could be during an enforced idle.

"Hands-off." I smacked the hand that was creeping across the seat.

"Just reaching for the water bottle," he lied, grabbing his drink and retreating.

My lips pursed against the smile that tried to break out. "Sure thing, Casanova."

That got a wounded-puppy look. "Doubtin' my honor?" He gave me his best Valdez impression.

I snickered. It brought a grin to his face. That brought a grin to mine. Maybe, I thought, maybe flirting with him was okay. Maybe it would be okay to let him woo me.

Maybe I wouldn't have to lose him, too.

"You're a lot easier to take care of sober," I jibed.

"That's not fair," he pouted. "You're easier to take care of unconscious, but I like you better awake."

"Do you remember anything of the mall?"

"Sure. I woke up one night with you snuggling up to me. But you left." His fingers twitched.

I stilled them with a stern glare. "You couldn't keep your hands off my waist, something about stopping my—my organs from escaping. I've never seen anyone so fascinated by a muffin top."

His fierce frown scolded me. "You have gorgeous hips. And you don't have a muffin top."

I shifted away from the finger pointed at my least-enviable features. "Weird hip fetish, I knew it."

He sighed. "Kel... Look. I'm a strength Power. So are my mom and my sister and all my aunts. You know what strength Powers look like, right?"

Since some of the biggest supermodels were minor strength Powers, I'd go with *yes*. They all had perfect figures; toned abs, sleek stomachs, not an ounce of extra fat. He correctly interpreted my look of *duh*.

His hand moved to my cheek. "It's really hard for strength Powers to keep extra weight on. Even sixth classes, and it's relatively easy for me. We've all got low body fat, but there's a reason normal women have a higher fat percentage than men. A lot of high-powered strength Powers become infertile, or have trouble having kids. My sister was devastated when she found out she could never get pregnant. She always wanted kids, but she was a second, like Dad."

Come to think of it, I remembered a history teacher lecturing about the collapse of Sparta, with such a high percentage of strength Powers for its time period, and how their population decline had been a major factor in their destruction. There'd never been a successful warrior-leader after that, either. "Didn't realize that." The flesh of my upper arm under my thumb was still softer than I would have liked.

He sighed. "Most women don't." And then his hand dropped down to my stomach, cupping the bulge at the edge of my waistband. "For the record, I think this is beautiful, the most beautiful part of a woman's body. It's healthy."

My face flamed. He pulled his hand away, but not his body. His eyes made me think of diving through an underwater forest, so very green and alive, so very airless.

Maybe it was the South after all—it was getting pretty warm in here. "C'mon," I said. "Let's take a walk."

He grabbed my arm. "Don't!"

"What?" My other hand rested on the door handle. "The butterflies are gone, Derik, and we're in the middle of the group. It's not like we're going off on our own or anything."

He glanced out the window and back. "We're on truck duty," he argued weakly. "Besides, Valdez—"

"Will understand the need to stretch our legs. Who do you expect to break in? Thieves looking for loot ever make it this far in?"

"It's deserting the post. You want to get court martialed?" If he had been able to meet my gaze, I might have believed it.

As it was, I rolled my eyes and cracked the door. "We're civilians, and if Valdez actually cares about having someone guard the truck, we'll turn around."

He cursed and followed suit.

The sergeant did send us a sharp look, but that turned into a grin when I wrapped my arm around Derik's and circled a finger in the air. Valdez waved a hand with a wink.

We walked through the others without interrupting them, keeping to the middle of the group. I can't say that Derik quite clung to me, but a Navy SEAL might have been less alert. On the other hand, it did finally let him achieve his goal of getting his arm around me.

We made it back to our post in one piece, surprisingly enough. He grabbed the door handle to my side. "Trying to put me up?" I asked.

His eyebrows waggled, and he spun me around. "Just keeping the lady safe," he said, putting himself between me and the rest of the world.

I rolled my eyes, but let him play knight. We might be on the edge of the group, but Valdez had posted lookouts after the rabid Lost. Nothing Mad would be getting close without a good warning.

The door *clicked*, and that's when I heard it... *Sa-sa, sa-sa, sa-sa.* I froze, grabbing Derik's wrist.

"Back... away... from the door..." I whispered.

His eyes were wide. I must have gone pale, because he nudged me away with his injured arm. I took a step to the side—

The door slammed open, knocking him over. I screamed.

Hind legs soared over Derik, hit the ground, and spun. Fangs bared in an long muzzle like a dog's, with a tiger's muscle in a greyhound's emaciated-looking body, and long legs ended in massive cat-like paws with claws no shorter than my own fingers. Valdez yelled something. I heard a gunshot, but it was already moving, circling us.

"Hey!" Elizabeth's voice sliced across from the other side of the truck. She held a squirrel in her hand by the back of the neck.

"No!" I shouted, but she'd already started running, and a snarling flash of fur ripped past us after her. Someone screamed. Derik lunged at it, but landed face-down over inch-deep claw marks in the dirt. Could I throw something at it, run after it, scream at it? Too many things I wanted to do, fear a fire in me, and all I could managed was three steps in that direction before it reached her.

The squirrel hit the ground and rolled to a stop against a tree stump, limp but blinking rapidly. A scream, maybe me, maybe one of the others. Elizabeth's shriek bounced as it dragged her over the ground by her leg between a pair of soldiers, her shoulder trailing red. One man leapt forward as the other dodged back, but she was already past their reach anyway. She grabbed up a stick off the ground and jammed it into the creature's side, pulled it out and hit it again. The creature didn't even stumble.

Another pump of a gun, and a spray of dirt into the air.

Dashing in that direction, I scanned the ground for a weapon, and scooped up a stick of my own. I dodged around the truck, but they disappeared behind a building almost as soon as I saw them.

Derik swore, not two steps behind me. There was a growing red spot on the bandage around his wrist, which he held his hand over as he ran after them. Valdez passed us before we got to the alleyway.

There was nothing there but a bloody streak and a torn patch of cloth. Derik knelt, grabbing the cloth and looking around.

I crouched beside him, tearing my eyes away from the bloody streak, and pressed my palm against his sopping red bandage.

It was just like she'd described it — a Hunter.

Shaking, I searched for a sign of movement. Nothing, no eyes watching us. We were alone.

I cried.

Chapter Eight

Derik had split a couple of stitches in the fall, but the medic got him patched up. The rest of us were much more concerned about Elizabeth and the Hunter. Echoes of Valdez's shouts carried to the Team as he squared off with someone over the phone, pacing around camp. When he wandered by, hand yanking on his dog tags and rifle slung across his back, I got a coherent whiff of the conversation. "So send someone else. I'm not leaving until we find her!"

Not surprisingly, he confined Derik and me to the truck. Derik agreed that he was going to stay crammed into the back, under lock and key, until we got back to Wisconsin. I didn't disagree. This wouldn't have happened if we'd stayed in the truck. But Valdez wouldn't even ream me out about it. For some reason he didn't think it was my fault; he seemed to blame himself, as if letting us go on a walk made it his responsibility. It'd been my idea, damn it.

"It's not fair," I argued, bracing my feet on the lip of my seat and resting my chin on my knees. "It was supposed to go after *me*.

It only attacked her after she grabbed one of the Lost. What if it goes after someone else?"

"Guess that's our sign to leave." He slumped into a seat beside me. "Pack up and hit the first truck north. Unless you want to head out alone?" His lunch sat uneaten, unopened, in the corner.

Leave was right. But not in a way that could get anyone else hurt, especially not him. I shook my head. "We'll stick to the group. I don't want those things catching you without backup."

Letting his head fall back against the wall of the truck, he pulled his sleeve over the bandage and played with the fasteners. "It wasn't angry about the bear, though. At least, it didn't come after me for that."

I dropped my feet to the floor and said, "You were also in the cab."

His withering glare could have killed all of Central Park. "It was in the passenger side." My side.

"You opened the passenger side first," I pointed out, because being the devil's advocate might get him home, get him safe. "How do you know it wasn't in the driver's seat?"

Valdez popped his head into the back. "We're headin' out. Get your asses ready. And by that, music lady, I mean keep your pretty head in the truck. And eat something, both of you." Then he was gone again.

He hadn't been able to finagle us time for searching. We were to go east along I-20 and US-238, and probably outpace the Hunter by days of rapid foot travel. Fifteen minutes into the trip, Valdez began to swear, a steady litany of curses that kept up a good five minutes. No one spoke after that, but I wasn't the only one shaking, or with a wet face. We drove a good three hours that evening before stopping to make camp.

I let Derik into the back of the convoy truck without argument. "Locked doors in a truck won't keep you safe," he said, "but I'll do what I can." Not that all the doors were locked. The air was too thick with stale magic to be completely closed in.

I might have argued, but he chose that moment to take his shirt off, and my line of thinking pretty much stalled in its tracks. The smooth grooves of muscle that disappeared beneath his waistband drew my gaze and wouldn't let it go, and my skin felt electrified, heat building inside me. What was wrong with me? Damn hormones; they didn't use to do that. But his hands on me would feel like heaven; I wanted to taste him, skim him with my tongue.

And I was a cold-hearted monster for even letting that cross my mind now. *Shock,* a distant part of me realized. *Not healthy, not a way to fix anything.* Another person gone.

I'd liked her. Elizabeth had been fun, quirky; I had thought we might keep in touch after getting home. But she'd been taken. She'd died because she knew me. Why did everyone keep dying? I closed my eyes and covered my face, breathing deeply. Only it came out as a sob.

He knelt beside me and wrapped his arms around me. "I'm sorry."

I shook my head. "You couldn't have stopped it." That was my responsibility.

The lines at the corners of his eyes and the purse of his lips told me he didn't believe me. Guilt. But there really wasn't anything he could have done, any more than Trax could have saved Mom and Dad by dying himself. *Even he wanted to leave me.* No. Trax had been grieving; he'd never wanted to leave me behind, hadn't really wanted to die. From his recaps of the things he'd talked about with his therapist, it was my shock talking, focusing my grief inward instead of coping.

But knowing better didn't stop the hurt. I wiped my cheek with back of my wrist and shook my head. "Don't blame yourself. I'm the one who killed the butterfly."

He sucked in a breath, and nodded. "My group therapy leader said the same thing once."

"That he killed a butterfly?"

A snort. "That I can't save everyone."

A shadow moved outside the tent we'd duct-taped over the open back of the truck. Valdez's voice came through. "Kelly-girl, I'm sendin' Derik to keep you company tonight. No arguments; that's an order."

Derik rubbed his eyes and winked at me with a weak smile. "Yes, sir!" he answered.

The sergeant cursed, unzipped the flap, and stuck his head in. "No playin' around, got that?"

"I think I can keep him in line," I drawled.

Valdez nodded and walked off, like that was that.

Derik kept me company in the aisle between the seats, snuggling his sleeping bag against mine. "You can trust me to keep you safe," he said, spooning his bag around me. "Anything that gets in here, goes through me first."

I just nodded, and said nothing. Strength Power didn't stop wounds from happening, not at any level. If the Hunters wanted me, they wouldn't hesitate to kill him. And I doubted they'd let themselves be distracted again.

If I wanted to keep him safe, I should give them what they wanted. There was a way to keep everyone safe, and as soon as they were all asleep, I could do it. This time, I could save everyone.

Voices murmured incoherently through my head, a chorus of songs and chirps and babble that had me tossing and turning between droplets of sleep. There was a dream that involved a grasshopper joining me for afternoon tea. "I don't suppose you could find me a Hunter, could you?" I asked, pouring a cup for the half-exploded bear beside her. It would be much easier if a Hunter came to me than if I had to sneak out of camp to find one. Then I opened my eyes, and there was in fact a grasshopper standing on my hand. She jumped off and away before I could say anything else.

It was the hour of the night when the darkness was so complete, morning seemed impossible. I heard the beat of Derik's sleeping heart: *sa-sa... sa-sa... sa-sa...* Letting my senses drift, to outside the truck, I heard more, the sleepers in their tents, the guards wandering around. And farther out, past the edge of camp in the city itself, a different heartbeat: *sa-sa, sa-sa, sa-sa.*

A Hunter. I don't know how I knew; I just did. And I thought, *It's time. Before they come for me.*

Extricating myself from Derik's sleeping form without waking him was a slow and careful process, but staying wasn't an option. I could wake him, and he would try to come with me, try to protect me. It would be so easy, just make an accidental noise.

I could let them come to me, and expect the guards to protect me. Could let men die to keep me safe.

No more Elizabeths. It was time for people to stop dying.

I slithered free and grabbed my shoes, not putting them on because noise they might make. Derik slept on. Reaching out, I *listened*, heard the guards' hearts moving around, waited until two of them drifted apart.

Swallowing, I slid through the bottom of our jury-rigged privacy screen.

Two of the in-camp lookouts were side-by-side, keeping a close eye on what appeared to be silvery shapes moving in the distance—deer? Their positioning left a gap in coverage that I aimed for, although how long it would last I didn't know. Had to move quickly. I slid through the tents without a whisper of sound. My bare feet, numbed by the bite of frost-laden ground, managed not to betray me to my companions. A tent inches from my feet rumbled with a whistling snore, uninterrupted by my passage.

It would be so easy to stumble. But this was my responsibility. No one else was going to get hurt because of me.

I ducked into a folded hill, a small dip in the park that hid a stream. To avoid being seen by the perimeter guards, I crawled on hands and knees through an old storm drain, the earth devouring the warmth from my limbs.

The trickle of water running through ancient concrete dampened the knees of my jeans, and the unpleasant chill became a sharp pain of cold.

I emerged on the other side of a street, the slope of the ground concealing me from camp. "Can't believe I actually succeeded," I muttered. Sneaking out of a guarded camp wasn't something I'd expected to be good at. But keeping people in wasn't the focus; keeping things out was.

I glanced back only once, as I took the time to shove my feet into my sneakers. My fingers were too numb to tie the laces, so I left them as they were.

It crossed my mind to wonder if I'd get to find out first-hand what happened to Elizabeth.

Barely a block into the suburban streets I found it. A pair of wiry-haired ears perked forward, and a few too many teeth grinned at me from a long, narrow snout. Large, dark eyes watched me through long eyelashes that would form a perfect shield from splattering blood, with no indication of mercy or emotion. It could rip me apart in a breath.

"I think you were looking for me." Holding out a trembling hand, I waited.

The jaw gaped into a grin, opening wider than I thought possible, wide enough it could fit my whole head if it so chose. My feet got in my own way and I bumped into a lamp post behind me, unable to see anything but those teeth. I couldn't do this. I couldn't—The whimper that came out of my throat choked all the thoughts out of my head, and I couldn't bear to look anymore, had to close my eyes.

Then a cold nose pressed into one of my palms. *Yes. We'd prepared to fetch you. This makes it easier, though. Follow,* it ordered.

The beast, as tall as a mastiff, a murdering machine with tiger stripes down its back, stood watching me without ripping me to shreds. I raised my hand to my chest and took a deep breath, feeling humiliation burn through me.

It impaled me with a sharp glance before turning and sauntering down the street. I considered running, or screaming. Then I thought about it again, thought of everyone in camp, listened to the steady *sa-sa, sa-sa, sa-sa* of its unlabored heartbeat.

I could do this. I had to do this. Everyone in camp would be safe because I did. So I began to jog after it, through a dead and empty city.

The exercise warmed some of the chill out, but not enough to banish the ache. So I was almost relieved when I saw a fire and a change of clothes. Wait, how were there clothes waiting, when it hadn't been expecting me?

Then I noticed the others.

Two Hunters waited beside the small trash-can fire. My guide nudged the backs of my now-frozen thighs. *Go. Change. Warm yourself. No death now, Kelly.*

I have heard more comforting phrases in my life. *"Give me all your money,"* comes to mind. The fact that it knew my name? My stomach churned, and I thought again about running the other way.

But the new Hunters weren't watching me at all, and I was very, very cold.

My fetcher waited until my shivering body was sufficiently close to the fire before moving to join the others. I did not doubt it was continuing to watch me, although its eyes were elsewhere.

The pile of clothes still bore tags on them, a gut-wrenching relief to me. They didn't fit perfectly, but they were warm, and the itch of slightly-stale fabric was much less uncomfortable than the ice of my newer, better-fitting, wet clothes. The leather gloves, at least, were a decent fit, even if biker gloves weren't my typical style. I stuck them in a pocket for the time being; the heat of the fire felt good on my knuckles.

An old flip-lighter beside the trash can answered a question I didn't dare ask. I glanced at the fire itself—trash, mostly, some paper and shattered pieces of wood. This was not the first time this can had housed a fire, either. A sun-bleached and well-frayed sleeping bag sat in a corner, tied in a roll with shoestring. Tucked under a plastic tarp were a pair of shoes and an open aluminum can, the label faded past all recognition.

Once, the homeless had gathered here. Now a raccoon crouched in an upended, rusty garbage can, eyes flashing in the firelight, watching the Hunters with a focus I hadn't seen on any other Lost. When I blew on my hands, its head swung my way. *Middle-hay?*

One of the Hunters spared a second to sneer at it.

Taking a shoe in its mouth, the raccoon scurried away.

I wondered if it considered the Tides an improvement, and decided not.

By the way their heads and eyes moved, the Hunters had to be talking in some fashion, but the ever-present chatter of the Lost was absent. The only sound I got from them was the beating of their hearts, and that was as steady as ever, unruffled and calm. How long, I wondered, until they decided to kill me? What did they want from me?

The memory of Elizabeth's scream made me shiver harder, and I bit the back of my hand, breathing deeply to quiet the urge to vomit. It didn't settle my stomach much, though.

When I was thoroughly warm, two of them disappeared. The third—the one who had brought me here, because it had a lighter coat—stared at me expectantly. I followed it.

The old pickup truck sat abandoned beside an equally empty house, a pile of expensive junk in the bed. I stared at the open door, at the keys on the seat. This truck hadn't been here long—

the rust of Tide-washed vehicles didn't mark the doors and wheels. It probably even still worked.

"The drivers?"

The Huntress grinned at me.

Two light *thuds* announced the other pair hopping into the bed of the truck. The lightest one just kept looking up at me.

I shook my head, stepping back.

Three pairs of eyes stared at me without remorse or forgiveness.

Someone—someone who was now *dead*—had driven that truck. I took another step back.

The Huntress growled.

I froze.

How useful was I, if I didn't give them what they wanted? And, I had killed one of the Lost. I wasn't sure they cared it was an accident.

Ants crept up my skin as I realized what I was going to do. "Oh, god," I groaned, and lost the fight with my stomach. Then, wiping my mouth, shaking and swallowing against the awful taste of bile, I climbed into the driver's seat of the truck.

The Huntress circled the truck and let herself in to the other seat. I watched the door open, watched her flow in, watched the door close, and still couldn't believe the utter lack of sound that accompanied her actions. The magic of these Hunters just *absorbed* the noise.

She curled up like a cat on a seat and placed a careful paw on my thigh. *Forward*, she said, and I realized for the first time that I was thinking of her as a female. Her voice felt muffled through my jeans, and although it was still deep and harsh, with the edges blunted it struck me as distinctly feminine.

I tore my eyes off the Huntress and grabbed the keys. My body shuddered violently; my stomach nearly emptied itself again. I bit my arm, and the urge to dry-heave quieted. When I could breathe again, I put the keys in the ignition and turned the car on.

Thank goodness it was an automatic transmission.

After the first ten minutes of driving through an empty city, I stopped thinking about it, the fear burning itself into a brainless numbness. I just went *right, left, stay straight*, following the terse instructions given me, dodging potholes and rusty cars. We headed due south.

We stopped off US-231 in a small town called Rockford. There I discovered to my great astonishment that gas had not decayed at the same rate as everything else stuck in the Tides. The abandoned tanker loomed above me, a large block on the road that had miraculously rolled to a stop without overturning or running off the road.

"How, exactly, am I to do this?" I asked, holding the small red container in my left hand and rolling a large plastic barrel with my foot.

Fill the barrel, the Huntress said, *and fill the gas can from the barrel. Use the gas can to fill the truck.*

I had the sudden feeling that the males in the back of the truck were snickering at me. I glanced over my shoulder. They were.

An hour later, the tank and all the spare cans in the truck bed were full.

Montgomery, AL sat right on the edge of the Tide. I was afraid we'd end up in the Tide itself, that they were planning on resigning me to the same fate as the Lost, but we swung sideways to run parallel to the Edge. We passed through subdivisions of white-painted houses, half the roofs stucco and half tile, and streets lined with leafless blue trees. Papers fluttered abandoned in the streets; a pair of faded pink rollerblades sat propped against an empty wrought-iron park bench. Once, we passed a pride of housecats lolling on a skateboard ramp, the light of dawn giving them cougar-sized shadows. They watched us pass by, and a few of them jogged after us until we drove out of sight.

Eventually, the Huntress gave me one final turn to the left. *Stop here*, she said. There was a *scrape* announcing one of the males leaping off the truck.

I looked up at the water tower we faced. "You've got to be kidding me."

Her fanged grin said she wasn't.

With a sigh, I let myself out and allowed the two remaining Hunters to herd me toward the tower.

The rungs of the fallen ladder looked more than a little rusty, paint peeling back in large patches. "Are you sure there isn't an easier way to do this?"

One of the males snickered, his grin showing many long teeth.

I sighed, and started climbing. At least they'd seen fit to give me gloves.

About halfway up, I realized that Derik's presence had significantly improved my endurance without my knowing it. Since he had a limited number of people he could focus on at a single time, I was surprised he'd bothered. But I wasn't an athlete. I shouldn't have been able to work my way up a 100-ft rusty ladder without help.

The Hunters climbing up below me didn't count as help.

Finally, I dragged my panting, trembling self onto the narrow walkway encircling the tank. Slipping off the gloves, I tried to massage the cramps out of my palms.

The Huntress gave me a dirty look through her long lashes as she slid around my feet, still flopped over the ladder. Her compatriot wasn't so subtle — a quick nip at my foot convinced me to roll out of the way. The male levered himself through the opening, snickering at my prone form.

"Screw you," I grumbled. "I don't do ladders."

His fanged grin forgave the insult, but only at my expense.

They waited as patiently as Hunters could for me to regain my breath. And considering that they were Hunters, that meant I lay panting under the intense observation of two predators on the cusp of a silent, deadly pounce. I recovered my breath long before I actually recovered my breath.

"Kay," I said, sitting up. "I'm good." My arms trembled slightly in protest.

The other side of the water tower sat only a few feet away from the edge of the Tide. The Huntress placed her front paws on the rail and looked out. I joined her and edged a hand out, as close as I dared, until she closed the gap with her paw. "What did you bring me here to see?"

Look.

I did.

Light distorted, shifted, inverted and spun. The Tide was a giant soap bubble, colors and shapes and images, pure translucency overlaying another world. I saw cars roll by, and crowds mill, and a woman screaming as she ran from something I couldn't see. I saw a child playing hopscotch, and a house burning down.

"I don't get it," I said. "I don't know what I'm looking at."

She looked over her shoulder at something. I turned.

The third Hunter had come back and made his way up the tower without letting me know. His fangs were surprisingly gentle as their cradled their still-fluttering prize. I would have backed away, but a soft *chuff* beside ordered me to stay.

I almost ran anyway. But I was more afraid of the Hunters — just barely — than I was of that butterfly.

Hands, the Huntress ordered.

They were quite willing to wait until I gathered the courage to obey. I was only human, after all. The male held it by a wing as I cautiously caged it between my palms.

It fluttered and dashed itself against my cupped hands, wiggling for escape. There were no voices in my head. I started to assume that a single insect did little harm —

Then, the Hunter let go.

Not my baby. Not my heart. I want my baby. I want, I want, I want my baby. Stay away. Run away —

I saw a flicker of blue light, a reflection of a butterfly-shaped light shimmering on black water, a black iron shackle clasping the wrist of a skeletal arm covered with a veneer of flesh. The hand twisted and pulled against the shackle, and the thought it might belong to something still living horrified me.

LOOK. The Huntress's voice shattered the vision and pulled me back to the here-and-now, cut through the chatter of the panicked flutter of the butterfly. With just one butterfly voice beating away in my head, it was bearable enough to turn and look.

Between the scattering of my thoughts, images began to form.

A woman in her mid-twenties cradled an infant in her kitchen, the marble countertops carefully clean. Her business suit hung open to accommodate the child's feeding. The soft light of a fancy lamp highlighted the clock: 5:36, it read. I assumed it was night.

A man walked in, said something, and she laughed in reply. He picked up the newspaper and began reading to her, words lost across time. I could only see the front-page article: Lorren's Oil Strikes Black Gold, it read.

Stroking the child's hairless head, she looked over the man's shoulder at the window. Eyes flying wide, she jumped back, but stumbled over a chair and fell, clutching the child to her breast and trying to shield it. Light swallowed the wall, the table, her husband. Ripples darted across the surface of the bubble, evaporating the woman whose mouth was still open in a silent scream, arms wrapped around the afterimage of an infant. The scene disappeared.

I opened my hands to let the butterfly go. She darted off, straight into the edge of the Tide, and went through. The Tide held no fear for her now.

"What was that about?"

It means nothing to you? The Huntress's eyes drilled up at me.

I shook my head.

Are you certain?

At my nod, the trio huddled together to exchange more silent glances. When one of the males stood with a red glint in his eye, I tensed. Claws gleamed in the early morning sun, and he crouched. *It's too far to jump down,* I thought, and wondered if maybe I should try anyway, because then at least I'd technically have a chance.

The Huntress shoved him aside with her shoulder and glared at him. He stared back, a full minute of staring, with them between me and the ladder. Then he ducked his head and turned around.

She stalked over and bared her teeth at me, paw pressing down on my shoe and claws sinking just far enough through the canvas to touch my foot without piercing skin. *You might not be as useful to us as we hoped, but we can still use you as a messenger, since you can at least understand us.* The subtle emphasis on *useful* and *use* sounded as if my fate rested on those words. *Tell the Teams to leave, and don't return. Their interference is not welcome any longer.*

Withdrawing the claw, she left me pressed against the rail, my knuckles against my lips and my shoulders hunched. One of the males stood and followed her.

The other waited until they were gone, and then stalked forward. I had nowhere else to back up, nowhere to go when a freezing cold nose touched mine, the smell of ozone overwhelming.

You're lucky, he said, eyes pale and grey and full of storms. *I've long forgotten mercy.* His claws screeched against metal, and I winced, cold metal of the rail digging into my back. He snickered once more. *But then, that's why she's in charge.*

And then I blinked, and he was three feet away, a canine smirk on a too-long mouth. Confused and shaking, I watched as the Hunter disappeared around the circle of the water tank.

When I got to the bottom of the water tower, they were gone. I waited for a few minutes. When they didn't show back up, I got in the truck, and drove north.

Chapter Nine

Nothing stopped me on the way back. Without my guides, I nearly got lost getting back to the highway, but it was pretty much a straight shot up US-231. I drove into the city of Stewartville, and by some miracle, managed to find the park once more, despite the haze the world around me had acquired when pure fear faded into exhaustion.

Sergeant Valdez greeted the arrival of my pickup truck with shouts, curses, and a bear-hug so hard I heard my ribs creak.

My return did what Elizabeth's disappearance hadn't: Valdez agreed to the orders to head home. He had me sit up front with him in the cab, but put Derik in charge of bringing us food. For every MRE I had, Derik would go through two, which he'd only eat with shaking hands after watching me start my own. But it was the only time anyone else was allowed near me on the way back to Memphis.

"I don't know what they wanted," I pleaded during the debriefing. "I think they wanted me for something, but I don't know what, and it seems like I wasn't as useful as they thought.

We drove to the edge of the Tide, they made me climb a water tower, I watched a family do family crap and then die, and then they let me go home. They told me to say the Recovery Teams should stop coming."

Hours of interviews turned into a week and a half. By the time I was allowed to leave the government cave they'd holed me up in, I'd been over every detail a thousand times, until I was half-positive I'd imagined the whole thing, like the soft-voiced man in a dark suit suggested before letting me go. "Maybe you're a little closer to third than you thought," he said before signing the release paper, giving me a final pat on the hand. "Anyone would have nightmares about Hunters after finding one in a truck. Take it easy for a while."

Perhaps the butterflies had driven me mad after all.

Maybe I'd fallen into the Tide, and was Lost.

Or maybe Derik and Trax had taken my sanity, now that they had me back in their tender mercies.

\#

Trax set the plate of pasta in the middle of the table beside Derik's amazing meatballs. "I'm just saying, maybe you should take a few more weeks off," my brother suggested, dark circles under his eyes. Dad's guitar was missing from the wall; its case now sat on a chair beside Trax's bed.

Derik plopped the glass of ice water beside my plate. I sulked at it.

"He's got a point," Derik said. "You said yourself that you don't get to see your brother enough. No point in wasting perfectly good leave time."

How they had become friends, I'll never know. It defied every supposed law about brothers and boyfriends I knew.

Not that Derik was my boyfriend or anything. I'd almost lost him, just when I'd started thinking dating him would be okay. Life couldn't give me a clearer sign than that, right?

"I see no reason to laze around at home," I argued. It didn't really matter. In the end, I was planning on going back to work the next day. They could vent their opinions all they wanted, if it made them feel better.

Trax twirled his fork slowly. "No one's going to comment. They're still getting compensated for your time." He shoved the noodles into his mouth to punctuate his statement.

"No, Trax." I glared at him.

"I managed to get two weeks," Trax whined, nudging a piece of garlic bread deeper into the rich, red sauce, a bracelet made of paperclips jingling with the motion. "No practice or anything, just so we could spend some time together. I was hoping you'd take me down to the lake. They said you *disappeared*."

The prongs of my fork paused on the plate. I raised an eyebrow at my twin, who looked up at me through his long dark eyelashes in the same way he'd done as a little kid, back in the coloring-table and watch-mom-work years. I'd been trying to convince him to get scuba certified since college, something we could do together without getting mobbed by fans.

"It's too cold for diving classes right now." I slammed my fork down and got up, started to stalk away, turned back long enough to grab my plate, and finished my exit.

Just because the little brat fought dirty, didn't mean I was going miss Derik's cooking. Had to get as much of it as I could while I still had the chance.

#

Sa-sa... sa-sa... sa-sa... The sound of my brother's heartbeat the next morning soothed my ears, made the new light splashing across my face almost bearable. It sounded like home.

Around ten, I fried some eggs with a dash of nutmeg, toasted some bread, and opened a can of collard greens—nothing as delicious as fresh collards, but beggars couldn't be choosers. Trax came stumbling in, rubbing his eyes, just in time for me slide a pair of plates onto the table. A cup of coffee made him coherent enough to regale me with stories from his New York tour, from the fan ambush at Fifth and Main to the new song he and the guys started based on the fortune cookies they got halfway to Boston. There was the cute red-headed singer he'd met when her band opened the Baltimore concert, whom he wished didn't live in California, and a recount of how his own band's drummer had become the official first grown-up of the group by proposing to his boyfriend. The light shows, the music, the snippy arguments on the road, the laughter, the music, the after-parties and the morning afters... my brother's world.

We ate a late lunch in a restaurant overlooking the lake. The heating bills alone must have cost a fortune, thanks to the floor-to-ceiling windows, but then again, the prices of the food more than covered it.

He took about twenty pictures of me being attacked by one of the tropical gingers surrounding our table, the worry lines at the edges of his eyes finally transforming into crinkles of laughter.

I finally stopped pretending it was throttling me when a flash outside the window caught my eye. Maybe it was just a passing car.

Or maybe it was paparazzi snapping pictures of famous Trax with his not-so-famous sister.

Concern crept back into his eyes. He must have caught a change in my expression. "What is it?"

"Food's here," I hedged, nodding to the arriving appetizers, and wishing for a moment that we hadn't been directed to the best seats of the house — the ones overlooking the lake, the little bubble in which all the famous guests were shown off to the world in exchange for a magnificent view. Trax was used to it. I never would be.

We watched the snow piling up on the ice outside, warming our mouths with ginger-laced delicacies. "Have you seen the otters?" I asked to break the quiet.

He shook his head. "My agent doesn't want me going out by myself. I brought my hat. Figured we could go check them out after we ate."

I smirked at him. "Babysitting you again. I think your agent owes me five bucks."

He rolled his eyes. "Sheesh. For a whole afternoon? Hold out for at least a twenty."

The ginger beer that almost sprayed him in the face? His own fault. Absolutely his.

His hat was a toboggan, thick and striped with the colors of the local football team. Paired with the matching sweater and sunglasses, the hat transformed Trax into just another college kid, an anonymous walker looking for exercise in the middle of a cold snap. His dark blue gloves matched the shirt hidden underneath his sweater, but nobody ever noticed gloves, anyway.

We skipped rocks across the ice of the lake, trying to reach the line where the ice turned to water. Lake Mendota was too stirred by the boat traffic to freeze over completely, even in weather like this.

"Yes!" Trax did a little victory dance as his pebble tilted over the edge with a *splash*.

I snorted. "Dork."

"You're just jealous because you throw like a girl."

I shoved him. He shoved me back. We wound up racing around the edge of the lake like maniacs, laughing and screaming like we were kids. We were gasping for breath by the time we reached Otter Point, the newly-dubbed little beach where the animals were most often seen.

Funnily enough, the McDonald's cup was still there, now frozen in a block of solid ice and half-hidden by a reflection of a Lorren's Oil sign.

Trax crowded me, eagerly searching the water. "Hear anything?"

I listened, closing my eyes to concentrate. *Shhhhhhhha* – the lake breathed. *Sa-sa sa-sa sa-sa*, Trax's heart beat. *Fwmp-fwmp-fwmp* a boat's propeller pounded. *Levy-lorry-lorraine*, a voice whispered, a voice that spoke of brown hair, chubby fingers, and cheesesteak bell peppers.

I stumbled, tripped, fell.

"Careful!" Trax ordered. "You'll scare it away!"

I opened my eyes in slow dread. The otter—small, just over two feet long—watched us from the edge of the ice. Little splashes further out suggested that it was not entirely alone.

It hoisted itself completely onto the ice and sniffed the air. Trax was kneeling. "Hey, little guy," he sang, offering his fingers.

Lily-litter-leafling, it chortled, and slid along the ice toward my brother's perfect voice.

"Don't." I grabbed my brother's hand.

It paused. Our eyes met. My throat ached.

Donna-ditty-due, it warbled, and skated closer, until its fur was within touching distance. *Dodge-derring-day*.

The wet tracks on my cheeks seared in cold fire. I shed a glove, reached out, and touched the wet fur. Ice shot up my arm.

Please, can you hear me? Please... Please remember me, Kelly.

"I can hear you," I whispered, my voice trembling. "I can understand you. Oh, god. No." And then I ran.

#

Trax caught up to me a good quarter mile down the path, back the way we'd come.

"What's wrong with you?" It was half accusing, half concerned. A worry, a plea, a dismissal.

I hugged my arms tighter around myself. "Lost," I said hollowly. "It's Lost."

My brother took a step back, rocked his weight away, and stood half-frozen with indecision. "The biologists say that otters returning to the lakes is a good thing," he offered hesitantly. "Pollution reduction, and all that jazz."

I shook my head violently. "Not lost. Lost. *Owen.*"

His hand slowly slipped the sunglasses off. Without them, his eyes were the same clouded blue as the lake, worry like silt under their surface. "Kel?"

I tried to force it out, to explain, to beg him to make it stop. But to say anything would make it real. So I shook my head and cried. Eventually, my brother wrestled me into the car, and took me home.

Derik met us at the apartment and hustled us inside. I could smell his sweaty gym shirt through his coat. "What happened?" He wasn't asking me.

Trax shook his head. "I don't—"

"Owen. It was *Owen.*" I locked the apartment door behind us. The men watched me warily. I clicked the deadbolt closed.

"Who's Owen?" Derik's voice had never been so deep before.

Trax shoved a score of music books off the sofa and pushed me onto the seat in its place. "It's okay, Kel," he whispered. "Whatever happened, it's okay."

I looked at Derik. "It was Lost," I said. "He was a Lost. The Lost are *here.*"

Chapter Ten

By the time they got a rational explanation out of me—pudgy, sticky Owen; Sandra's dating expertise; the Lost in the South; hearing Owen's voice from the otter—they were as overwhelmed as I. The three of us sat on the two-person couch, sharing warmth.

"Go take a shower, Derik," I ordered suddenly.

He looked at me, at Trax, and nodded mutely, quietly disappearing out of the apartment. He believed me.

Trax was a different story.

So I showed him the pictures, the ones from the trip that I'd taken every now and then in an effort to document the places I'd been. Most of them had been edited out, zapped off my memory drive and hidden by the government. But there was one of the Lost, a cat in Elizabeth's hands from the shopping mall, staring at the Santa hat on her head.

And I told him about the squirrels, and the ants, and the butterflies. I told him about the Mad, and Derik's scar. I even told him about the Hunters, which the government had expressly forbidden me from doing.

Derik came back to hear me detailing the visions at the water tower, rubbing his hair with a towel. He didn't comment, just perched himself on the arm of the sofa and listened.

I felt better for the telling. I couldn't have told anyone else, but this was Trax. He went to his room, grabbed Dad's old guitar, and began plucking at the strings, unconsciously falling into one of Dad's old working songs. Thinking.

Trax needed a little space. Derik had tossed his towel across the back of a chair by one of the heat vents. Straightening it to dry better, I leaned into Derik's warmth, sampling the smell of his soap. It was fresh, clean, just a hint of spice. "Sorry for pulling you away from work."

His arm wrapped around my shoulders. "They did just fine without me while we were in the South."

"I don't want to get you in trouble."

He snorted. "I'm the boss. They'll deal."

Wait. I leaned away. "You're the boss?"

The tilt of his eyebrow called me an idiot. "I own the place. What do you think I do? Wash towels? Come on, you've seen the suits I wear for the business stuff."

I picked my jaw off the floor. "I didn't know you *owned* it," I muttered. "Most guys brag about that crap."

He snorted. "You're not implying that I have bad taste, are you?"

My lips twitched. I grabbed his hand and pulled him into the kitchen, raiding my icebox. Over the errant melody of Trax's thinking, we chopped and diced and simmered and stirred, until the smell of Mexican filled the apartment.

"I want to know what's going on." I tested the pico de gallo, and decided it needed more Serrano pepper. "Why they're here."

His grunt of agreement said he'd expected as much. "You're going back to work tomorrow."

I nodded. "Find out what I can about the otters. We've got a couple of reporters doing human interest stories on them. I'm sure Sandra will share. Then I'll go investigate. I've still got the press pass—"

"Not alone." His hand deftly took the knife out of mine before I could start on the second and third peppers and scooped the small handful of diced chilies into the bowl. I pouted at his back, but put the extra pair back in the fridge before he could turn around.

The music stopped.

Trax walked into the kitchen. "He's right. You're telling us everything."

I goggled at my brother. "You were listening?"

He shrugged. "I'm not deaf." He snatched a chipful of pico de gallo and perched himself against the doorframe. "Needs more spice."

Derik rolled his eyes. "Try not to burn the kitchen down."

We dragged our dishes to the table, pico de gallo as it was, and sat.

#

I went to work the next day.

My boss badgered me, my coworkers welcomed me, and someone mysteriously produced a cake out of nowhere for an impromptu welcome-back party. My government-approved photos and articles were handed in, circulated, and set aside for close inspection before publication. My desk managed to walk across the office, apparently all on its own, and had to be relocated back with the help of three possibly guilty sportswriters. Somebody's Chihuahua named Lucifer got loose in the office after gnawing on the company accountant's designer heels, an article about an editor being devoured by zombies appeared in my inbox, and an ad for "Strynge and Unusual Plynts" was posted right under my nametag.

I almost missed the deathglares. Almost.

But after I finally chased away the worst of the office mischief, I turned to Sandra and perched my hands on my hips. "Is something wrong? You've been shooting daggers at me all day."

She *huffed* and *tcktcktck'* ed away.

I crossed my arms and tapped my foot. *Tptptp-tp-tp...*

"Fine!" She pushed away from her desk and spun in her chair to send me another hope-you-die-with-a-pen-shoved-through-your-eye glare. "You ran him off."

I searched my brain. A nagging suspicion — the otter's voice — I inhaled in realization. "Owen?"

A curt nod. "He was just trying to fit in, finally putting his life back together. Getting himself back together after his sister and niece... well. Got a job and all, and then disappeared right after you left. What did you do? It must have been *something* horrible."

I planted my palms on her desk and leaned down. "Disappeared? What job did he get?"

She rolled a few inches back, regarding me warily. "It's not like you don't know."

"I don't." I pushed up. "I swear, Sandra, I had no idea that he left. I didn't talk to him at all after that lunch. But I think this is important. Where was he working?"

"What do you mean? Important how?" Like a dog to bacon, her nose honed in on a story.

I shook my head and stood back.

She got up and followed. "Something's up, isn't it? You *know* something."

I glanced around. "Just a suspicion. Tell me where Owen worked. I swear to you, I'll let you know if it turns into a story."

Her arms crossed, and she leaned back against her desk, chin in the air. "I get an exclusive."

I nodded. "Fine."

Her mouth opened. She shut it. She opened it again, and this time her voice was worried. "And you'll call the police first, if Owen's in trouble?"

I glanced down at the floor.

"Oh, god." Her hands covered her mouth. "He isn't—"

"Not dead," I hedged. "I mean, probably not. I don't think so. But—" I shook my head and turned to face the wall, then turned back. "Just tell me everything you know about him, about what happened after that lunch. I think it might be a clue."

She nodded. "But you have to tell me, too."

Could we involve someone else?

I could use the help. "Come over tonight, after work. To dinner."

She sent me a file that afternoon. I forwarded it to my personal e-mail, and left.

#

"Lorren's Oil."

I nodded at Derik's statement. "They just started drilling for oil in Lake Mendota. Hired a bunch of locals—it was absolutely terrific for the economy, after the influx of unemployed."

Sandra sipped her tea and pulled over the sheaf of papers, flipped through, and stopped at another article. "They were drilling in the Gulf, too. It was a big deal. A lot of environmentalists were terrified there'd be another oil spill, and undo all the progress they'd managed to make."

Derik's glass hit the table with a *tunk*. Water splashed over the edge and soaked the tablecloth. We all stared at the growing stain for a moment.

"And now they're drilling in Lake Mendota," Derik finished.

Sandra nodded. "But we have every reason to believe that they're following regulations. Ever since the BP spill all those years back, safety has become the PR 3-ring circus. That's not where they're cutting back."

"Do you think they hit something besides oil?" I asked. "Or were they just unlucky?"

She shrugged. "The first step, I guess, is to check out their operations."

I nodded. "But that's not one of your columns. How would we get permission?"

She smiled, the forest-green of her gel nails glinting against her iced tea. "Leave that to me." Her eyes dodged to the empty hallway. There was no one there to impress.

I nodded, pretending not to notice. Trax was practicing with his band, since I'd gone back to work. He wouldn't be home for hours.

I might have suggested he go try out the drummer's new video game afterward, too.

"We should go back to Otter Point," I said to Derik. "See if we can find anything." I hadn't told her about Owen.

Neither one of us needed to think about that right now.

He nodded. "After work?"

"I'd rather go while it's light. How about lunch?"

A disagreeing grunt. "Got a client. Man pays for a strength Power, can't leave him hanging."

"We can take a late lunch, maybe."

He thought about it, pouring himself another glass of water. "Yeah, that could work. Is two o'clock okay?"

"Sure. I'll take a snack. Sandra, can you cover for me, if it goes long?"

She waved her fork in the air. "Bribe me with that peach cobbler you stashed in the kitchen, and it's a deal. I haven't had peach *anything* in months."

Chapter Eleven

"I told you not to come." I slammed the door and glared up at my brother.

He shrugged in false innocence, pretending his sunglasses and hat made up for hanging out in the parking lot alone.

"It's not like I'm wearing blue, Kel."

I growled at him, but let it slide. "Whatever. Derik's running a few minutes late. His client wanted to do push-ups."

Derik's car chose that minute to round the corner. An apology and a short walk later, the three of us were back at Otter Point.

Trax knelt down. "I don't see anything."

I tilted my head to listen. "They're here." My eyes scanned the surface of the lake.

"There." Derik's voice brought my eyes around. It was behind us, and scurrying over quickly.

I wasn't sure until the tiny paws pressed against my calf. *Please, please!* Owen's voice sobbed in my head.

"Hey, Owen," I said, kneeling. "No, don't move. I can't hear you unless you're touching me."

Trax knelt down beside me. "All I'm hearing is squeaks."

Derik looked over our heads, keeping an eye out. "Higher-level Powered can hear them, too. But she's the only who can understand them."

Help me, Owen begged, all but crawling into my lap.

I sat down on the cold grass. "I want to," I said. "I don't know how. You have to tell me what happened."

Little black eyes goggled up at me. *Help me,* he said.

"What's he saying?" Trax laid a hand on my shoulder.

I shook my head.

Kelly, help me. Please.

"You have to tell me what happened," I told him again.

You remember me. I need you to help me. Why aren't you doing anything?

"I'm trying, Owen! But you have to—"

Pleeease. I'm so cold. Why can't anyone hear me? Just like all the others.

I looked up at the guys, my eyes hot and wet. "I don't think he can hear me," I said, and my voice trembled.

Trax's hand rested on my shoulder. "You said that the Lost could. Try harder."

I cupped the furry face between my numb hands and stared into Owen's eyes. "Come on, Owen. Tell me. Tell me what happened." I said it. I *thought* it. I put everything I had into it.

Help me, Kelly. Help me.

Valdez had once said no one outside the Tide Zone could hear the Lost. I could, but that wasn't enough, not if they couldn't hear me. There had to be a way. If only he wouldn't panic.

"I'm going to try to calm him down." A warning, so they wouldn't freak out when I spaced out to concentrate.

I *listened,* and heard the *sasa-sasa-sasa* of his fluttering heartbeat. *Tcktck-tcktck-tcktck-tck-tck — tck-tck — tck...*

No effect.

Why won't you help me?

It was like I was trying to soothe the ocean. The Power touched him, and then disappeared, swallowed whole without effect.

I tried again. And again. Nothing. "It's not working," I finally admitted. "It's like he's absorbing the Power, when I try to use it directly on him."

We tried writing it down. We tried having Derik and Trax say it. Trax sang it. Owen liked to listen to Trax's voice, but he didn't understand either of them, or the writing, or the hand gestures. It was like he was halfway in another world, able only to recognize us, but not hear us.

"You need to get back to work," Derik finally said, his voice raw and deep.

I nodded, shivering and pulling his coat tighter about me.

Trax reached out to touch Owen. The Lost huddled deeper in my lap.

Don't touch. Don't know you. Don't leave me. I don't want to go back below.

I paused, midway through pushing him off. "Below? What below?"

Please help me.

"Kel, we have to go." Trax tugged at my arm. "You're turning blue." His coat joined Derik's over my shoulders.

"He said—"

"We can come back later," Derik replied. "Trax is right. We need to get you warm."

Reluctantly, I dumped Owen from my lap, and let them lead me to the cars.

Trax shouldn't have given me his coat. The battered leather of Dad's old trench—Trax had stolen it years ago, in high school—had hidden his blue sweater.

He always wore blue.

And I looked just like him.

It took the women a single double-take to figure it out. The joggers paused in their tracks, stared, and squealed.

"It's *Trax!*"

I tensed. But Trax stepped in for damage control—he raised his finger to his lips and grinned. The women took this as an invitation to run over.

"Oh, my god. I am such a fan. Won't you sign—er—" One of them latched onto his arm. The other patted herself down, searching for a pocket that wasn't there.

I shuffled through my purse for the pen I usually carried. "Here," I said, shoving it at her. She grabbed it from my hands like I was a convenient desk caddy, and offered it to Trax with a flourish.

Derik stood straighter and folded his hands politely in front of him, eyes narrowing and scanning the trail in both directions. He looked suddenly as out of place in his jogging pants and puffy jacket as a lion wearing jeans and a slouchy T-shirt.

I passed Trax back his coat, and he shrugged back into it with a pretense of checking the pockets for paper. His too-charming smile at the lack produced bodyparts that had no business being out in this weather. With an apology to me in his eyes, he signed the women and sent them off.

"Gack," I muttered as they jogged away, all giggles and conspiratorial winks. "I was terrified they'd bring a swarm down on us."

Trax offered me back the pen. "I'm a little better than that." He sounded offended, like I'd insulted him or something.

Derik snorted. "As soon as the tits came out, I was sure we'd be mobbed."

My brother smirked up at him. "I'm sure you hated it."

Gaze dodging in my direction, the whites of his eyes showing, Derik took a step back. I raised an eyebrow. He gulped. "Uh. Didn't notice."

Trax winked. "Of course not. Great rack on the brunette, though." Sly dog. I swear, sometimes I wanted to kill my brother.

But Derik didn't take the bait. "Really? I was busy watching out for more fans. Hope you enjoyed the show."

The two men stared off. Then Trax nodded, a slight acknowledgement of something or another, and they both relaxed.

"Where'd you learn to go all bodyguard like that?" Trax asked a moment later, as we walked back to the cars. "*Bam.* Like a damn light switch or something."

Derik just smiled darkly. "Family business, of sorts."

"Thought that was the gym," I prodded gently.

He shrugged. "My uncle's. But he's based in Boston. Figured we'd start a franchise up here—better business, better location.

He's probably going to sell the Boston one and open up on the other side of town."

Trax nodded like this was common sense.

"Wasn't the rest of your family was in the army?" I asked.

Derik grunted. It wasn't an answer. Then, "Fort Bragg. My uncle, Dad's brother, is a sixth, like me."

Fort Bragg, North Carolina. Heck, we'd probably gone to the same beaches as kids—I wondered if he'd hopped along the dunes of Kitty Hawk as I once had, or followed I-40 until it panned out in Wilmington.

I could ask, but nobody liked remembering everything he grew up loving was gone. The silence hovered among the three of us, heavy in the air, broken by our footsteps. Great. Now I'd gotten the past stuck in *all* our heads.

Trax's voice cut the awkwardness. "You know they've moved into remaking the Korean games from the early 2000s, right?"

"What?" I looked at my brother in confusion. He was looking at Derik.

Derik settled his hat a little more firmly over his ears. "Video games," he explained to me before looking back at Trax. "Guess it makes sense. Got to be running out of the American games."

Rolling my eyes, I unfolded my arms from around my shoulders and rested them on my head. "Of course you play them, too."

"Who doesn't?"

Trax yanked on my sleeve. "Everyone but her."

I pushed him hard enough to make him stumble. "Brat."

"Nerd." Pulling the keys out of his pocket, he began fishing for one to his car. "Anyway, I got the latest release this afternoon. Want to come over and try it tonight?"

Derik grinned. "Sure."

#

I stumbled into the kitchen the next morning, rubbing remnants of exploding bears from behind my eyes and Elizabeth's screams out of my ears, and tripped over the sofa when I saw Derik sitting at the table, dressed in his khakis and spooning cereal into his mouth.

"Did Trax let you in? I didn't hear you knock." I *knew* he and Trax had stopped before ten last night; I'd heard him leave. I'd have heard him come back in. Right?

Derik poured another bowlful. "Ran out of breakfast; door was unlocked so I assumed you were up. Ever thought about switching to whole wheat or granola? This stuff won't last you through lunch."

My feet froze. I watched him slice an apple and eat a good half of it before words came to me. "You just came in?"

"Nah, a good ten minutes ago."

Not what I'd been asking. "But you knocked, right? Trax let you in?"

He cocked his head, eyebrow raised in question. "Doesn't he usually sleep pretty late? I didn't want to wake him up."

"But— you— ah." Communal living. Dear god, I was too tired to deal with this now. I should probably be screaming at the idiot, except it was too damn early. "If you'd been a few minutes earlier, I'd have still been in a towel."

His eyes lit up. "I'll be earlier tomorrow?"

The heel of my palm hit my forehead. Abso-freaking-lutely clueless. "You can't just walk into someone else's apartment, Derik. Not even … especially not mine. It's not okay."

His cheeks grew red, and he stood up so fast the chair behind him toppled. "Uh. Sorry. I just assumed—we always locked while we slept—I'll go—er—" Bending to pick up the fallen seat, he hit the spoon, and it went flying, milk splattering everywhere.

I drew in a deep breath, padded over to the kitchen, and grabbed a paper towel. "Just knock next time. And wait for one of us. Unlocked door or not."

He wasn't able to meet my eyes on the drive to work, or the drive home, where he dropped me off before running to a group therapy session. But when he knocked on the door that evening with a grocery bag full of fruit, granola cereal, and Greek yogurt and grinned hopefully at me, I sighed and gave him a small smile back before waving him in.

He crowed with delight to see the new knives I'd bought over lunch, and hidden in my purse on the way home. "Ceramic?"

Nodding, I grabbed a chopping board from counter. "Didn't feel like getting the others sharpened. And, you know, dull knives

94

are dangerous." Besides, I didn't want him to think I was mad at him or anything.

The huge grin stayed on his face even after freeing the knives from their clamshell prisons.

"There's something below," I said over dinner. "That was the only thing of use I got, that there's something below the surface."

Sandra pushed a bowl of salad over to me. "I've been researching the drilling. The main site is perfectly legit; their environmentalism is great, and the location is carefully monitored. But it's also not the same place that Owen was working."

I paused. "It's not?"

She shook her head, taking a plate of gnocchi from Derik's hands. He glanced down at his empty hands in surprise, then sighed and went back to the kitchen. Sandra put the dish down in front of me. "I drove him to work a few times. We couldn't go in—he said there wasn't any parking, so they all met up at the company lot and got driven in. But he pointed the area out to me. Nowhere near the official drills."

"Wouldn't someone notice that?" I asked. Derik was coming back with a second plate of food, holding it high in self-defense.

Sandra shook her head. "No, they were drilling underwater. Thanks, Derik. You're a sweetheart. Just put it right here." She patted her placemat.

Derik looked down at the empty spot in front of Sandra, at his food, and back down. His shoulders slumped in defeat, and he surrendered the plate.

I thought about the logistics. "But, the silt, the equipment..."

She shrugged. "A clean drilling site doesn't cause much of a surface stir, not with the new technology they use, and on top of that they hired a bunch of Powers to keep pollution down. The containment bubble holds it all in, and usually buffers most of the vibrations."

"Wow." I grabbed the pepper as Derik sat down, cracking a light layer over my meal. He hovered over his plate, like he was afraid someone would take it away or something. "I hadn't realized they'd come quite that far."

She took a large bite of gnocchi, and hummed in appreciation. "This is really good. It's too bad your brother had to miss it."

Derik grunted and stuffed a bite into his own mouth.

I swallowed. "He's got to practice. His band is working on a couple of new songs, so he'll be away most nights."

"Oh. That's too bad." She took a long drink. "But I guess it's part of what makes him so amazing, isn't it?"

I took a word from Derik's vocabulary, and grunted.

Derik swallowed and left his fork in stabbity-position over his plate without attacking. "We need to figure out how to get in."

I glanced at him. "It's underwater. I'd bet anything their entrances below the surface are relatively easy to get into. The best way in would be to dive, but... I don't have a suit." Not anymore. I'd always figured I'd be doing my ocean diving down in Carolina during my vacations, so it had made more sense to leave the bulky drysuit, designed for cold-water diving, with Mom and Dad.

Oh, hindsight.

That brought a raised eyebrow to his face. "I can snag a suit from Travis at the gym. He does the classes for scuba—brings us in a bunch of money." He punctuated his words by stabbing his meal and taking the bite.

"Really?" That would solve a lot of problems. "Grab two, if you can. I want to go."

Derik opened his mouth to argue. Sandra blanched, and he hurriedly shut it, swallowed, and tried again. "Scuba isn't something you just do, Kel. You have to be trained."

"Yeah. I know." I waggled my eyebrows at him. "I've got hidden depths to me, too."

"What kind of diving have you done?" He looked like one of my old teachers, stern and exacting.

"UNCW teen SCUBA courses, then went on a couple of wreck-diving safaris in college. Graveyard of the Atlantic and all; I couldn't resist." I speared a forkful of salad and stuffed it in my mouth to hide the smirk. Bet *he'd* never swum over the deck of the Alexander Ramsey.

He raised an eyebrow, but laughed. "Okay. Travis has a couple of suits in women's sizes. Probably for the best, anyway. He won't ask questions if I say it's for my girlfriend."

He realized the goof about thirty seconds after I did. We stared at each other, then both looked down and away.

Sandra glanced from me to him and from him to me, and wisely said nothing.

Chapter Twelve

It had been four years since I'd last wiggled into a scuba suit, so Derik insisted on taking me out to check my certification. The drysuits he begged off his friend were no different from the ones I'd learned in, with the notable exception of being much better quality. He seemed a little disappointed that I shrugged into it without a problem.

Neither the pool nor the open water of Lake Mendota gave me any trouble in our nice, controlled, instructor-supervised class. So Derik was forced to admit that my certification—now officially renewed—wasn't just for show, and that he had no real reason to bar me from a potentially dangerous outing.

"We don't know where to look," he finally stated, walking with me back up the stairs. "We're not going out until we know where we're looking."

I couldn't really argue with that. But I'd earned my victory fair and square, so I was satisfied. At least, as far as diving went.

"Derik..." I hesitated.

We stopped on the second floor's landing. His shoes were still covered in slush, ice slowly dripping off the laces and onto the rug. "What?"

I pulled my hat off and kneaded it in my hands. "When you said you were telling Travis that you wanted to take your girlfriend diving..."

His boots abruptly pointed at the wall. "Erm. Sorry."

"No, it's okay. It was the logical thing to do." I stopped beating up my hat to jam it back onto my head. It covered my eyes. "Just wanted to make sure you didn't think we were, uh—"

"No!" He walked quickly past me, and up the stairs. "No, just friends."

"Yeah. Good." I followed him up. He didn't walk me to my door like he usually did. Which was sensible. Because he wasn't my boyfriend or anything. Boyfriends could break up with you, leave you. But Derik was a friend, which meant I could count on him to stay. Just a friend.

I was *not* disappointed about that.

Really.

He also didn't come over that night. "Where's Derik?" Trax asked, seeing me with my head in the fridge. "It's not his group therapy night."

"Busy," I muttered. Poking around behind the milk, I pulled out a glass bowl of leftover gnocchi. Should I eat it or not?

I wasn't really hungry.

But it smelled like Derik's cooking.

Except he wasn't here to cook. Something—something warm—was missing from the kitchen, making the walls seem barren and hospital-cold. Maybe I should have soup? Derik made a barley stew a couple of days ago, and there was still some left.

Nah. Not hungry for that, either. There really wasn't a single thing in the entirety of the fridge that looked appetizing.

"You gonna hang out there all day? Because we can open the windows if it's too warm in here, save a little electricity."

I stuck my tongue out at Trax and shoved the pasta back into the fridge. There was some fruit in the bowl on the table.

He took my spot at the refrigerator door and grabbed the dish I'd returned. "There's still some gnocchi left. Want some?"

"N'thanks."

His head popped out of the fridge. "Something wrong?"

"No." I sniffed the apple, trying to convince myself to bite into it. It smelled… too fruity.

Trax grabbed a ceramic plate from the cupboard to nuke the pasta on. He kept stealing glances at me as he waited for it to beep. "You and Derik have a fight or something?"

"What?"

Digging through the silverware drawer, he made an ambivalent *mmm* sound. "Dunno. You just seem off. Like you're fighting with your boyfriend or something."

I slammed the apple down onto the table. "He is *not* my boyfriend."

He pursed his lips and made a smooching sound. Then he ducked as I feigned like I was going to chuck the apple at him. Snickering, he dodged the kick I aimed at his shins and dashed into his room, plate held in front of him. I thought about following him for a little tormenting, but he was just being a brat. Not really worth it.

I rolled my eyes and looked at the now-bruised apple. He made it sound like I was moping or something.

Digging through the fridge, I pulled out a still-passed-the-sniff-test pouch of deli meat and tossed a couple of slices on a plate, then sprinkled on some cheese and nuked the whole thing. The slices I rolled into meat tacos, something Derik would probably have a heart attack if he caught me eating, and shoved one into my mouth.

I didn't mope. Moping was for lovesick teenagers. I was a grown woman, and perfectly capable of forcing myself to eat even if I wasn't hungry. Which had absolutely nothing to do with Derik.

#

Sandra dropped the article into my inbox the next day. It looked just like any other article needing edits, except that "Otter It Be Pointed Out" contained a list of dates, times, ship names, and a link to a file on the shared network that contained pictures of construction workers in a boat.

I printed off the 'article' and the file, and sent the article back with the dreaded "Rewrite" label.

Ten minutes later, "Otter It Be Pointed Out" was a short documentary on the improvement of Lake Mendota's pollution levels, as gauged by local wildlife.

I retitled it "Otters Up, Pollution Down!" and sent it on.

#

He'd invited her for dinner. Without telling me.

I groaned, seeing Sandra's car in the parking lot beside Trax's. Derik, who'd skipped our carpool that afternoon, wouldn't have brought her over without asking. And she wouldn't have come without an invitation. That left my brother, feeling guilty about chasing off a fan.

"Hey, she's home!" Trax shouted as I walked in the door. I grunted, tossing my coat over the back of a kitchen chair and kicking off my shoes.

As I'd expected, Sandra was all but hanging off my brother. He bore it admirably, the three inches of space she'd allowed him more than enough room to pretend she wasn't going all fangirl. They were sipping some muscadine wine that had probably cost half Sandra's holiday bonus. She tilted the bottle at me, but I shook my head. Most Powered didn't drink; inebriation fizzled a person's ability to use magic.

Derik popped out of the kitchen. "Get my text?"

"No." I pulled out my phone. "Sorry, no mozzarella."

He disappeared back into his domain. "I'll make it work."

Trax waved to a pile of papers on the coffee table. "Sandra found a bunch of leads. She's got a list of all the docks around the lake."

I dropped down on her other side. "Even the private ones. Nice. That must have taken all day."

She shrugged. "Not really. Google maps, you know. We're pretty well covered in the satellite photos."

"That's creepy."

She gave me a grin. "Aren't you glad illusion Powers can't fool technology?"

Trax pointed out a couple of circled spots on the map. "Lorren's owns these." He bit his lip, spinning the map this way and that. "I don't think they'd do something illicit on their own property, though."

I pulled out my own day's work. "I've researched the owners and head members of the corporation."

My brother held out his hand. I surrendered the files and went to check on Derik.

Both his hands were full of spinach. He barely glanced at me, just pointed toward the stove. "Grab that pot for me?"

I rescued the orzo before it could boil over, stirring it back into submission. "You never told me where you learned to cook like this."

He grunted, eloquent as always.

I played sous chef in silence for the rest of the preparation, waiting for him to say something, to make the awkward go away. He didn't. But by the time I was pouring the orzo onto the serving dish, he was wearing his usual cooking-grin.

It was like last night had never happened.

He plated the chicken, adding a few sprigs of parsley and a drizzle of juice. I wasn't allowed to plate the meat dishes; it was eat them out of the pan or let him arrange them to his satisfaction. I assumed this was punishment for the nights I refused to let us serve ourselves out of the pans. It was a punishment I was willing to endure.

Sandra and Trax met us at the table. Derik surrendered the chicken to Sandra and sat himself down. "My first job," he said, "my sophomore year of high school. Mom wouldn't let me join JROTC, the military-sponsored program my siblings were all in, so I figured I'd get an afterschool job instead. I started out as a bus boy. Then two of the chef's assistants eloped in the beginning of my senior year, and the kitchen was desperate. Cooking was a lot more fun than busing tables. I would have earned more waiting, but I would have had to deal with the customers, so I stayed in the kitchen."

Trax heaped a little more of the orzo on his plate. "Couldn't deal with the kids?"

Derik grinned. "Couldn't deal with the full-grown kids. Not many tykes, but I would have had to wear a suit all the time."

Sandra accepted the serving dish from Trax's hands, ignoring my brother's gag of sympathy. "Sounds fancy."

"It was." Derik dug into his meal. "I learned to cook, though."

I showed my appreciation by grabbing a second serving, gesturing to the coffee table after I put down the bowl. "What did you guys think?"

"I think you're right." Talking with a full mouth got my brother a glare from Sandra. He swallowed. Her eye lingered on him for a few seconds longer to get the point across. He swallowed again for good measure before continuing. "I can look into Rogers tomorrow morning, before practice."

Sandra nodded. "I'll search the county records, see if he owns any of the lakeside property."

Derik was frowning, looking back and forth among us.

"Lorren's Oil is a corporation," I explained. "The chairman is Aaron Surry, but he's really into environmentalism and such. I don't think he'd be for a side project like we're thinking about. Thomas James Rogers has been on the board since before the Tides, on the other hand, and he's got his hand in a lot of things. Especially the pockets of politicians. Was up in New Jersey for a meeting when the Tides hit, lucky for him, but he'd been overseeing the drilling in the Gulf personally during that time period."

"And he's given a lot of grants to research centers, too," Trax added.

Sandra pointed her fork at him. "That isn't all that suspicious," she said. "I'm all for funding research."

"What kind of research?" Derik asked.

Trax answered for me. "Powers, mostly. Understanding how they work, where they come from. He gave a multi-million dollar grant to a university trying to link seismic activity with Power development."

Come to think of it... "You know," I said, "there was a building at Mechany's named after him. I know most of the other students were given the option of joining research studies to discover the cause of their disabilities."

Derik glanced at me. "Not you?"

I shrugged. "I'm tone-deaf. That one was easy."

Trax snorted.

"Shut up."

"I said nothing." He smirked at me from across the table.

I couldn't kick him without getting either Sandra or Derik, so I settled for waving my knife at him.

Sandra frowned.

"Sister's privilege," I defended, and stuffed my mouth full of chicken and orzo.

Derik took a long drink of water, and only choked a little.

He and I took our turns going through the papers while Sandra and Trax cleaned up. My brother, thank goodness, refused to let Sandra kick him out of the kitchen. Even if she was horrified that dishwater might destroy his hands.

I heard Trax pointing out that the dishwasher worked just fine.

"Most of the docks are for private homes," I said. "I don't think Owen would have gone on something *quite* so suspicious as leaving from a house."

"So we should be on the lookout for privately owned, respectable, and somewhat public-looking docks," Derik interpreted. He scanned through the list of addresses Sandra had printed off. "What about this one?"

I glanced. "Too public." I knew the street—right beside a bunch of restaurants.

I grabbed the second sheet of the list from the table. Most of them were worthless as leads—in the restaurant district, beside the school, in the state park. One, I noted down on another sheet of paper—a fairly discreet dock lodged between two other semi-private commercial properties.

Between the four of us, we narrowed our search down to handful of sites. "I guess now, we just research who owns what," I said.

Trax offered Sandra her coat. "Text me if you find anything important," he said, and I winced.

She smiled at him, a softening to her face that made her look years younger. "You've got practice again tomorrow?"

Trax's "yeah" brought a disappointed look to her face, but she didn't pout. Derik left right after, his own list in hand.

"Sorry about Sandra," I apologized when my brother and I were alone again.

"Sorry for what?" he answered, and headed for his room.

#

I heard him moving around some, heard his music turn off about 3am. I figured he was going to go to bed.

The door opened and shut.

I sat up and cursed.

The note taped on the door said that he'd gone to stake out one of the sites. I texted him immediately. *Get your a$$ back here.*

He didn't respond. Or answer his phone when I called.

He also didn't come back.

Chapter Thirteen

I called his bandmate again during my lunch break.

"Geez, Kel, he's not here. Wouldja let it go? He canceled practice; he's probably *fine*."

I thought about calling his agent. If he was fine, he'd murder me.

So I went to Sandra instead. "He still hasn't answered."

She looked up, her eyes dark with worry. "I forwarded you the text, right?"

I nodded. He'd sent her a site last night to mark off the list. He hadn't said which one he'd be going to next, and he'd taken his list with him.

I bit my knuckle. "If he's not back after work, I say we go looking for him." *Not Trax, not Trax*, the litany in my head begged over and over. Was this some bizarre revenge for the Hunters?

Sandra's gaze moved to her master list on the corner of her desk. About half the addresses were crossed off. She would go with me. I paced away without waiting for her to give a verbal answer.

#

Derik called as Sandra and I were about to get off work. "I've got the suits," he said.

"Coming by to pick you up now." I hung up the phone. "Want to carpool?"

Sandra shook her head. "The more cars, the better. We can split up if we go in separate vehicles."

I gave her a hard look. "If something happened to Trax," I told my middle-aged friend, "I'm pretty sure it could happen to you, too."

She grabbed the list off the desk and handed me the copy. Her knuckles were red, tooth marks indenting her fair skin. "I'll follow you both back to your place."

Mom used to chew her knuckles like that, too, when she'd been worried.

Derik stuffed the gear into my trunk and let me drive in silence. Trax wasn't back yet. Derik and I searched his room, but there were no clues.

Sandra had more luck with the list. "I've narrowed it down to five likely choices." She'd numbered them, too. "You guys take three, four, and five."

Derik raised an eyebrow. "You're going by yourself?"

She shrugged. "I'll call you if I see anything suspicious. Promise. I'm not going to get myself hurt. I'm going to number one first."

I took number three.

My phone rang almost two hours later. I fumbled it open, almost dropping it through my mittens. "Sandra. Find anything?"

"Trax's car."

She was at the second site. She'd called Derik first. I scrambled into my own car and took off, dialing as I went.

Derik got there before me. He was parked across the street from the address, by a co-op built in a refurbished warehouse. I pulled in beside him and got out. "Where is she?"

He shook his head. "I didn't find where she parked." We looked—we looked for two hours, driving up and down the streets in the dark. I called her phone. She didn't answer.

I called Trax's agent next. Told her that Trax had gone out last night, and wasn't back yet. She asked if he'd told me when he was planning on being back.

"Well, no, but it should have been sooner than this."

"Probably having a one-night stand." Her voice was calm. "Don't worry about it. If he doesn't come back by Monday, then give me another call."

"There's no girl! He was going to look at a piece of property—"

"Happens all the time," the witch interrupted me. "He's a star. Look, if he doesn't show up by tomorrow, I'll call his number. How about that?"

"I'm calling the police," I announced.

"Don't you dare."

Apparently, mysteriously disappearing stars were normal. And police were bad publicity—when the stars turned up fine, that was.

I hung up in with a huff. Derik saw the situation in my eyes. He stopped me from throwing the phone into the wall. "You might need that," he suggested gently, prying it out of my fist.

I grumped. Derik politely ignored my attitude.

He drove us around and approached the address from another street, past the building Sandra had described. Sandra's car was nowhere to be seen, but he parked beside Trax's on a side street. Instead of investigating the property immediately, Derik and I swung wide, making like we were going to the co-op. His hand wrapped around mine. For the facsimile, I allowed it. It did feel nice.

We re-emerged from the co-op with a single shopping bag and a pair of fresh sandwich wraps. Derik stuck the bag in the trunk, wedged between the two scuba tanks—we weren't particularly worried about the bread or goat cheese freezing. Delicious food was not the primary objective.

At least the muscadine grapes wouldn't go bad. The half-pint had cost as much as caviar, but I hadn't been able to resist. And Derik had been more than willing to make sure they didn't reach the car.

He slammed the trunk shut and gave me a mischievous glance over his shoulder. I raised an eyebrow. Then I shrieked, because he'd grabbed my hips and spun me between him and the car.

"Just for show," he whispered, and leaned in, a brush of lip on lip. He was slow, methodical, his eyes closed and his hand firm immediately below the nape of my neck. I pressed back into him, *for show*, and let him lead. I could always take revenge later.

With the ice-cold bumper against the backs of my knees, and his hand on my spine, and my breasts and belly against the firmness of his body beneath the pillow of his long coat, and the sweet aftertaste of the grapes filling my mouth—I forgot to breathe.

The warmth of his lips disappeared. "For show," he repeated, and I nodded, perfectly dizzy and content to enjoy the seaweed green of his eyes.

"For show," I answered, and decided that the red in his cheeks was the bite of the winter cold.

I caught my breath, and pushed him away. It really wasn't the best time to think that Derik was an excellent kisser.

Although I didn't really think I'd ever be able to avoid the thought again.

Like lovers, we ambled along the road. I leaned left, as if stumbling, and pulled us into the alley beside the next building over. We rattled our way along the gate to the waterfront.

The alley spit us out with a view of the lake. I curled under Derik's arm and absorbed some of his body heat. "Are there any security cameras? I think we're out of sight," I whispered, the road not visible from this point.

His breath stirred my hair. "Just look at the water." His lips touched my cheek, and he stepped away, his fingers still in mine. He made no secret of scanning the buildings for inhabitation—the rub of his thumb over the back of my hand was all the motivation a witness would need.

There was a *splash*.

"I think we're safe." He didn't argue when I retrieved my hand and stepped closer to the edge of the water.

Dotty spotty hottie?

I knelt down to greet the Lost while it pulled itself out of the water. It sniffed my fingers. I scratched the thick fur. "How'd you find us, Owen?"

You came back. Knew you'd come back. The others said you were here. Not the usual place. You're looking for them? The boy who looks like you, and Sandra. You're going to help them. I think. You are, right? You know they're gone, right? Why won't you answer me?

"Yeah, we're looking for them," I said quietly. "Where are they? Are they in trouble?"

Nobody talks anymore, he whined. *Not even the Powered.*

Derik knelt beside me. "What's he saying?"

I shook my head. "He saw Sandra and Trax. They need help. But..."

He placed a hand on my back. "Can you get him to show us where they are?"

"He can't even understand me."

His grunting reply echoed in the alley. I pulled my hand away from Owen long enough to bring feeling back into my fingers.

"Have you tried your Power again?"

"I don't know what to do." I couldn't use it on him.

An idea sparked.

He must have seen it, because he backed up to give me a little more space. "What are you going to try?"

"Can't do it on him, but..." There was nothing to stop me from trying it on myself. Using it through my voice, like a real music Power.

This time, when Owen's words filtered through my head, I focused and began twitching my foot. *Tap, tap, tap.*

I heard the song of the lake: *Shhhhhhh* –

I heard the *thump* of boat's propellors.

I heard the beating of Owen's tiny heart: *Sa-sa, sa-sa, sa-sa...*

And I interrupted his gloomy babble.

"Owen."

-!?

How do people speak? There's a rhythm to their words, a beat to their voices. A lilt is a step away from a song; a song is only speaking in rhymes and beats, and to the Lost, rhymes and beats don't matter. I'm no singer. But this day, I sang. "Owen. Listen. Where's Sandra? Where's Trax?"

He stood up on his back legs.

I hear you. You're speaking to me!

110

"We want to help. Show us where my brother is. Show us Sandra. I can hear you when you touch me."

He dove for the water.

A few minutes later, he came back up. Walked over. Put his paw on my ankle.

You didn't come.

Focus. Tap. "Meet us in the water. We will need to change. Scuba for the water."

Oh.

#

Open-water diving in Lake Mendota was too tightly regulated to work from a boat. So we drove a few streets away, stopped by an alley in a shadowy area, and unloaded. It was starting to get dark. An asset, for us.

Sneaking into an abandoned warehouse at night was about as clear-cut a crime as I'd ever committed. Derik took one look at the padlock and snorted. He led us around the side to a poorly lit gate, also locked, the steel lock almost black with age. He pulled a paperclip from his pocket. "Thought I might need this. Hold the flashlight?"

I almost dropped the light when he yanked the gate open seconds later. He knew what he was doing. "What the hell, Derik?"

"Just go in."

There was no doorknob; it was one of those number-code electronic locks. I expected him to kick down the door or something, but instead he shucked his shoes, set his fingers into the mortar, and pulled himself up.

He got about three feet off the ground when his foot slipped, and he went tumbling to the ground.

"You okay?" With a glance over my shoulder to make sure no one had heard his fall, I knelt beside him.

"Ow. Yeah. Fine." Grunting, he sat up. "That is not at *all* like climbing a rock wall in a gym. Do you see anything I could use to give me a boost?"

Squinting, I saw the second floor window he pointed to had a partially missing pane of glass, the hole about the right size for a rock.

"Uh. Do you know how illegal this is?"

"You want to leave our stuff out here?"

We found a plastic trashcan down the alley. He climbed onto it, with me steadying it as well as I could. It still wrenched out of my hands when he jumped, but I managed to grab it and stop it from making too much noise in the fall. I looked up to see how he was doing. Hanging with one hand to the sill, Derik pushed his weight upwards with his toes just enough to reach in and unlock it. A yank on the metal, and it swung up and open, plenty wide enough for him to squeeze through. All I could think as I waited was how criminal I must look, standing there by the fallen trash can with all our things. Then the door opened, and he had me hold it as he pulled the equipment through.

I balked the minute we got out of sight. "How the hell do you know how to do that?"

He locked the door behind us. There was no shyness to him as he started changing, but then, we were putting on dry suits. The process involved more 'adding clothes' than removing them. "Didn't you ever watch Scooby Doo?"

I shook my head. "Don't you dare give me that crap. Since when do you break into abandoned warehouses like a born cat burglar?"

For the first time, he hesitated. Something dark flashed across his eyes, memories that sat heavy on his shoulders. "I don't. Padlocks like that are damn easy to break into, if you know how." He shook his head.

I dropped my bags. "And?"

"Kel, I need you to start getting changed now. We can talk about this later."

I ripped my coat off and slipped into a tight-fitting fleece vest. "Give me the short version, then."

He shook his head. "Look, it's..." He stopped. He thrust his hands into his hair. He growled. And then he gave. "When the Tides hit, my parents and my siblings were mostly at Fort Bragg. I couldn't handle it. I had a college scholarship; was in a good school. But losing my family? Suddenly there was nobody telling me what they wanted from me, no one living through me. I was in control of my own life, and I didn't know how to be. I cracked; I stopped eating, got down to a thousand calories a day."

Pacing away from me, he rolled one of the tanks with a foot. "You ever seen someone starve? Your body cannibalizes itself for energy. Protein's easiest, so muscles go first. Strength Powers, we don't have much fat, and our bodies don't really like sacrificing muscle mass, so they start nibbling away at important muscle like the heart and diaphragm after a few weeks, just so they won't have to eat as much bicep. In a way, it's a good thing it happens so fast—the habits never really had a chance to get stuck in my head."

His hands fell away from his hair, hooking onto his belt. "They sent me home after my roommate found me half-dead, when my heart got so weak it couldn't sustain a regular beat. To my uncle, the only other sixth class in the family. He stayed with me in the hospital for the first few days until my heart healed— wouldn't have worked if it was my kidneys, you know, but the heart's a muscle. At home, he had some old family friends who were crashing with him and working at his gym until they could find something better. The guys, they were ex-mil, they'd seen my shit before, and worse, too. They paid him back by putting me back together, teaching me the basics Mom had never let me learn, helping me connect to the memories. Worked with me until my head was back on straight, asked me to cook for them. I always loved to cook. They never called me weak or got mad at me when I broke down; just ate whatever I made and gave me something else to focus on instead."

Leaning over, he picked up his toboggan. "I came up here last year to start over, to open the new gym, and hired anyone military that showed up. Moved again when I started making enough profit for a place of my own, after my group leader said I was probably ready to be on my own." He sighed. "It was almost like having my family back, bunch of jarheads crashing around everywhere. Not enough jobs in this damn city anymore, but I make sure anybody that knew my family has a place to go. There were... benefits to living with ex-mil. Like pissing contests over breakfast on who knows the best way to break into buildings without being noticed, and lock-picking lessons when everyone's bored and no one wants to bring out the beer around the recovering alcoholic."

Jamming his hat over his head, he turned to find his hood.

I stared down at my hands. Then I reached for my gear.

Slipping on the hood, I turned around. "I'm sorry."

He shook his head and waved a hand. "Don't."

My gloves had to go back on under the suit's gloves. I'd left them for last. "I just... I didn't know what to think. I'm scared. Do you think they'd come with us if we asked them? We could use the help."

A sharp green glare. His hands grabbed the zipper by my neck and tugged, double-checking it. "Yes," he said, "they would. But we're not asking." His voice had the finality of a concrete wall at the end of a road.

I looked down. The silence stretched until I had to fill it or go crazy. "You never seemed like the military type."

"Most strength Powers get more or less drafted, but Mom always wanted me to go to college. Sixth class; I could do it. She was so determined that I would. Wouldn't even let me do martial arts as a kid." He turned around, and I began double-checking his seals. "The guys saw it right off: military shit reminds me of them, and I didn't want to forget. Doesn't make me a soldier, though."

"Is that how you got into the Recovery teams?"

He nodded. Turning back around, he caught my well-insulated chin with his hand. "Don't worry, Kel. We'll get your brother back."

He pulled his facemask on, and clopped through the empty warehouse.

Owen ran circles around us as we walked out, our fins *flip-flapping* against the concrete.

By the time we were in the water, the sky was dark. Owen dove fast and sharp. We followed at a speed we could maintain.

Our flashlights struggled to pierce the soupy water. A well-used lake like Mendota, even half-frozen, was full of particulate. Fish darted across our vision, and I had to pause once to chase one out of my light.

Something sleek and large butted up against my leg. I glanced back, and saw another otter. Derik's light fell on me, and circled. We were surrounded by them—a family of otters, fifteen or twenty of them, escorting us through the water.

Owen's voice echoed in my head. *Dolly polly holly,* he scolded. I assumed we weren't moving quickly enough.

Derik slid through the murky water, and I followed.

The dome was half-sunk in the dirt, the operation excavated into the muddy lakebed. It was dark, a blister on the lake floor, round and rank.

Derik's light gestured. I looked where it led, and saw a hatch. Owen scratched at it.

The hatch wasn't locked; underwater, locks could be more hassle than protection. We swam through and closed it behind us. There was a narrow passageway leading up.

Kicking upwards, we emerged into an air chamber, a bubble of a room that stayed aerated by pressure. We pulled ourselves up onto the ledge and stripped off the clunkiest of our gear.

"What is this place?" I asked softly. My voice echoed.

"Dive chamber. Probably for maintenance."

Owen tugged at my leg. I shed a glove and offered him a hand.

It's quiet here at night. Most everyone goes home. Only a few security guys and some of the higher-ups stay. You should be able to go out the door without anyone noticing. There was something in his stance that hadn't been in the dripping pita-pocket holder, the way his fuzzy jaw thrust forward and the way light glared in his beady black eyes.

"Thanks, Owen." I translated, and Derik nodded.

The paperclip worked equally well on the door to the inside.

Chapter Fourteen

We were thirty feet up on a narrow platform that twisted and twined around the inside of the dome. Floodlights pounded the inner hemisphere with false daylight. Rails and pipes emerged from every imaginable point in the dirt and flowed up to converge in a single bundle at the apex of the dome, disappearing into a tube.

"I think I played this video game once," Derik muttered, and stalked on cat's feet down to the ladder.

A pressure on my ankle, as an otter leaned against it. Owen's black eyes glittered up at me, a strange wistfulness behind them. *Last I saw my niece, she was two. That was three years before the Tides. I'd been planning on starting her on her first video game this year. Thought I'd never get the chance, but... Guess I could go visit her now.*

He shook himself viciously, then hopped into Derik's waiting arms, avoiding the *skitter* of claws that I was sure would have resulted from trying to climb the ladder. I followed.

Without our fins, our steps were quiet, but three layers of socks weren't enough to keep my feet warm. Derik made me stop to let a guard pass by below. I think he was afraid I'd do something clumsy, like slip. I wasn't sure I wouldn't.

Owen was right in that the place was virtually abandoned. Even the guards were unobservant, probably more from being fifty feet underwater than any lack of training. Their hard hats didn't seem to help, either. I wondered if any of them were flight Powers. Security guards who could fly, even for short distances, would have an advantage here.

Thump. Thump. Splat. The three of us dropped, one by one, onto the damp ground below. I laid my hand on Owen's back. "Which way?"

The fur under my hand shivered. *We need to go in toward the center.* He shook me off, the mud slurping at his paws. Baring his teeth in a grimace at the mess, he danced through the muck like a cat in snow. We followed.

"Mph—" I ran into Derik's shoulder. He looked back long enough to lay a finger on his lips.

Squch, squch, squch. There was someone coming. Derik shoved me behind a pipe. I peered around. He was crouching behind another.

A body slouched past. I thought we were in the clear. But then the man glanced back and saw me. He grabbed for a whistle around his neck.

Derik jumped.

Fwack.

Splorch.

The man fell into the muck, Derik holding his stun gun and shooting it before the guard's eyes could uncross.

After he stopped jerking, Derik rolled him over onto his back and checked for a pulse. "Unconscious," he whispered, sliding the man under a bent pipe. "This thing's useless now, though. One charge." He dropped the stun gun onto the guard's chest. A moment of pocket-rifling later, he pulled out a keycard.

The main building was in the midst of the pipe jungle. Owen led us straight to its door. *Drill's in there. Upper floors have the offices. I think we need the offices.* A single *beep*, and we were in.

The floors in here were concrete. Dark gray walls arched overhead, hundreds of pipes and scaffolding and gauges everywhere. In the middle of the room, a steel cage *ping*'ed with residual heat.

Tump-tump tump-tump. I grabbed Derik and gestured. He dragged us behind some of the mechanical debris until the footsteps had passed.

We padded through in the guard's wake, peeling off at a sealed glass door. Stairs.

I don't know which one, Owen admitted at the top. *We weren't allowed up here.*

Office doors lined the circular hall. Marble floors, well splattered with dried mud, echoed every sound threefold.

"Can you stay here? Hide here and wait? We'll need your help, to head back out."

His furry face nodded, and he nudged open the first door. It was a small broom closet. Derik closed it silently, tucking a piece of cardboard into the catch. Owen would be able to get out without help.

"We'll follow our ears," I whispered. "Trax won't be quiet for long."

Derik's eyes looked doubtful. "Let's look behind the doors, just in case," he suggested.

I tapped my ear. "I'll tell you if there's something worth hearing behind the door. Just remember, I won't be able to hear the halls at the same time."

He bowed slightly. "Lead the way."

I had to concentrate. It was slow going. The first door was empty, as were the next four, but there was someone in the fifth. Not Trax. I heard paper shuffling around, coffee being slurped. One heartbeat. I shook my head.

Three doors further, Derik opened it and pushed me through. "Someone's coming," he mouthed.

The office was cluttered, a bureaucratic nightmare. Papers littered the desk. Coffee mugs left rings on most of the furniture. File folders hung open, and the distinctive smell of take-out Chinese wafted from the trash can. Old take-out Chinese. I wrinkled my nose.

"Since we're here," I muttered under my breath, and plunged into the papers.

Thirty-five minute breaks, lazing about, late. Absent. Underproduction. It was HR stuff, discipline and pay docking. I was about to give up when I found a folder hidden at the bottom of the pile: *lost*.

Cory Lewis. 37. No family in the area. Lost November 14.

Pat Skatowski. 29. Had roommate. Lost November 16. 3 calls sent to roommate. Roommate reported missing persons.

Owen Hammers. 30. No family in area. Lost November 20.

There were seventeen in all. I slid the folder under my vest.

Derik motioned us out.

There were several more occupied offices, but none of them by more than one person. No one was sleeping, and no one sounded restrained. I kept us going.

We got lucky right before the doors turned to glass offices. *Glass*, I thought, *would let people see prisoners. Witnesses.* Even in an illegal operation, extra witnesses would be inconvenient.

The heartbeats were steady and quick, just two of them. Both of them were awake. Why were they so quiet? Pressing my ear against the door until the rim throbbed with pain, I dropped deeper into listening.

Scrch. A rubber shoe shifting on a hard floor. *Phhhh-phhh*, someone breathing through her nose. *Hphhhh-hphhhh*, someone breathing nervously through his nose. *Shff.* The slide of cloth over skin.

My lips stretched. They were on either side of the door. Waiting. "Trax," I murmured against the wood.

A moment. I risked a slightly louder murmur.

Clothes rustled. "Kel?"

"Yeah. Shh. Let us in."

The doorknob jiggled, rattled from the inside. "I don't have a key. We're stuck."

Derik raised an eyebrow at my curse. He tried the knob from outside. Also locked, but there was no keyhole, just a card slide. He pulled something out of a pocket. The keycard.

A red light flashed when he slid it through.

"We can't stay here all night," I said.

He shook his head. A *V* had formed in his brow. "Do you know who has the key?" he asked.

Sandra's voice answered. "Caucasian, about 6'2". Blond, gray eyes, square jaw. Thin build, but not lanky. Answers to Jorgen. He was on the phone with T.J. Rogers." Trust Sandra to give a policeman's answer—a reporter's answer.

The door didn't muffle the quaver in her voice as she added, "They're going to kill us."

Derik's lips thinned. "No, they're not." He'd break the door if he had to.

Tempting. But it would be loud.

"Check the offices?" I asked.

Derik considered it, shook his head. "Wait here. Or..." He tried the next door over. It was unlocked. He pushed me inside. "Safer here. I'm going to go scout."

I thought about arguing, but he was right. He'd had little training, which was still more than I'd had. So instead I repeated my past performance: I turned to the desk.

There were a couple of invoices laying on it, which I added to the file already stuffed into my shirt. Productivity reports and a thin notebook apparently detailing the results of a lab experiment were neatly stacked beside a warm cup of coffee to the side; I pocketed those, too. A brand-new pack of pens and a handful of paperclips were in the top drawer beside a picture of a grey-eyed child and two tubes of lipstick. And then there was the locked bottom drawer.

It was a safe bet that the most useful information was in that drawer, but this office, unlike the last, was tidy. Wiggling the handle on the solid oak drawer did nothing more than demonstrate the sturdiness of the woman's lock.

A *clack clack clack* caught my ear, heels in a hallway. "Crap," I muttered, and squeezed into the a gap between the bookshelf and the wall. There weren't many places to hide in here.

The door opened, and her heels *clacked* their way to the desk. She stopped. *Clack. Clack.* Beeping as she dialed someone. "Honey, did you borrow anything off my desk? ... Yes, some papers, the Kline-Roberts report, a couple of invoices."

The phone *clunked* onto the table. I breathed in and tried to disappear in my tiny corner.

No use. Her voice was commanding, strident. "Stay where you are. Security is on their way."

I knew she'd seen me. I knew she was on the other side of the desk. I knew I was almost worthless in a fight. But Trax was here, and I'd come to get him out. So I whirled and snatched the first book at hand, and threw it.

It didn't even cross half the distance of the room, but the flimsy pad wasn't enough to do any kind of damage, anyway. I grabbed another, a scientific dictionary, and charged.

Dodging under my swing, she kicked up and fell back. "Help!" she shouted, twisting out of reach. Thank god, someone as pathetic at fighting as I was.

Muffled shouts and banging through the wall cheered me on. "You shouldn't have taken my brother," I growled, jumping on her. Her manicured nails raked at my face. One caught my cheek. The sharp pain sparked a red-hot anger in me, and I grabbed for her hair, yanking.

"Psycho!" she screeched. "Get off me!" I slammed her head into the desk.

The door burst open and a yeti of a guard rammed into us, pinning me against my unlucky victim. The shaggy giant wrestled my elbow back, wrapping his other arm around my waist.

It dug into my ribs. My feet left the floor: he was a flight Power.

I clenched my fist and got a handful of blonde hair and a scream.

The satisfaction was short-lived. My parting kick swished through the air. "Let me go!"

The woman screamed again. *CRACK!* The yeti let go, and I fell onto the floor, banging my funny bone on the rebound. For a moment, all I could focus on was the pain shooting through my arm.

Derik yanked me up by the armpits. The shrill screeching behind us was better than an alarm, but Derik didn't bother to shut her up; he set me on my feet in the hall and angled his shoulder at Trax and Sandra's prison door.

"Back up!" I shouted, rubbing the fading pain from my elbow, hoping they'd hear.

I knew Derik was a strength Power. I knew he was rather large, tall, broad and built. But none of that prepared me for the human-bull that charged the door and smashed it right off its frame in an explosion of splinters.

He stood in the doorframe for a second, holding his shoulder. Trax and Sandra appeared from behind the desk.

My brother flew. I was in his arms, getting the life squeezed out of me. "Trax!" I gasped, and he let me breathe.

"No time for that," Derik ordered. "Move!" He ran.

I shoved Sandra in front of me into my brother. He pushed her in front of him and grabbed my hand. Racing down the hall in Derik's wake, we all but tumbled down the stairs. "Hide, Owen!" I shouted, and immediately remembered that he wouldn't understand me.

The closet burst open and an otter leapt out in my tracks, joining the train.

"Owen's here?" Sandra shouted in confusion. "We can't leave him!" The otter stumbled over her foot as she tried to stop.

"He's with us!" I answered without explaining. "Keep running!"

A guard rounded the corner and took Derik's fist to his face. Derik grabbed the stun gun from his hand and kept going.

"How do we get out?"

Trax's question was a good one. Derik fired the gun once. I didn't see what he was aiming at, but he gestured for us to duck beneath the criss-crossing pipes. A small can of something or another landed in the mud beside us.

"Hold your breath!" Derik pushed us away from the gray smoke rising from it, out from under a sheltering overhang. Too late. Something sweet and thick clogged my throat, and I stumbled, choking.

But whatever it was, I could still move, still see. A little dizzy, that was all.

Thwup. Thwup-thuwp-CLANG. Rocks perforated the mud and ricocheted off the pipes, propelled by telekinetic Powers. Sandra squeaked.

Derik grabbed a pellet and threw it back at someone, kneeling in the muck. I scooped Owen into my arms, staggering as the world spun to the left and straightened. He thrashed once, bit, then realized it was me.

Sorry, sorry.

"We need to get out," I said-sung, and then had to repeat myself when I realized my concentration had been shot the first time.

He muttered something, but it sounded foggy.

I followed the point of his nose, although the ground tried to run away with every step. "That way," I slurred.

"Grab her," Derik ordered, one arm over his nose and the other throwing another stone. "I've got you covered."

The ground was gross, but Trax pulled me forward in a half-crouched scramble that ended at the double-doored elevator. A pipe directly overhead sheltered us from view, providing some cover, and the framework supporting the pipes created a couple of low-to-the-ground hiding holes nearby I thought I might be able to slip into, if only I could make it that far. Trax let me slump into the mud beside him so he could jam the elevator button with his palm, slapping it rapidly. "C'mon, c'mon," he muttered.

I blinked. Derik was gone. No, he was behind us, heading our way, throwing another stone. If I could use some magic, maybe I could distract them, make someone panic —

The ever-present fizzy feeling of magic was gone. Completely gone.

Owen squirmed. I closed my eyes and tried to hear his mumble in my head. Nothing. Sandra gasped and shrugged her shoulders, staggering. "Telekinetic Power," she muttered. But it would take at least a third class to pin somebody; living things didn't take well to being pushed around.

Then something heavy seemed to be sitting on my shoulders, a great weight pressing down, more than just dizziness. Everything around me started to grow dark — an illusion Power, too? Or maybe not; my arms trembled and shook. I dropped Owen, and things got a little lighter, more resolute. No, not an illusion Power. Just some damn drug, cutting me off from magic and making me dizzy.

Derik was backing up toward us, duck-cover-step. He stumbled, coughing hard, and I felt my heart stop. But then he raised his hand again, and I breathed in relief; he was still moving. I couldn't bear it if I lost him, too.

It never occurred to me that the biggest danger might be from the pipes. Guns made Powers far less useful; I should have wondered why they weren't using them.

A man in a suit raised his hand, holding something black. The shape of it wormed into my fuzzy mind; a split second passed between seeing it and identifying it as a gun barrel. A second too long, because it fired before I could shout warning.

A bullet slashed through a smaller pipe behind Derik, just enough to release a tiny spray of fine gray mist. He stepped back.

Loudspeakers boomed a command—"Code white. Repair patch to the elevator!"

Derik took another step. Into a mist that was congealing into a soap bubble.

He fell to his knees, mouth gaping but nothing coming out, and I could see him shrinking, an arm shifting forward to the front of his body as his shoulder *changed shape*. Fingers sucked into his palm, nails curling up into points and poking out from what used to be knuckles, hair stubble poking out from the backs of his hands and growing into short, wiry brown fur. Then his eyes— green eyes still, despite their different shape—widened, a sound like radio static whimpering out of his mouth, and he collapsed into the mud completely, barely missing an overhanging pipe. His twitches pushed him under the framework supporting a pipe, into the shadow beneath it. One leg thrust back out at a right angle from his body and hit metal with a clang; the flesh dwindled, almost skeletal, and then he writhed again and it was gone.

I screamed. Started screaming. Couldn't stop.

The elevator *bing*ed. Slid open.

Guards poured out.

#

"Someone shut her up."

A flash of movement. *Whooomp*. Pain shot through my middle from the boot that had buried itself in my gut, forcing every ounce of air out of my lungs in a single fell swoop that abruptly cut off the loudest noise in the area.

Trax was yelling. I was on my hands and knees in the mud. I couldn't breathe.

124

There were hands on my shoulders pulling me back to kneeling, Sandra's hands. She wrapped me in her arms and held me as I choked air back into my lungs.

Derik.

Owen was paw-deep in muck, burrowing into the lump that had been Derik on the ground. Derik moved, a slithery glide along the pipe and under an intersecting pipe's framework, and then there was only Owen, lurching around and growling and biting at the air.

He was alive. Derik was *alive*. A reflexive sob of relief strangled out as a whimper.

"Shhh," Sandra murmured, stroking my hair.

Trax stood between us and the guards, hovering protectively. Not much he could do against the bristling armory leveled at us.

"Your sister?" The speaker was a blond in shirtsleeves and black pants, a perfect match for Sandra's description. Jorgen. "That simplifies things."

He stepped forward, his leather shoes still a spotless black despite the grime of this place, white-gold watch and white-gold ring far too shiny for a place like this. He stopped on the other side of my brother. "You've been asking too many questions," he said with a smug little smile. "I appreciate your consideration in joining us in person."

I spat. It landed in mud. I wasn't very good at projectile spit, and the ache in my stomach was like someone had kicked me all over again, and my knees couldn't figure out which way gravity was pulling, but the bastard had kidnapped my brother, and Derik—

It was the thought that counted. And all I could think was that I wanted this guy to die.

A person in a shiny white suit approached with a roll of duct tape, maneuvering around the pipe and carefully patching the leak.

"Won't hold for long," Jorgen commented, "but it'll do until the proper patch is ready." Moving to our left, he eyed the mud distastefully. Owen now huddled miserably in the muck, coiled as small as he could get. Covered as he was, it was hard to see anything of him but the teeth. "What have we got?"

The soldier leaned over for a better look. "'Nother otter."

Jorgen turned to us. To me. "You're a troublemaker. I don't like troublemakers. And I really don't like people messing with my facility." He nodded at the soldier. "Get rid of it."

Bam.

Owen's blood splattered across the mud.

I would have screamed his name, but could only come up with a strangled, unintelligible gasp.

Sandra did it for me. "Derik!" she shrieked, and tried to run to him. I felt cold and wet along one side, saw I'd fallen in the mud. One of the guards grabbed her before she could get to him.

Derik.

She thought he was Derik. She and Trax had been standing; unable to see the change from their angle. They didn't even know that Owen had gotten us down here.

Sandra didn't even know that Owen was Lost.

The shadows under a distant pipe moved, stilled. If I hadn't been looking for it, I would have never noticed.

"You bastard," I slurred with the first breath I got back. "You murdered Derik."

Chapter Fifteen

My head began to clear soon after, while they were putting me in a chair in a windowless office. This time, guards stood outside the door. The woman packed the last of her files in a box, including the ones the guards had pulled off me. She smirked at me as she walked by, and kicked me in the shin on her way out. Jorgen stopped her at the door for a fleeting kiss, and she gave him a half-lidded smile before disappearing.

I yanked my wrists against the zip-ties holding them together behind the chair. It didn't do much good. The three of us were well and thoroughly tied.

Jorgen perched on the desk, dialing the phone. "Rogers. Yes, I got them. It was the boy's sister and her boyfriend." He picked up a keyring from the desk, *my* keys, which they'd frisked from my pockets. "Boyfriend's dead." The phone lodged between his ear and his shoulder as he used my apartment key to pick clean one of his nails. The white gold of his ring flashed in the bright office lights. *Cute couple.* I found myself hoping he and his wife shared a horrible STD. "Yes. Easily. I'm handling it. Just wanted to update you." A second check must have revealed clean skin, because he put the keys back down on the desk. "Right. Tomorrow. I'll be there." He hung up.

Sandra yanked at her bonds until the chair rattled. "You can't get away with this. He's a celebrity." She nodded to Trax.

Jorgen chuckled. "And you're his number one fan. That's exactly why we'll get away with it."

Trax glowered. "You have no idea how many people will be looking for me. There's nothing you can do that will get you clear of this."

Our captor snorted. "You. Out at night, visiting the lake." Running a finger along Trax's shoulders, Jorgen laughed at the screech of my chair legs on the floor. Trax had flinched, damn it. What the hell had happened before I got here?

Holding the back of Trax's chair, he pointed a finger at Sandra. "Her, your number one *crazy* fan, sees you. She's been planning this for years; she only had to get you alone long enough to make it happen. She pulls her gun and orders you go with her."

He circled behind me. I flinched from the hands that clamped down on my own shoulders. "But you're not alone. Darling sister, always worried about her beloved brother, has followed you. She sees the gun and tries to tackle it away from you."

I yanked against his hand, and he let go. "Everyone knows we work together," I countered, nodding to Sandra.

"All the more reason for you to know how dangerous she is." He patted me on the head. I growled at him. "The gun goes off, and hits brother-dearest. He falls in the lake. You get the gun away from blondie, and turn it on her."

Sandra cursed at him. "I would never hurt Trax. Ever."

Jorgen shrugged, spreading his hands and adopting a tragic expression. "With the death of her last living relative, sweet sister can't take it anymore, and runs off into nowhere, never to be seen again." He frowned and leaned against the desk, pressing the back of his hand to his forehead. "It's the tragic story that graces the covers of magazines for months. I'm sure they'll put together a lovely tribute."

"I'm sure they will," Trax growled out through clenched teeth.

"No one would fall for that," Sandra argued.

Jorgen turned to me expectantly. I said nothing. "Well?" he prompted with a raised eyebrow. "No dire promises of failure and retribution? No cliché 'you won't get away with this' to follow my evil monologue?"

I let my glare answer him.

He smirked. "Someone knows how the real world works." He patted my cheek. "I'm going to go arrange your date with Rogers. He can always use another Powered for his research." Giving himself one final check in the mirror mounted on the wall, he straightened his tie. "Be good," he admonished, and left.

I closed my eyes, and listened.

"You shouldn't have come," Trax scolded.

"Shh." I didn't have to tell him twice. He knew when I was concentrating.

The guards shifted and muttered jokes to one another. Jorgen was on the phone with someone. His wife was setting up in one of the glass offices further down, tapping a nail into the wall. Guards were weaving around the building, inside and out.

It took half an hour for him to get to the door, long enough for the mud on my clothes to dry into a crusty mess.

"What was that?" one of the guards outside our door asked. *Shhhhhf.* "Rex?" The *click* of a gun safety being removed. *Thmp.*

Then nothing.

The door opened.

"No," I gasped.

Derik grinned. A Hunter's grin.

Sandra and Trax's strangled gasps reminded me that they had no idea. "It's Derik!" I hissed at them.

Sandra stared at me, eyes wide. "But—"

I shook my head. "That was Owen." My throat caught on his name. Derik glided up to me, slit the ties with a single claw. "He—he must have..." I placed a hand on Derik's head, hot streaks falling down my cheeks.

Ordered me to get moving. Told me to hide. Knew what he was doing. His voice in my head was deeper, rougher than the one I knew. Different. His eyes were green, though. *I understood him,* he added unnecessarily.

I nodded. Of course he had. Seemed like the Hunters understood everything.

Shaking off my tear that had splashed on his snout, Derik cut both Sandra's and Trax's bonds. *Is there any evidence left?* he asked as they stretched.

I shook my head, pocketing my keys. "They took it all."

Never mind. Getting out is more important. Tell them to take off their shoes and carry them.

"How are we going to get out?" Sandra's question stopped Derik in the doorway. He looked over his shoulder at her and then moved forward again. I'd expected to have to step over a pair of bodies as I exited the room, but there was nothing. We followed him left, down the hall past the offices.

Two of them had open doors. Both of the open offices were empty. The rest had their blinds drawn.

Of course. Who ever heard of a private office with the blinds open? Corporate giants liked their privacy.

Derik must have hidden the bodies at this end, because the only sign of guards was a fine red splatter across the patterned marble floor. He'd put the key in the plant in the corner. At his direction, I fished it out and slid it through the elevator card slot. The light activated.

We breathed as lightly as we could, the three of us trying to huddle behind a spindly indoor palm.

We weren't hidden. But we were out of the line of sight when the doors opened.

Never had I seen an expression more terrifying than Derik's evil grin. He was a Hunter, and already moving before the people in the elevator could even shout.

There was only one strangled, muffled scream. One man threw himself out, his right arm split in two from the elbow to the hand. Wide eyes didn't even register us as he scrambled for a handhold, gasping and pulling at the slick marble floor, a thick stream of blood gushing from his neck.

Paws landed on his back with the *crunch* of broken ribs. Derik leaned down and *breathed* on the man, a vaguely visible miasma of distorted air. And then Derik stood on nothing but marble.

His eyes raised to meet mine. There was an apology in those green eyes. Right above a mouthful of razor-sharp fangs. I shuddered.

A door opened.

Trax pushed me toward the elevator. I stumbled. Sandra grabbed my arm and tried to pull me back. Trax shoved both of us with a strength I'd never known he had, and we slid forward, my stockinged feet slipping and sliding.

Derik stepped out of the elevator, staring down whatever witness waited behind us. Sandra *eep*'ed at the half handprint on the wall. It only had three fingers. She turned Trax toward the doors, away from it, her hand over her mouth.

"Don't look," she said. His hand settled on her shoulder, turning her as well.

Grayish tan wasn't a good color for my brother. He reached for the door-close button with the arm not holding Sandra, his jaw set.

"Derik!" I hissed.

Trax's lips thinned. He pressed the button. A red light beside the door-open button flashed off.

Derik swirled in between the sliding doors, twisting to send one final glare at the blonde woman with a bruise on her forehead. The doors closed. And we were going up.

#

We reached the top in about two minutes of silence, more quickly than my diver's ear was comfortable with but slowly enough for safety. I'd never ridden a diagonal-motion elevator before, and I was pretty certain now that I'd never want to try again.

"The pressure regulators must be terrific," I observed when the soft chords of the elevator music ended.

Derik *chuffed*, and I realized he was laughing.

He ran out the doors as soon as they opened. There was no one waiting for us. The guards who knew about this entrance must have all boarded when the unauthorized-access alarm sounded.

The floor under our feet was carpeted, but the small office's walls were clearly metal.

"I think we're on the Lorren's Oil official drilling platform," Sandra said.

The elevator doors closed behind us. I turned, and couldn't see them. They were the exact shade and shape of the wall panels. Not even a button betrayed them.

Sandra patted the seam in the wall. "How do they open?" she asked.

Trax shook his head. "I don't know. We need to get out of here, before someone comes."

I looked down at Derik. "Got any ideas?"

His Hunter's grin said *no*.

Taking a deep breath and releasing it, I ran through the likely options in my head. "If there's an alert—and there's been enough time for one—Jorgen won't want to give away the entrance. He'll go to great length to hide it, even. So if there's a report out about us, it won't direct them here."

"That means we have time, right?" Trax squatted, his gaze on the place where the door met the floor. "We have to figure out how to sneak out."

Sandra bit her knuckle. I found myself staring at the bags under her red eyes as she spoke. "Mm. I did an interview… They ferry the workers in from shore, but there are tons of lifeboats, just in case. I bet we could steal one, if we were careful." She kicked off her heels, picked them up, and then stood staring at the shoe in each hand, fingers tightening around them. I heard a strangled sound, half-whine and half-choke.

Placing my hands over hers, I bowed my head, and felt her forehead come to rest against my own. *Owen*, I thought, and the hot splash against my hand could have come from either one of us.

"Guys…" The word from Trax skirted our hearing, soft and hesitant, but unwilling to leave.

Breathing in deeply, I met Sandra's gaze, rubbing my thumb over the back of her hand. She sniffed hard, transferred a shoe to the other hand, and squeezed my hand, and then wiped her face and nodded.

"We'll have to move quickly and quietly," she said, and if her voice was deeper than normal, her words made sense.

I turned away to touch the wiry-furred shoulder as tall as Trax's hip. "Derik, can you scout for us, as soon as I say it's clear outside the door?"

He nodded.

Closing my eyes, I dropped into the worlds of beats and rhythms, and *listened* once more. The rush of oil through the central pipe, and a *whooosh* of air through the ducts. A rumbling of the platform's engines, and a hum of electricity. Feet in a room above us, stomping back and forth. Rubber-soled boots down a hall not far away, the rustle of nylon accompanying them.

I waved to Derik and cracked open the door. "Try not to kill anyone," I whispered to his back. He paused in doorway and looked at me, snickered, and disappeared off.

He hadn't been gone long when the boots rounded a corner and started cracking doors on our hall.

Clutching Trax's arm, I pointed in the direction of the sound. Wide-eyed, he looked from me to where I was pointing and back, then waggled two fingers back and forth like legs walking. I nodded, and Sandra covered her mouth, going pale.

We had to find a way to hide in the elevator. Striding across the room, I ran my hands over the woodwork once more.

Thump-thump – thump-thump…

Sandra fell to her knees and ducked under the desk. Her fingers scrambled over the woodwork.

Muffled voices not far off: *"Clear. Check the next; I'll cover."* Shit. They had to be next door.

Trax threw himself at the small bookcase in the corner, hands sliding up and down the sides.

Something clicked. The elevator door slid back open.

We scurried in on tiptoes, my finger jamming the *door close* button. Thankfully, it didn't announce its presence with a bell or a ding; Jorgen valued his secrets, apparently.

With my ear pressed to the door, I could hear the man slam his way into the office. "Clear," a deep voice said, and the boots stomped off.

With sighs relief, we piled out into the empty room.

Derik returned not long after, the door swinging open for him despite his lack of opposable thumbs.

"How do you *do* that?" I asked.

A snicker. *I found a way off,* he answered instead. *Follow me.*

We ducked down the corridor from which the searchers had come. It didn't take long for me to realize that the trio of guards who'd ridden down on the elevator might have been as much night duty staff as the platform could manage.

Dawn, I thought, felt closer than the previous dusk, and my feet felt heavier. Trax put a hand on my arm and offered me a weak smile, more wish than form. He looked pretty tired—no. Squeezing my eyes shut and shaking my head hard, I revised the thought: *He looks damned exhausted.* Better.

If we had been less tired, we might not have walked right past Derik, standing with his shoulders bunched forward and legs bent. I might not have ended up nose-to-nose with a surprised-looking lone guard.

Trax, half-conscious and stripped to his blue long-sleeved shirt, did what he'd been trained to do when cornered by an unknown member of the public: he lifted his chin to catch the light on his profile, displaying his limp Mohawk, and gave his best surprise-photo PR grin.

Recognition flashed in the guard's eyes, and the shout forming on his lips tangled over confusion to come out as a quieter, "You're...?"

Something flashed beside me, and there was a loud *Klunk,* and then I had to slow the guard's slump to the floor as he fell, Trax grabbing for the gun so it wouldn't clatter to the ground.

Derik's nostrils flared. Nudging my thigh, he looked up at me through the top of his eyes. *You asked me not to kill another one,* he said. *Getting knocked out like that isn't exactly safe, but he's not dead.*

I didn't ask for clarification on that statement. *Owen,* I thought, and pursed my lips to suck a breath in through my nose. "How much further?" I asked, and hoped the tightness in my voice didn't give away how much I had to atone for.

Almost there, he said, and a few twists and turns later we were slipping into a mostly sheltered-from-view lifeboat whose securing cords had been cut but for the single one left tethering it to the platform. Derik pulled a large dark blanket out from a corner, and we draped it over ourselves and the boat, edges trailing in the water. In the darkness of the early morning, we were as camouflaged as we could be.

"If we can get far enough out and throw off the blanket, then start the engine," Sandra said, "we'll be just another set of boaters."

Tie a rope to me, Derik ordered.

"But the cold —"

Won't bother me now.

With shaking hands, I tied one of the ropes he'd cut around him. He slipped into the water with barely a splash, and then we were huddling under a blanket that was growing wetter and colder by the second, getting towed by a Hunter. By the time we cast the blanket off, the sliver of a moon sat low on the horizon, and by the time we reached shore, the stars had faded on the cusp of the coming dawn.

Chapter Sixteen

My car was where we had left it, apparently untouched. I opened the door.

"My question," I said, "is how we're going to change you back."

"And my question," Trax piped up, "is how long it takes them to concoct a story against us. I don't think we should go home."

Sandra groaned.

"ATM, cash, and hotel?" I suggested.

We slept through the morning at a cheap motel. Sandra disappeared for a while and came back with a pair of shoes in my size and Derik's geriatric car. "They saw yours and mine," she explained.

"Now what?" I asked over one of the pizzas she'd brought. "Police?"

Trax dropped his chin into his hand. Our cell phones had been frisked away, so there was no calling his agent for her advice — fat chance she'd be of any use, anyway. "Maybe."

"Worth a try, right?" I blew on my slice before taking a tentative bite.

Sandra shook her head.

Since my mouth was full, I rolled the fingers of my spare hand in the air in a silent request for elaboration.

"How long do you think an operation like that can stay hidden?" she asked. "For one thing, we committed half a dozen crimes last night ourselves. For another, chances are that there's an insider or seven, smoothing things out with law enforcement. You don't just build a huge operation like that and hope nobody notices."

Trax stretched out on the bed he and I had crashed on. "I can say something to the public," he suggested.

Derik dropped the remote in my lap. I turned on the TV.

"Good point," I admitted a few minutes later.

An interview with Thomas J. Rogers was progressing in the foreground. "Power is as much mind as body," he said, as the news ticker rolled. *Singer Trax and sister missing, wanted for questioning in the death of local resident Derik Holskerski,* scrolled across the bottom of the screen. *Local reporter Sandra Collins suspected.*

"Guess that eliminates the police, too." Sandra stood up and began to pace. "So what? The Internet?"

"We'd be labeled as nutjobs." I crossed my legs and reached for another piece of ham-and-pineapple.

"At least the message would be out," Trax argued.

"And where are we going to get a computer?" I asked. "The library? With the city searching for us?"

Derik lay down against my hip. *If they're trying to implicate you for my death...*

"Nobody knows what you are," I said. "And I'm the only who can understand you. There's no official pictures or reports of Hunters, and I wouldn't trust them not to hurt you."

Trax sat up. "We need to change him back."

#

I don't want to involve him in this, Derik argued.

"And see how great that worked before?" I answered back, settling myself on the couch. "If you'd called on him earlier, would we even be in this mess?"

Probably. Probably be worse, he grumbled. But he lay his head on my lap.

I made sure both of my hands were visible when the door opened. The man still had a gun out of the breadbox quicker than I could move. "Give me one reason I shouldn't kill you right now," he growled. The gun was pointed at the monster in my lap, not me.

"Derik's still alive," I answered. "And he needs our help."

Valdez lowered his gun. "And that thing?"

"Is Derik."

#

"I think we need to go south," I suggested after updating him. "The key lies there, I'm sure of it."

Valdez poked Derik in the ribs a third time. "What's the difference is between a Hunter and a normal Lost?"

Derik flashed his fangs at him.

"Besides that. Why *you*?"

"He has a point," Sandra put in. "And what about that guy that — that disappeared?"

Derik looked up at me. *One of the guards became Lost. But most people just disappear. It's like I've got a piece of the Tides in me.*

My hand was too numb to feel the texture of his coat under my fingers. I'd gotten used to being cold. "Sandra, wasn't Owen Powered?"

She nodded. "Earth Power, low level. He was pretty sure he'd find a construction job up here. Do you think…?"

I wrapped an arm around Derik's neck and studied the patterns in the ceiling tiles. I wasn't sure what to think.

Valdez sprawled out on the floor. "I'm with Kelly-girl. I say we go south. Hook lover-boy up with his southern cousins and find some answers."

Trax popped a bottlecap and passed him a beer. "They can't know more than anyone else. Don't you think they would have told her?"

Sandra wiped her fingers on a napkin and then grabbed another piece. "The Tides are coming in. In another two weeks, they'll be back to full."

"Which is why," Trax said, "we have to go now. Pass me a slice of the pepperoni."

Derik sneered at the cheesy slice of deliciousness as it passed by his nose. I had the feeling he rather disapproved of pizza. Why had I never known that?

I already missed his cooking.

"I've never been to the South." Sandra's face was pale, and the pizza she held by her fake nails was shaking, but she wasn't arguing.

"How are we going to get there, anyway?" Trax took a swig of his drink, the bottle coming away from his lips with an audible *pop*.

Valdez looked at Derik. "I've got a truck. How do you feel about horses?"

The bared fangs were probably a joke.

#

The horse-trailer attached to the half-rusted deathtrap Valdez called a truck was the serious kind, secured with heavy bolts to the hitch, two steel stalls closed by thick, dingy white rear doors. Half-gates inside the doors allowed for cooler unloading waits, and for ventilation were mesh windows with metal locks. The rubber matting had been graciously lined with blankets and pillows instead of straw, although the dusty scent of old bedding lingered, and the wall dividing the stalls was thick metal mesh. Under the smell of dust was a vague, mildly pungent odor that reminded me of old grass ad fresh dirt; I eyed the streaks on the door and decided it could be worse.

"Guess we're housebroken horses, to get pillows to sit on." I crawled into the right side. "Where'd you get it?"

"Friend of mine has a pair, a gelding and a companion pony. The pony likes to bully the gelding when it gets stressed, so if he doesn't want bloody noses he's got to keep them separated, but they both freak out if they think they're alone. I'm gonna leave the windows closed. Stay quiet if we have to stop."

Trax slid in behind me. "I'm not going to argue. It's bad enough smelling like horse without being chased by the police." We had enough room to sit elbow to elbow with our feet on the divider.

Derik's face appeared on the other side of the bars separating the two sections. I hadn't heard him get in. Valdez bolted the door closed behind Sandra. "You kids comfortable back there?"

"Neeeeeigh," Trax answered.

A snort of laughter, and then Valdez was moving away to climb into the cab. The truck started with a *clung* and backed out of the driveway with a *ratta-tatta-tatta, fhwomp-fwomp-omp*. The gears screamed *aaargh* as he put it into first. I shared a pained look with Trax. This was going to be a noisy trip.

It started a mile out, before we'd gotten out of town. The soft *clang* of claw on metal, half-buried beneath the *rattle-grind* of the truck's running song. A little scrabble. A quiet whimper.

"Derik?" I asked, trying to peer through the mesh. For a moment, I didn't see him at all, hidden in a nest of blankets. Then he sat up. His mouth hung slightly open, his breath coming in short pants.

We hit a bump, and he shuddered at something other than the whimper of metal.

I pressed my fingers against the divider. "What's wrong?"

He edged over until short wiry hairs poked through to prick against my skin. *Hurts,* he said. *Deep pain. Like a twisted muscle or —* The trailer bounced, and he lurched. It took him a moment to get back up. *Don't worry about it. Probably why the Lost don't leave the Tides. It'll be better when we get there.*

Come to think of it, why hadn't anyone ever experimented on the Lost? I didn't think the Hunters could catch *everyone*. Someone had to have tried.

"I don't like this. We should head back." They wouldn't have said anything if all the subjects had died.

Sandra shifted over. "Is he okay?"

I shook my head. "He's in pain."

Derik tossed his head and growled.

"It's his decision," Trax interpreted, and turned to the bars. "Can you deal with it?"

A panting nod. And then Derik lay back down.

"Let me help you sleep." Kneeling so my forehead almost touched the metal, I tried to see him. I couldn't. But I could hear him: *Sa-sa sa-sa sa-sa*. The quickest I'd ever heard a Hunter's heart beat. I tapped. "Relax. Don't fight me, and I'll see if I can help you sleep through it. Like the truck driver, remember?"

He panted, which wasn't a disagreement.

Tng-tng tng-tng tng-tng. My finger against the metal, the feeling of Power pulling through me, the rattling and bumps of the road trying to make me miss the beat. I wouldn't. Not if it stopped Derik's pain. *Tng-tng, tng-tng, tng-tng, tng-tng... tng-tng... tng-tng...*

Sa-sa sa-sa sa-sa. Every drop of the magic disappeared, flooding into him without making an ounce of change. I *pulled* harder. As hard as I could, until a fire began to throb behind my temples.

"It's not working." My voice came out in a panicked squeak. And then I remembered Owen. "It's not going to work."

Derik sat up enough to touch his nose to the divider, and then lay back down.

It got worse. He made an effort not to make noise, I could tell he was trying, but he'd lost the silence that had been a part of his very being. Scritches, scrambling claws. Panting and spasms. These segued into quiet whimpers and thrashes. By noon, his cries had become loud enough to be heard over the screams of the truck, and no matter how much magic I tried to funnel into him, it didn't seem to make a difference. I banged on the metal, hard, hoping they'd hear us in the cab.

Valdez pulled over in some middle-of-nowhere side road, *cruuuunch-rattle-ping* on gravel. The latch twisted with a groan. He opened our stall first.

"That sounds worse than Bessie. What's going on?"

Pain in my hands made me realize my nails were biting into the skin of my palms. "We have to go back. I think it's killing him." My throat hurt, raw and tight.

We dragged ourselves out. Trax glanced at me before going into the woods for a bathroom break. Sandra put a hand on my shoulder. I bit my wrist.

Sandra pulled on my arm. "C'mon. We should get down there as soon as possible."

I winced at a *clang* of claw on metal. "We have to take him back."

A snarl from the stall.

"We're as close to the Tide Zone as we are to home," Valdez said. "Turning around now won't help."

I let Sandra take me into the woods.

Chapter Seventeen

In the final hours, I was afraid he'd gone Mad. The steel was graded for protecting full-sized horses in case of an accident: good, solid metal protection. Shame filled me when I realized I was comforted by its presence.

Trax clutched me in his arms, trying to cover my ears and wiping the tears off my face. He'd grabbed my hands to stop the tapping, to stop my magic and to keep me from wearing myself sick after I nearly vomited on his shoes. There were people who used their Powers all day long without stop, but endurance like that took years of long, hard work. If he hadn't forced me to take breaks from the useless magic I wouldn't stop throwing, I would have spent the last few hours unconscious instead of merely sick to my stomach.

Might have been an improvement.

My last solace had come when Valdez stopped for gas, and Derik had had enough mind to quiet down. That was four hours ago.

Four hours can be an eternity.

But Sandra sat up against the steel wall, crooning a lullaby, ignoring the clatter of claws across the fine grill of air holes. The deepest part of me wanted to join her; the rest of me couldn't move, could barely breathe, ached from exhaustion and numb fingers that kept escaping Trax's hands to tap the floor.

Trax didn't sing either. In those final hours, as Sandra wet her throat from water bottles and croaked out a Shenandoah solo, her shaky notes half-buried beneath the agonized death throes of a truck that wouldn't actually die, I loved her music more than I'd ever liked my brother's.

We didn't stop in Memphis. We barely even slowed down through the unmanned checkpoint at the gate marking the boundary where civilians supposed to turn back, a good mile out from the highest point of the Tides. But Derik was quiet now. Was he in less pain? Was he dying? I slid away from Trax and knelt by the divider.

"Derik?" No answer. The slow scrape of a claw on metal. "Derik, are you all right?" Nothing. "Derik!" *Bang bang bang.*

"Don't," Sandra begged, grabbing for my arm. "You're going to hurt yourself."

No. This couldn't be happening. *I could not be losing him.* My fingers couldn't fit through the fine grill, but I had to see, had break down the barrier; my cheek burned with cold as I stood to press it to the metal, and my fingernails screeched against the steel.

Hot hands wrenched me back. Struggling, I kicked and nearly unmanned Trax when a bump in the road tossed us the wrong way, but he did that damn pinning move he'd figured out when we were kids wrestling in the backyard, and my stomach pressed into the floor where we'd tumbled. What was wrong with Derik? "Let me up!" Stupid brat; from this angle I couldn't get a good kick in, could barely turn my shoulders enough to glare at him.

"Just stop. We can't do anything right now." His face was wet, though, and his cheeks splotchy. Lower lip red—he often bit it when trying not to show frustration—he held me down until my thrashing turned into sobs.

We pulled over five minutes later, not far past the beginning of the mile-wide Tide zone, the area where the oncoming Tide's magic soaked into the land ahead of its inundation. With a few final gasps and sputters, the truck settled itself into a full stop. Valdez swung open the latch and opened our door. "There's a car here with a license tag from this year; don't look like it's been through the Tides yet. Empty, though. Doubt the driver's comin' back. I figure that's as good sign a sign as any, bein' as we want company."

"Come on," Trax urged me. I shook my head, burying it between my knees. I didn't want to see. He hesitated, then crawled out. A *clang* as Valdez unlocked the other door.

Silence broken only by the *ping* of the settling truck.

"Derik," I whispered. He was too quiet; he might be *gone*. Why did everyone get taken from me?

Sandra put a hand on my knee.

"He's still breathing," Valdez announced at last.

A sob caught in my throat. I pushed it down and wormed my way out. The least I could do was sit with him.

They'd left him in the other half, the door open but the half-gate closed. I tried to pull him out, but Valdez stopped me. "He might not be himself when he wakes up," he said. They wouldn't let me climb in with him, either.

Derik lay there, his sides moving slowly (and hadn't I wondered if the Lost even breathed? But clearly he did). Pounding didn't wake him up. Neither did screaming. So I put my head against the metal and waited.

It wasn't until the sounds stopped that I realized the others had been setting up a camp with the supplies Valdez had crammed into the truck bed. At the complete silence, I turned to see what had made them stop.

The others had frozen mid-motion among the fledgling tents, a thin pole jutting six feet in the air from Sandra's left hand. Her lips were pale and thin, her gaze trained to a spot at the edge of the road.

It sat out in the open, just watching.

Guards aren't really needed at the checkpoints, I thought, and then, *it's a Hunter.*

"Help him."

It looked at me. I stepped away from the trailer. "Help him!" I pulled the handle that latched the inner gate to the other stall. "He's like you, damn it! *Help* him!"

He was on his side, the brown-black fur matted with sweat. Everyone else faded from my view. I crawled onto the stall, reached in. His fur was definitely wet. But it was a lukewarm damp, cooling. And he was so quiet.

"*Please!*" Desperation pulled me out of the truck, put me right in the face of the Huntress. "You can fix him. He's one of you. I know you understand me, dammit!" I grabbed her ears and stared into her startled eyes.

Her fangs bared. *How dare she — wait. Since when do they know we understand them? I wonder…*

"Hunters took me to the border," I answered. "Made me watch the butterflies go through."

Kelly? Her head tilted slightly.

Sandra gasped. Six more had appeared out of the grass.

"Do something!" I shouted at one of the newcomers. "You have to."

My captive Huntress shook her head, her ears flapping free, and looked at one of the others. It gave me what I swore was a skeptical expression before going toward the truck.

The trailer sagged under its weight, but the magic of its abilities silenced the metal's groan of protest. Prodding Derik with its nose, it sniffed around his body, nudging him. He didn't move.

Sticking its head out the back, it summoned one of the others. I bit my knuckles as they leaned over him. Broke skin when they breathed on him, that miasma of deadly power that had evaporated a guard.

The ice spearing through my thigh stopped me from going to him. She looked up at me. *You love him very much.*

They were saving him. I wasn't going to argue. I nodded.

The pair jumped down and came over, stood for a moment, then moved away. *He'll be fine. He's already recovering. We don't know him, though.*

"Do you know all the Hunters down here?"

She nodded.

"It happened in Wisconsin."

And so I had the privilege of shocking a Huntress off her feet.

#

The ones who'd run off after my announcement returned with others. At first Valdez tried to keep us humans together, but then there were just too many Hunters, some wandering around and ignoring us altogether, others watching with avid curiosity. I was quickly herded away to tell my story in the center of a circle around an abandoned Ford—the one with the up-to-date license tag, which I thought might bother me, but was surprised when all I felt was a moment of relief at the possibility of having an actual *seat*, should we happen to drive home. The other humans stopped freaking out when it became clear that the Hunters were more interested in talking than hurting me.

Camp got put up in relatively short order. Trax actually pushed his way through a knot of them to bring me food. More surprisingly, they let me go with him afterwards. *Rest*, one of them ordered, and nudged me toward Valdez's truck.

Derik still lay somnolent in the back. He wasn't breathing. I touched his side and froze in panic. He was cold, ice-cold; he was gone. No. No, he couldn't be. "Derik! Derik, wake up!"

Green eyes glittered sleepily at me. *What?*

I choked. "Ah... you're cold..." And not breathing.

A Hunter's laugh from behind me. The Huntress had followed me in. *He's Lost. What did you expect?*

"Oh." I laid a hand on his shoulder. He let his head flop back down.

Tired, he said. *Just a few minutes more.*

The Huntress whapped him with a paw. His head popped back up. Their gazes locked for a moment, and then he sighed and rolled up into a sitting position. She left.

I'm fine now.

"Are you?"

He nudged my shoulder with his nose and slunk out of the truck, silent and graceful.

I wanted to follow. But I'd already panicked and made a fool of myself, so instead of chasing him away with hovering, I helped Valdez finish setting up camp. He didn't comment on my red cheeks.

#

By morning, the two dozen had multiplied to six dozen. Breakfast consisted of Valdez tripping over ruthless, fanged nightmares as he dropped just-add-water pancakes onto our plates. The nightmares seemed somewhat nonplussed at being tripped over without being screamed at.

I passed Sandra hounding a particularly badgered-looking Hunter with yes-or-no questions on my search for Derik. Finally I found him in the center of a circle of Hunters, the ones I immediately thought of as the leaders. There was one, lighter than the others, that looked familiar, with her dark eyes and long eyelashes. The Huntress I'd met on my first trip down? I wasn't sure. They made room for me, letting me perch on the bumper of the Ford with Derik by my side. "Does this thing still work?"

Derik nodded. *Assuming it has keys. Hasn't been through a Tide yet.* He cocked his head. *Yeah. We can get them if we need to.*

If he wasn't going to mention my freak-out, neither would I. I stretched my legs out for the others to touch if they wanted to chime in directly. "We might. What have you found out?"

None of them were at the point of origin, Derik said. *We confirmed their theory that it was Lorren's Oil that started it, but we're not sure where to go from here. There's something that keeps them away from the Gulf, that stops them from investigating. They always seem to get turned around before they reach the coast.*

"Why the Lost? Why Hunters? What's the difference?"

He shook his head. *They don't know.* A hesitation. *They've put me in charge, you know.*

The Huntress placed a paw on my knee, and her voice confirmed she was the same Huntress I'd met before. *The youngest always gets the lead. They remember the most, still fight to remember. No one wants to talk about before, about what we lost. It hurts, literally. Even thinking about it hurts. Instead we protect the Lost, and guard the Tide Zone. Not guarding hurts. So we guard, and over time, forget who we were.* Her paw dropped back to the ground.

Derik's snout bobbed in agreement. *I asked before you got up and they all said the same thing. None of them can talk about who they used to be, not out here, not even their names. And they all feel the need to leave the Tides when they're in them. But they were all Powered; only the Powered become Lost. Everyone else —*

Vanished.

I should get Trax out of here.

Derik nudged me with his nose. The tip of his fang scraped against my jeans. I'd gotten him turned into a Hunter; he was already mostly lost to me. Or was he?

There was a piece of this puzzle I was missing. Something big, something fundamental.

"They don't know how to reverse the process." It was a statement; if the Hunters could fix themselves, I was sure they would have. One of them nodded anyway. Moving closer and offering him my hand, I stared toward the horizon, toward the south.

"What's it like behind the Tide?" I asked.

Silence, at first.

Cold, he said. *Only place I ever feel cold.*

Not cold; magical, another brushed him aside to refute. *The heart of Power itself, and it rips you apart.*

Jostling, then, as they all tried to get in a say. *Viscous without impairing movement.*

Loud silence. Colors that are sounds and sounds that are colors and nothing really makes noise, but you can hear everything. Everything is different. But everything looks just like it did.

Nothing works the same. We're ghosts. There's Power everywhere, all over, and it's death to touch. You can't use your active magic at all. People burn out, or run for the Edge and go Mad.

Other way around, doofus. Go Mad and then run for the Edge.

It's lonely.

Crowded.

Millions of people, but none of them can see you, all stuck in their own worlds.

They're not really there. Just shadows. Remnants.

We're all Lost.

Nobody's Lost. Everyone's human.

No one behind the Tide is human. Not even us.

I couldn't solve this here. There was too much information missing, too much I couldn't figure out. I stood up.

"I need you to take me to the Edge. Get the keys."

#

I lied to Trax. Valdez traded me his keys for the Ford's, which had more gas and could fit four, and promised to take care of the others while he unhitched the trailer. He also promised to get them out of here if I didn't get back that night. There was an angry glint in his eyes when I made him say it. "It's not the first time I've mysteriously vanished," I said. "And it's not like the Hunters can't protect me."

He spit. And turned away.

Trax tried to get in the truck with me. So I made Sandra get in instead. "I need to see the edge of the Tide again. Sandra's better at taking dictation. I don't think you'll be able to see what I'll see at all, so I need her skills." He grumbled, and stalked away from my window. Two minutes later, there was a *screech* as someone leaned on the tailgate. And then another as the truck bed raised back up.

The bed was full of Hunters. No room for stowaways.

The clatter of the truck meant we couldn't talk. Sandra had to wait until we arrived before she could ask her questions. "At least I'll have an exclusive," she said as we sat, staring at the swirls of nigh-invisible color.

"For what?"

Her eyes said she knew. I sighed.

"I don't want Trax to see this."

"How is leaving him wondering any better?" She pulled on a twist of her hair, her nose scrunching up in distress. "You'll break his heart. Leave it to the Hunters. They can do it just fine."

"They can't get close enough to the center."

The raised eyebrow, the angry glare said she disagreed with my logic. "What makes you think you can do any better? You'll be wasting your life. And what good will knowing what it looks like inside do you?"

I yanked the keys from the ignition, the key chain whacking against my thigh. "I don't know, Sandra. I don't. But it *can't* be plugged from the outside. God knows, they've tried. We've got to go to the source, and I'm the only who can hear them. If I'm different enough for that, maybe I'm different enough to make a difference. I have to at least try."

She rubbed a naked fingernail, its artificial shield long lost, and said nothing, although a tear rolled down her cheek. I slammed open the door and jumped out.

"It's beautiful." Sandra opened her car door and climbed out, keeping it between her and the Edge. "Horrifying, though."

Yeah. I turned to the dozen volunteers. "Just a few seconds each, that's all I need." The first of the Hunters slid under my hand. My eyes turned to the barrier.

A violent burst of color consolidated into a man holding a child's baseball bat. A boy sat beside him, tossing a baseball between his hands. The boy's lips moved to the words of a song, and the man watched out of the corner of his eye, a half-smile on his lips.

Then the boy pointed up. The man turned. His eyes widened, and he hefted the bat, and charged.

Light. And then it was over, the Hunter walking back out.

Another Hunter replaced the first. A woman grabbed a gun and began to shoot.

The next Hunter who went through, I saw a police officer shove a handcuffed man behind him and pull out a baton. The fourth, a warehouse manager drove a truck with a determined glint in his eye, and I could have sworn I heard the rumble of the engine as the truck barreled down at the barrier, but the sound faded before the vision did. The Huntress stayed by me to direct the others—the same Huntress who had taken me to the water tower, I was sure of it now.

I heard a car door close nearby. *Sandra must be getting bored.* Or could she see what I could? I put a hand on the Huntress's head, watching another walk in.

The back of a short-haired woman wearing a karate gi appeared on the Edge. She was teaching a child, no more than six. The child pointed, and she turned. Shoving her young student away, she turned and leapt into the air, snapping a flying kick at a force that couldn't be stopped.

The image faded. The Huntress looked up at me, her eyes dark and serious.

"Okay," I said. "I know what to do."

Are you sure?

I closed my eyes. "Yeah."

Okay. Meet you there.

I knelt by Derik. He nudged my hand, and I settled it between his ears. My mind replaced the knobby skull under my fingers with calloused fingers wrapping around my own. "You're coming, right?" I couldn't do it if he wasn't.

He nodded. *That was the plan.* He nudged my arm and then followed the Huntress through.

Sandra was crying when I pulled the tire iron out from behind the drivers' seat. Moving away from the open passenger door of the truck, she opened her mouth, but no words came. She glanced sideways, down the road, where half a dozen cars sat long-abandoned. One looked like the one we'd left behind in camp, rust invisible from here. But they'd have had no reason to follow us; I'd promised my brother I was coming back. And I'd surely have noticed the only other working car in the area if they had.

I hugged Sandra. "Take care of Trax," I said again, and turned.

And then I charged the barrier.

In the last couple of steps I remembered having heard a car door close. I tried to stop, but momentum, the Edge—

"Kelly!" Trax's voice followed me through.

Chapter Eighteen

I remembered my mother.

The best hours of my youth were those I spent watching her work.

As an editor, she would spend hours working on the computer, *tump-tump-tumping* away, or else sitting with her eyes dancing and her mouse *click-click-clicking*. When it was "Mommy's work time," she'd place my brother and me in our play zone with crayons and paper, put on a pair of headphones connecting to her cranky old music player, turn the volume to midway, and start tapping out the tune of the music on her collarbone as she read.

As I got older, I discovered that I could judge her clients' work by that tapping. *Tump-tump-tump*, regularly to a beat I couldn't hear, meant they were doing well, that she didn't need much concentration because there wasn't much that needed fixing. When the beat dissolved into a rapid flutter, I knew she was enraptured, on the edge of her seat as the novel gripped her and wouldn't let her go. When that happened, sometimes she wouldn't remember to make dinner, or hear Dad come in. She'd always hear us if we cried, though; she never forgot her kids.

When she ran into something that made her think, the beat would lapse into silence, and her lips would curl into a moue. These were the moments she loved the best, even more than being swallowed by the story. Mom liked a good challenge, and so when she found a passage that came *so close* to being perfect, if only she could figure out what it needed... Sometimes, if she really had to think, she'd pull the earbuds out and stare at the screen in silence. Her nose would scrunch and scrinch and squirm around her face, and her eyes would take turns squinting and rolling around. She was always in a good mood after a day like that.

I could tell she'd be in a bad mood if the rhythm slowed without stopping. *Tump... Tump... Tump...* it was the Imperial Death March, the ominous sound of funeral drums. But worse were the occasional e-mails—the ones she despised more than anything, when a once-favored writer was snatched away by a larger publisher. That usually led to squeaky vituperation and the dramatic *crack* of Mom mercilessly kicking the tiny, battered trashcan under her desk. This was usually followed by more high-pitched cursing, as Mom rarely wore shoes, and the trashcan sensibly chose to fight back by being metal. We typically ate out on those nights, because Dad was a terrible cook.

In actuality, Dad watched us more often than Mom did. Mom's job might let her take her work home on Monday and Tuesday afternoons, but she often had to travel, seeking out new clients for her company. Dad's job was a little more flexible. As a fourth-class music Power, he went from clinic to clinic, hiring himself out by the hour to sing away patients' pains. As a subcontractor, he got to choose his hours; as a father, he tried to keep his schedule as regular as possible for the patients' sakes, but his own kids came first.

It was Dad who had taught Trax and me how to swim. The first time I was under water, I was six. I can still remember how I opened my eyes and saw a world undulating and distorted, peaked with sparkles of sunlight and folded at strange places. My eyes had burned in a way I hadn't expected, water and chlorine making themselves known, but I'd been so distracted by the sights that the pain hadn't bothered me.

It bothered me now. Not a pain-burn, but that almost-headache I'd become used to during diving class, looking out of the water into a world that would never quite focus. Was I diving? No. There weren't office buildings in the ocean.

I wasn't underwater. I was in the Tides.

I was different. I was the same. My hands flickered, danced, morphed, refracted into a caricature of themselves. But they were still hands. Somewhat transparent hands, but still hands.

I'd like to think I gathered myself quickly. I didn't. My hands, my legs, my feet: they fascinated me more than the suburban city around me. My legs were long and pale through the haze of my jeans, and I could see the texture of the pavement through them.

My feet stood on the pavement; I walked three steps, and felt a slight viscosity, less than water but more than air; I picked my feet up and gravity forgot to pull me down. The word *plasma* came to mind, an old memory from magic class: not quite gas, not quite liquid. Paddling forward moved me faster than walking, the white lines on the street blurring with each smooth stroke.

Street. I was some place. Some place important. Oh. In the Tides. I had a purpose. People to protect. To save. I looked around, taking in the rest of the world.

If the Earth were made of smoke, that would be the buildings around me. People swam through the inanimate like water, and wavered through each other as if they were on separate levels of existence.

Most of the bodies were faint, more ghostly than myself, and completely unaware of my arrival. Threads of light hinted at people I couldn't see. But one person stood out, someone swimming toward me. Her large, dark eyes met mine. She was my height, maybe a little shorter, a pretty African American woman with beautiful long eyelashes, still sporting the utilitarian uniform we'd worn on the Recovery team.

"Elizabeth! You're—you're alive?"

She nodded, a wry smile on her face. "Yeah. Sorry. I'm the Huntress. I couldn't tell you that before."

"I thought you were—" I covered my mouth. "You're okay?"

"Mostly." A glance down over herself. "I always miss hands, when I'm in the other form, out there guarding everything." An apologetic grin twisted onto her face. "I bet I worried you guys."

Worry? "I was half out of my mind. I thought you were fucking *dead*, because of me." I wanted to hit her. I wanted to throw my arms around her and celebrate. God, I didn't know what to think.

"I did want to say something—I kept the others from attacking you, but I couldn't make myself say it was me. I mean, I couldn't. Like the words wouldn't even form in my head." Pressing on her temples with the heels of her hands, she stared at me through long eyelashes.

Her thoughts couldn't even form? "What, like how you wanted to leave the Tides when you were in it?"

Tucking her hands back into her armpits, she nodded. "It's hard to explain. Being a Hunter, it changes how you think. Messes with your mind, and the way you feel about everything... I dunno. Elizabeth kind of *is* dead, outside the Tides. I only think normally here, inside, except the need to leave. It's so cold here, I can never wait to get out."

"But the midnight drive, the oil rig—I was scared out of my mind. You *laughed* at me."

With a duck of her chin, she turned partway away from me and shifted. "I know. I can't even say why, because I don't know. It was me, and yet I wasn't me. Like I'd forgotten the concept of compassion."

Reeling, trying to stop the feeling that she'd lied to me, to quiet the memory of that truck ride to the water tower, to quiet the memory of her human self in the jaws of a Hunter, I wanted to sit down. My knees gave out, but instead of falling, I continued to hover. "Why did you do it? Why did you save me?"

"Grandma was always about saving people." She wrapped her arms around herself and shivered. "If it helps, I really am sorry I couldn't let you know I was still around."

She was alive. She'd kidnapped me. She hadn't been herself, and magic could corrupt her thoughts. Probably couldn't have helped it, but that didn't make the bloodstain on my memories go away. A pressure built inside me, anger and fear and confusion, an explosive level of emotion that left me gasping. Stars fluttered across my vision, and I wondered if I would — if I could — faint.

I had to think of something, anything else. A distraction, something to focus on. Anything. So I said the first thing that came to my head, jerking my head at a man swimming through a nearby door. "They can't see us."

"No," she said. "Hunters can see other people, but we're the only ones. We're more solid, more real than the others. For the rest... it's like they're in their own world." She pointed at something off to my side. "Look."

Blond hair floated around a figure kicking toward us, a determined look on the newcomer's face. Frozen with too many things in my head, I watched him approach without moving. "Kelly," he said, stopping, his hair floating around his face.

I reached out to touch his cheek, shaking. My hand passed through. "Derik."

He cupped his hand over mine, and our fingers merged. "I want to touch you," he whispered, and I bit my lip to keep from crying, because I wanted him to touch my hand, too.

"We should go," Elizabeth interrupted. Her eyes were looking past me, but when I started to look over my shoulder, she snapped, "We've got things to do."

She wanted me to follow without seeing something. Of course, I looked to see it.

They were frozen as they'd hit the field, the story clear as day. Sandra had lunged at the Edge. Valdez had grabbed for Sandra to keep her back, but his momentum hadn't been enough, and Sandra had hit. The slight momentum they'd had on entering had sent them drifting at a snail's pace, so that they floated forward inch after inch, unimpeded by friction or physical objects.

Sandra must have had a reason to charge the Edge. She wasn't suicidal or a fool.

There was only one reason she would throw herself at the Edge.

"No," I whispered.

She'd been trying to grab him, to pull him back. Her lunge had tripped him, sending him stumbling into the Edge face-first with his hands cast out to protect his head. And so he floated along at a 45-degree angle, a demented superman careening aimlessly through ghostly fire hydrants and trees.

"No!" My hands passed through Trax's body, wisps of blue clinging to my arms. "No. No, no..." He wasn't supposed to even *be* here. He would have had to—Why would he *do* that? Why would the Hunters have let him?

First Mom and Dad. Then Owen. Then Elizabeth and Derik, but they were Powered and alive, so I had them back. But now Trax, Trax who was helpless in the Tides. No.

"You can't wake the un-Powered," Elizabeth said, watching my arms flail to cling to him.

I stopped, palms falling to my knees. My hands did not pass through my own flesh. But for the first time I felt the cold, because my knees were not, were skin-warm to my own touch.

Unlike everything else.

It was ice, pure ice, a pain so deep it became numbness, and I hadn't noticed. My brother was gone. I was—

Lost.

The Powered were Lost, and I was Powered. The Lost absorbed Power on the other side of the Edge, but now we were *in* Power, instilled with it from all around, *made* of it. What use was it, if I couldn't bring him back to me? *They go Mad*, the Hunter had said, and I cast the thought aside, because I'd rather be Mad than lose Trax.

Maybe I was already Mad. Maybe I was crazy, and stuck in living hell. A tantalizing hope, because then none of this would be real.

For years my brother's heartbeat had been the first thing I'd heard in the mornings, after the alarm clock. For years, I'd reached out to hear him, to hear him breathing and living and still existing. It was the first sound I could really recall, the beating of his heart, and it was an echo of my own, my twin.

Fuck it. I refused to accept this reality.

"No," I said again, and this time, it wasn't a plea. Life wouldn't take the only family I had left away from me. I wouldn't let it.

The wraiths were those who weren't equipped to handle Power, but Trax was my twin, and I was only barely Powered anyway; his genes were half mine so he surely couldn't have been far off from being so too. It was so simple, there in my mind: *Make him just a little closer.* Whether it was a prayer or a plea or a demand or a direction, I didn't know. But I wanted it with every ounce of my soul, *bring us back together*, so I closed my eyes and *pulled*, reaching deep for the all-encompassing fizz of magic.

No one ever doubted what the Tides were. They were pure and simple Power, uncontrolled and uncontrollable. But I was part of them now, and they answered me, pouring into me more Power than I'd ever experienced before.

Is this what it's like to be a first-class? It filled me, broiled me, burned me alive. All of this un-world was warping around me, Power twisting with me at the center of this whirlpool, until the faces of Derik and Elizabeth spun away in swirls of light and flutters of color.

Voices. Noise. The colors took shape, forming animals and Hunters and mostly butterflies. Bodies being dissolved and reformed, people shrieking and running, morphing. Flesh bulged, shrunk, reshaped into translucent wings. I saw butterflies.

The butterflies were being consumed by Power. *I* was being consumed by Power.

I didn't have the strength to control it. I was going to burst; I was going to die.

I could feel this; I accepted this. My mind hurt so badly I stopped feeling pain, lost the capability to comprehend it without a body to remind me of what it meant. But I had a mission. I couldn't die until I'd completed it.

So I reached out in the direction that Trax had been, and *listened*, listened for the heartbeat I knew as well as my own. *It should sound like this*, I thought, and tapped two fingers against the back of my other hand. *Tmp-tmp, tmp-tmp, tmp-tmp...*

And then I let go of all the Power that had pooled itself into me, told it the rhythm I wanted and let it go.

My vision darkened, distorted by magic into a nightmare.

Butterflies and half-monstrous people and Derik and Elizabeth and Sandra and Valdez spun around me, whirled, faded.

An ocean rig. Behind them all, I saw a rig in the middle of the ocean, drills pumping. The air around it wavered, something like gas spewing out from a door.

There was a light emanating from that rig. It grew brighter and brighter and brighter.

Then it shrunk, the light pulling in on itself, being swallowed by a pair of ice-blue eyes in a face caught in a rictus of pain. A scream sliced across my skull from the inside of one ear to the other.

Fire ringed my wrists, boiled the flesh off my skin down to my elbows, my chest, my body. Coils of blue light reached out to wrap around a patch of air, where Trax had been.

Make him like me. A prayer. A command. A whimper.

The fire surged through me.

And it burned me out.

#

Sa-sa, sa-sa, sa-sa, sa-sa...

Was someone holding my hand?

A warm hand. Everything else was icy. But the fingers around mine were warm. I could feel callouses on the fingers, built from years of guitar playing.

"Please," Trax whispered, "open your eyes."

It was my dirty secret. I never could hold out when he begged.

He was leaning over me, his eyes red. A hiccup exploded out of him when he saw I was looking, something that could easily have been a sob if he'd been crying.

I could see a tree through his head.

Oh, I remembered, *we're still here.*

I sat up. "Trax," I said, and hugged him. Held my twin tighter than I'd ever held anyone in my life, because I could hear his heart beat.

He was holding me back in the same way. My ribs could just deal with it.

"I thought I'd lost you," I said.

"You wouldn't wake up," he muttered.

When I opened my eyes again, I saw green eyes staring at us with a need so virulent it made me gasp. Derik watched, just watched.

I held out a hand to him. He tried to grasp my fingers —

160

And his hand passed right through mine. Again.

Trax wasn't crying, because tears could not be cried here. I bit the back of my hand, and despite the warmth of my mouth, I tasted no flesh on my tongue, smelled no faint scent of skin. It didn't even hurt.

Not even from the magic that I had felt searing it. That had left no scars at all on my skin.

Disentangling myself from Trax, I stood up.

Nothing had changed besides him. Guilt made me glance toward Valdez and Sandra. They were fading. After all they'd done for me, they were stuck like this in an unending nonexistence. Why? Because I'd led them here. "I have to —"

"Don't even think about it," Elizabeth interrupted. It shouldn't have surprised me to know she was still here, but it did. "You shouldn't summon your Power here."

"I have to." I reclaimed Trax's hand. They were *dying*. Or whatever happened to the wraiths that disappeared. My fault.

But he held me back, strangled my arm. "Please," he said. "You faded. You almost *disappeared*."

Derik was standing by Valdez, or what was left of him. They'd known each other for a while. They'd been friends long before he'd known me. "Derik," I appealed.

"No." He shook his head. "Don't."

"How can you —?"

Derik moved so fast he didn't seem to move at all. "I thought you were dead," he said, hovering beside me. "Don't try again."

I opened my mouth.

"Please." Fingers reached for my lips and passed through.

They were *dying*.

The look on my face must have been terrible. Elizabeth's shoulders dropped half an inch; her weight shifted from her toes to her heels. "They'll fade, but they don't go away completely," she offered. "If you look closely, they'll always be there."

I tore my hand out of Trax's and stormed over to the wraiths who had been my friends.

The way I'd brought Trax back had been by our genes. I could try to bring them back, but they weren't my twin, not my kin. The chances of it working were almost nil.

My own sanity was worth saving them. But throwing it away when I was pretty sure it wouldn't work? Elizabeth couldn't have stopped me, but that thought did.

I had to bring down the Tides. It was the only chance of saving them.

Sandra's blonde hair curled forward in long wispy strands. I watched it pass through my arm, and noticed that at some point she'd lost two of her fake nails, cracked a third. "I'm sorry," I whispered.

Her hand moved.

I gasped. "Sandra?"

She swung herself up, moving through Valdez like he didn't even exist, like she didn't even see him. "Trax?"

"He's fine!" My voice was raspy with nonexistent tears.

"Trax?" she asked again.

"He's right there." Pointing, I waited for her to look in the right direction.

She didn't. She didn't even see me. And she was so transparent, I was having trouble seeing her. I watched her wander aimlessly, calling for my brother, for me and for the others. "She can't hear me," I said, and covered my mouth with both my hands.

An arm wrapped around my shoulder, trying to draw me away. "We need to go," Trax said softly, the one solid touch in a wasteland of ghosts.

Sawing at my bottom lip with my teeth, I reached out for someone I'd never be able to touch again. She didn't notice my fingers passing through her cheekbone. All I felt was ice on my frozen hands.

I wrapped my fingers around the only warmth in this hell, squeezing his hand, feeling him squeeze mine. He rubbed the back of his other hand over his nose, lips pressed into a pale, thin line, and cringed when she called his name. She'd come through for him, and he knew it.

He'd come through for me. He should never have been able to do so. They should all have been safely back at camp.

"Trax. Why are you here?"

No apology in those blue eyes of his. "You're my *sister*," he said. "I know when you're lying to me."

"How did you even know where we were? You would've had to follow us; the Hunters would have seen… you…" I turned to Derik.

He looked away.

So did Elizabeth when I swung my gaze to her. Shuffling back and forth, she hunched her shoulders and gave Derik a sidelong glance. "Told you to tell her."

"He's your brother," Derik muttered. "It was his right."

His *right*?

He had no right to die. None of them did. *Their choice* my ass; they were supposed live and let me face this alone, alone with the man who was already stuck beyond humanity.

Derik was already Lost. Now Trax? My family. My whole family. How could they let this happen? How could *I* let this happen?

Suddenly I couldn't stand it. I couldn't stand them; I couldn't stand myself; I couldn't stand this anti-world. A thousand arguments and protests and screams tried to cram themselves through my throat, and all that came out was a rough choke. Trax let me stumble away, probably assuming I couldn't go far, but screw him, screw them all. I had to get away.

I looked as far as I could see and *pushed* myself.

By all accounts, it should not have worked. I was a music Power, and a broken one at that. There was no sensible reason to assume I could use a travel Power, no reason to even try.

But it did work.

Chapter Nineteen

I turned around on the top of the old office building, alone.

And I cried tears that didn't fall.

I shouldn't be here. I should be—

Outside. Out of Tides. I needed to get out, protect them, drive out the intruders—

No. No, that wasn't it. Pushing the stray thought aside, I focused on the vision I'd seen, an oil rig in the ocean. I needed to be...

At the coast.

At the Gulf Coast. Wasn't that where Lorren's Oil had been?

I'd never been to the Gulf Coast before, but I knew it was south, and I knew that south was away from the Edge. I should go there and figure out what had happened.

A ghost swam by. Long dark hair drifted around her face, her sharp cheeks tight with fear and worry. She was about the same height as Mom had been. Of course she couldn't see me, but I followed her anyway, the gravel that coated the roof not bothering to crunch under my feet.

My parents' home wasn't that far away, was it? Maybe half a day or so of travel by car.

I didn't have car, or a map, or a GPS. Even if I could get home, eventually, Mom was a wraith. Dad would be a wanderer, like this lady, so chances were he wouldn't even be home.

I'd brought Trax back. It would be worth it, if I could have Mom, too. But she wasn't Powered, and she didn't have Dad's genes in her, so what I'd done for Trax wouldn't work.

We were all dead. Or as good as, anyway. The ghost and I had wandered to edge of the roof. Her mouth moved, calling for someone. Silence swallowed her words.

She cupped her hands around her mouth and shouted so hard it bent her at the waist, and I still couldn't hear a thing. How far up were we? Thirty feet? If she fell, would she hit the ground hard enough to feel it? I leaned forward, searching the alley for signs that someone had tried it.

Elizabeth appeared beside me. "Don't bother. You'd just drift slowly down. Congratulations, by the way. You've figured out how to travel like a Hunter."

Apparently rooftops weren't great hiding spots. "It's not fair. If I can travel, why can't I use my Power? I should be able to bring them back. Like Trax." Butterflies in my head, and fire.

She looked at the ghost, still shouting, and shook her head.

I didn't want to admit she was right. It hadn't been like *using* Power; I hadn't pulled it into me. It was just part of what I was.

"I should." They deserved to live, too. "Maybe I could. Maybe I could think of a way, if I tried hard enough."

"Not without going Mad."

Would I? Would the visions consume me once and for all? "You can't be sure."

The silence that answered me made me wonder what she was thinking. Her eyes were closed and her brow furrowed, her lower lip caught between her teeth. Sorrow, maybe, or possibly anger. Maybe both.

But then she stepped back from the edge of the roof and began to walk away. "Do what you want. But we Hunters came here because we thought you were the best chance at bringing the world back. You break the rules. That makes you the closest thing to hope we have. And Kelly? It's cold here. Turns out, I hate being cold."

She passed through the door without opening it. I reached a hand through and felt nothing, so I stepped after her. Walking through walls should have some kind of unique feel to it, but there was nothing, no sense of otherness or extra cold or anything. "I haven't a clue what I need to do." A lie; I knew where to start. *Go south*, my instincts nagged at me. I just didn't know what to do when I got there.

Waiting until I fully emerged, Elizabeth stood rubbing at the goose bumps on the back of her neck. "Well, that's fantastic. Neither do I."

Sandra, Valdez. They'd followed me. My fault, my responsibility. Whether I knew what I was doing or not, I should try.

No, I *would* try. But what if it didn't work? I had to make it work.

I was a broken music Power. Was I really qualified to save the world?

The stairs passed a door. She paused at the landing, and then walked through the door. On the other side was an office, a cubicle farm that vaguely reminded me of my own workplace. Something was odd about the desks, though.

Stepping into one for a closer look, I walked through the desk and stood by an empty rolling chair. There was a piece of paper and a red pen in front of the chair, but no computer. Maybe not much like the Daily Grind after all, then. What time had it been when the Tides had hit? Five, six. Possibly someone had been working late, lost before she knew what was happening. She couldn't have seen the Tide coming in this little box.

"Promise me it will bring them all back. I'll find a way to bring the Tides down, but you have to give me everyone back."

Elizabeth said nothing, her fingers brushing over the pen. Despite being a member of the Teams, she'd been fully accepted by the other Hunters. Shouldn't she be capable of negotiating for the magic that held her captive? Didn't they get that right?

I turned my face upwards, screamed at the wavering ceiling. "Promise me!"

But no one answered. Frustrated, I kicked at the chair, and screamed when my foot passed through it.

Elizabeth didn't follow me when I stormed out.

Whoever had laid this building out had been a moron. I wove through a maze of cubicles that sprawled in twists and turns, and ended up at a different set of stairs. These went just one floor down into another maze, and the stairs at the end directed me to another. Finally I found the door. The flagstone streets stretched away in all directions. *What city uses cobbled streets these days?* I must be in a renovated downtown. That would make sense, as there weren't any cars around, either.

Between two buildings was a swath of green. The park was small, just a block's worth of field with a few benches and a soccer net. Derik lay in the middle of it, staring up at the sky.

He looked up at me as I knelt beside him. "Are you okay?"

"You let him in."

He didn't rise to my accusation. "Yeah," he admitted. "Because he's your brother. If it had been him, you'd have done the same."

"He's all I have left in the world," I said.

"You're all he has left."

Damn, the man could argue. I couldn't think of anything to say to that.

He laughed, suddenly, and it shattered the silence. Flopping onto his back, he ran a hand through his hair. "Besides, what am I? Chopped liver?"

I glanced at him out of the corner of my eyes. "You were—" I looked down. "Lost."

I guess he hadn't been expecting me to meet his humor with gravity. A moment passed before he answered. "Kelly," he hesitated, "you didn't... for me, did you?"

"I was sort of hoping... You were Lost. I was human. As long as Trax was fine, I mean, does it really matter?"

He sat up, his hands punching into the air. "Yes, it matters! Why would you *do* that?"

I pushed up to my feet. "Excuse me for caring! So I got used to you. You invited yourself over, stole my kitchen, and ate my food. And I *looked forward* to it! I even stopped thinking you would

go away, didn't want you to go away. I just—I just wanted to…"
To have you with me forever. My words petered out.

The Hunters had been right. I was in love with him.

And he was the one who'd allowed Trax to come with us. To wind up here.

He would never touch me again. Being a ghost was a sudden, vicious satisfaction.

I wanted to cry again.

He stood up. "Kelly?"

I waved him back, refusing to meet his gaze.

Of course, he came closer. "You wanted to what?"

"They died because you didn't tell me that he'd followed us. You should have stopped him, let me stop him. Damn it, Derik, I would have done *anything* to stop him."

He crossed his arms. "Like it or not, he's got a choice."

"Not *that* choice."

"Not the choice to live or die? Not the choice to decide whether or not he even wants a future?" Derik turned away and ran a hand through his hair. "You have no idea what it's like to not have a choice."

The words bit into my heart, made me hiss. "What do you know of it?"

Half-turning, he glowered at me. "What do you think I am? A damn music Power? Hell, Kelly, I'm a *strength* Power. If I'd been more than a sixth class, my only choice would have been *which* branch of the military to join. Instead I got my mother deciding I wanted to go to college."

"But you did want to go."

"How do you know that?" He threw a hand up and stomped a few more feet away before suddenly stopping. "I had no idea what I wanted. I never figured it mattered, so I never bothered to think about. I always knew I *wanted* to want something, but it was hard to think I had the right to complain when everyone else in the family was getting so much more screwed."

There was a bench not far away. I sat down and put my face into my hands. Through my fingers I could see his feet flash by, knew when he sat down beside me. "You would have stopped them if they'd tried to kill themselves."

He didn't answer right away. I got up. His hand raised, palm out. "I don't know." The hand dropped to his knee. "I don't think I can ever take away someone else's choices. Sometimes I still wish my uncle hadn't taken away my right to die, back when they sent me home from college. God knows I wanted to for a while, because the only thing I knew *how* to control was myself, was my body. But then again, I don't regret what I've done with my life since then. I don't regret living, and I don't regret meeting you, and I don't even regret being changed, because it meant I could save you."

His knees shifted. "I don't do well without someone telling me where to go, without having a goal." His hand hovered over mine, and when I met his gaze, I saw yearning filled his eyes. Dropping his head back, he stared at the sky again. "I didn't stop you from coming through. Hate me for that, too. You wouldn't be here at all, if I thought I had the right to take choices away."

"I do. I do hate you." I had to cover my mouth to say it, couldn't look him in the eyes as I did so, but saying it gave me a sharp stab of satisfaction. Even if his pained little grunt brought a throbbing tightness to my chest and the memory of a bad taste in my mouth. I *pushed* myself away, and he didn't follow.

Trax still stood beside Sandra, playing with the paperclip bracelet on his wrist. He didn't look at me when I appeared beside him, but his words said he was aware of my arrival. "She'll come back when we drop the Tides."

"You don't know that."

He stuck his bratty nose in the air. "Yeah, I do." But then his nose fell, and his lower lip quivered. "I killed them."

"No." I did. "Derik should have told me you were following us."

Trax rolled his eyes. "He should never have let you come. But when exactly has he stopped you from walking into danger?"

I propped my hands on my hips. "He respects me enough not to coddle me."

"Good to know that you don't think he should respect me."

There was nothing I could say to that. So I looked back to where I'd been, and *pushed* myself back to the rooftop. It was a quick way to move, faster than running. That was how we'd get to the Gulf. I sat and waited and stared into nothing. I figured they'd come. Eventually. Trax was the first appear.

What have I done to him? I wondered as he blinked into existence. Whatever it was, I wasn't sorry about my Power experiment. I still had him.

"We're going south," I ordered, not meeting his eyes. "I'm going to find a way to fix this. Get the others, and let's get started."

#

We stood at the edge of the Gulf of Mexico, looking out over an ocean of water. The real tide was low, the scent of brine heavy in the night air, and something reverberated in the distance. Despite the hour we could see fairly well, so either the Tides made their own light, or there was a full moon hidden by the distortion of the magic. Derik scratched his chin. I stepped into the water.

The Lost couldn't feel the world around us; we weren't really alive any more. It would make sense that nothing could scare us.

But the ice of that water cut through everything, cold crashing through me and making me queasy, my head abruptly clearing. It was like I'd just woken up from a nightmare and rammed my head into a too-low ceiling, and a distant sound became a deafening pounding in the back of my head, a slow and steady rhythm that reminded me of a screaming face and fire under my skin. I jumped out.

"We can't swim it," I said, and so Derik tried sticking his own foot in.

I looked at Trax. He looked past me, staring blankly into the horizon. "I'm sorry."

Jumping, he blinked hard a few times, and then focused on me. "Yeah, me, too." A pensive frown. He held out his hand, and I took his wrist.

"I don't know what to do."

He bared a couple of teeth in a half-hearted grin. "Me, either."

Shifting my weight, I looked up at the sky. It was light again, daylight. The hours of traveling had passed through dark skies into day and back again, a blur in my mind. I'd told them "south, to the Gulf," and Derik had pointed in a direction and led the way. We didn't get tired, or hungry, and we hadn't stopped to talk again. I could only remember following blond hair, feeling trees and buildings whizz by, nodding when Derik pointed and just moving forward. It was like a haze had filled my head, and a time or two I even forgot where we were, what we were doing.

But Derik kept pointing, and he looked like someone who knew where he was going. So I followed.

Trax and Elizabeth had copied my every move without question or comment, but then, Derik hadn't done more than grunt a time or two. Every time I had looked up to see him watching me, he'd looked away. Not much talking.

So we'd made really, really good time.

"I've always wondered how we do it. Traveling, that is. I was a heat Power." Her voice cut through my thoughts. Elizabeth squatted in the white sand, marred by no footprints but our own, flexing her fingers and rubbing her wrists, more alert than I'd seen her in hours. Alert enough to be curious about what we did, apparently.

The study of Power wasn't a common elective; most people took it for granted, like electricity. Being a remedial student put me ahead of the curve on this subject; we'd had to study the theory in hopes that it would improve our abilities.

"Power is bound by our genetics," I answered. "The method in which we process the natural energies of the earth can take a multitude of forms. Not everyone can tap into Power, but of those who can, a series of biological processes determines the way Power translates into the physical world, and thus determines our abilities."

"What?"

"Power is always the same; it's how your body processes it that determines the type of Power you have." I waved a semi-transparent arm at her. "We don't have bodies anymore, in case you haven't noticed."

She rolled to her hands and knees to poke at the foam left by a receding wave, shivered and scuttled back when the next wave splashed over her hand. "Which means?"

"Bodies are a limitation. As long as you don't try to force the Power through a body that doesn't exist, you should be able to do just about anything."

Derik kicked at the sand. His heel passed through it. "Except be human again."

Trax's fingers brushed by my elbow. "Yeah," he said, "except that."

Her hands settled on her hips. "Doesn't that mean we can fly, too?"

Oh.

I'd forgotten about that.

Kids usually got flight Powers and travel Powers confused, although they weren't the same. Travelers could "jump" through space; flight Powers defied gravity and had to transverse every meter.

It took a little more effort to forget gravity than to forget travel time. Traveling was like driving long distances alone on flat highways, where time blurs and just seems to disappear between one place and another. Flying was more jumping into the air and forgetting to fall, something that doesn't really happen to most people.

But finally we all managed it, wobbling and imagining that gravity didn't exist to pull us back down. I jumped out over the water. Not wanting to fall into it made it easier to stay up.

"Anybody got a GPS?" Derik cracked.

I ignored him. We were going *that* way. Even without my feet in the water, the constant noise was loud as thunder, and I wasn't actually trying to listen. *Dhhhhhhrm – dhhhhhhrm – dhhhhhhrm.* That way.

They followed.

Pretending I was dreaming made the trip go faster. It felt like a dream, only with the noise cutting through my head keeping me awake. The others didn't seem to have that focus; Trax even got bored and tried to fly upside down and ended up zooming toward the water. I caught him and whapped him across the back of the head.

He tried something similar once or twice more. I was about to take him to task when I heard Derik shout at Elizabeth, and turned to see her eyes glazed. She'd begun to drift downwards, but at his bark, she snapped back up.

Trax's eyes had been the same, each time he'd started to dive.

"Sorry," he muttered. "It's just... I keep forgetting where we're going."

How could he forget? The sound thrummed through my body like a beacon. I met Derik's eyes, and they were as confused as mine.

"It's why Hunters can't get close." Elizabeth thumped the heel of her hand against her head a couple of times. "Some never come back. Others... just say they forgot what they were doing on the way." She wrinkled her nose and stared at me over it, rubbing one of her forearms. "I have to admit, I've just been spacing out as we've traveled. Following you since halfway to the coast, except for the stop on the beach when you woke me up to talk."

Trax nodded.

Derik, however, scratched his head. "I'm fine," he said. "I guess I'm immune." And me, I couldn't drift off like I had on the trip down, not with that sound in my head.

Two of us, two of them. "Keep an eye on her," I ordered, and waved them forward, toward the source only I could apparently hear.

"What's that?" Elizabeth asked when the sound had gotten so loud I thought it might burst my ears.

"The drills," I guessed. "You can hear it now?"

She nodded. "Is that what where we're going?"

Of course it was. Where did she think we were going, the Florida Keys?

She read my expression and sighed. "Yeah, that's what I thought."

The light began to change. It was subtle, like rays of light dropping down from the sun, only these rays were being pulled in instead of cast out. Yet the shape that appeared on the horizon was dark, darker than night. Strangely enough, the noise was getting quieter and quieter, fading as we approached.

"What is that?" Trax swerved up and down, trying to get a better look.

Derik spun out to the left. "It looks like a platform."

"An oil platform," Elizabeth guessed. "Lorren's Oil. That would make sense." She pointed to a blotch of white off to the side. "That looks like an oil tanker."

They'd set it up as a clean drilling site, with all the major parts contained far under water. The reinforced lines would have been brought up to the surface in a secondary tube, emergency shunts periodically placed in case of breakage, and earth Powers hired to sense for the changes in the metal of the pipes that would indicate leaks.

But on the surface was the square platform, a tiny floating town. We circled overhead, getting a better look. I could imagine easily a hundred people or more living here full time, in the long buildings on the left. Now it was empty, completely devoid of life. To the right—

I couldn't really see much on the right side of the platform. That was where the darkness centered, sucking in light and letting nothing escape. I assumed that the drills were on that side.

Movement at the corner of my eye told me the others were going in to land. I joined their swoop. Trax was the first to ask the pertinent question: "So how do we get down?"

I met his gaze. I looked at Elizabeth. Elizabeth was looking at me. She turned to Derik. Derik shrugged, slowed to a hover, and grinned. "Wiley Coyote, anyone?" And looked down.

It *was* like a cartoon classic, a sudden reassertion of gravity that sent him sprawling onto the platform with an audible *clang*. Trax laughed and started to descend closer to the metal. I grabbed his shoulder. "Wait."

Derik was staring up at us with wide eyes. "I can feel it."

The platform was solid.

Clang. Elizabeth dropped down. Splaying her hands over the ground, she smiled, tears in her eyes. "Geez. I missed this so much. I'm not even cold anymore!" And she kissed the dirty metal plating, the knees of her loose gray pants collecting a brownish sheen, almost the same color as the hands on her tiny clock-face earrings.

I grabbed Trax's hand. Together we dropped, flopping gracelessly over. I scraped my knee on the rough surface. Best skinned knee of my life.

Then hands whipped me up, hauling me by my waist and tossing me into the air. Derik caught me before I could do more than squawk, his deep rumbling laugh vibrating right into me and stealing my breath away. A giggle of my own bubbled out, and I buried my hands in his hair and dropped my head to his chest, feeling his heart beat.

I could smell his sweat. It was glorious.

And then Trax wrapped his arms around Elizabeth, who was hugging him back, and Derik was tilting my head up. The heat of Derik's breath brushed my lips; Trax's joyful shout hit my ears.

I pushed Derik away, and stumbled back.

Kelp-forest green eyes regarded me with confusion. And then he looked at my brother, and bit his lip and turned away.

I wanted to go to him; I wanted to kick him in the nuts and run away. The stabbing pain in my chest was making it hard to breathe.

So instead of facing him, I walked toward the door.

If I couldn't figure out my own feelings, I could at least get started on figuring out the Tides.

Chapter Twenty

I stopped in the first room, a common area. Battered vinyl sofas faced a big-screen TV on the other side of the long room; closer by was a counter blocking off a square kitchenette, stocked with snacks and sodas. A can of soda was spilled across the plastic-topped counter of the kitchenette, cola dripping slowly over the edge and onto the floor. Battered books and sheaves of paper splattered the furniture at random; an old hardcover titled *The Dragon Reborn* lay face-down on a sofa. Towering piles of letters sat randomly around the room, one pile nearby on the counter.

"We need to find the offices and find out what happened," I said.

Elizabeth grabbed a stack of papers off the bar. "Letters. There might be something useful here." They were unopened; three of them were written in children's scrawls.

"You think?" Trax took one from her and started tearing into it.

"Trax!" I grabbed them from his hands. "That's someone's mail."

He lifted an eyebrow at me. "I don't think they're going to mind."

"He's right. This isn't the place for privacy laws." Elizabeth snatched it back from me and pulled out a paper.

And then something growled.

"You don't think," I said slowly, "that there's anyone left on the platform, do you?"

Trax's face was white. Even his lips were bloodless. "No," he said quietly, his hand reaching for mine. "I don't think there are any *people* left on board."

The envelope fell from his other hand. And he grabbed me and yanked.

We dove together, tumbling to the ground. Derik shouted. Something barked. There was a *smack* of flesh against flesh, and a howl of pain. Metal clanged and a bone snapped. Trax tried to jump up, but I wrestled him back down and threw my arms over his head.

And then it was quiet.

I sat up and turned. Elizabeth held a metal lamp in her hand, the stand dripping with dark red.

Derik wasn't visible.

"No!" Jumping up, I leapt over the sofa.

He was pushing the body of a seal off his knee. Its face was caved in, as was the back of its head. Derik raised an eyebrow at me. My face grew hot, and I turned my back on him to see if anything was around.

"The Mad," Elizabeth said, her voice strangely calm and collected. "We're inside the Tides. There shouldn't be any Mad here."

I grabbed another lamp and stripped off the cord and the shade. "I don't think the rules work right here."

Talk about the understatement of the century.

A laugh pitched a tad too high made me look back at her. "Rules? The rules haven't worked right since you first crossed into the Tide Zone. Congratulations. You broke the world."

Either she was getting hysterical, or she was right. I handed the lamp-turned-club to Trax, and grabbed another. "Maybe I did," I said. "Maybe I didn't. But if the rules change around me, I say we take advantage of it, and change them how we like."

Derik's head appeared. He pulled himself up with the sofa, and flexed his leg carefully. "Not broken," he muttered. And louder, "We'd better hope that there are no Hunters on board."

Trax touched my arm. "I don't think it was alone."

There were six of them, creeping in from a door on the other side of the room. And they didn't look like they wanted to watch us from afar.

Two of them were seals, like the first. They were a good six feet long, brown fur tinged yellow on the underside. Their mouths hung open, fish-capturing teeth bared.

The other four were octopi. Not more than calf-high, their long arms waggled and dragged their damp bodies in our direction. The pebbly flesh slowly changed colors as they crawled across the floor. *Schlop-schlop-schlop*, the sound of boneless arms dragging them toward us.

"To the door," Derik ordered, motioning us back.

I looked over my shoulder. The door was gone. "I don't think that's a good idea."

He glanced back, and a scowl settled across his face. His feet spread slightly wider. "You two, behind the bar. I'll take the seal on the left. Elizabeth, you get the one on the right." The opening was narrow, but there was plenty of room to swing. The seals wouldn't be able to get over the counter. The octopi, on the other hand...

Well, I'd never particularly liked calamari, but maybe it was time to develop a taste for it. This was downright surreal. I was about to fight *octopi*. Octopuses? Octopodes? Unreal.

These were the Tides. Nothing was real.

The thought felt more solid in my hand than the lamppost, and I found myself wanting to giggle. I didn't. That would be inappropriate. What sound did an octopus make when you hit it with a lamppost?

Trax's gaze met mine. His lips were white, and his eyes wide.

No crazy octopus was going to kill *my* brother. Not while I was still standing.

His hands tightened on his lamp, and he nodded back at me. I couldn't help but wonder what thought had just passed through his head.

As one, we jumped behind the bar. "I want to point out," he spat as his feet hit the floor, "that those guys don't exist."

"What?" I couldn't help it—I took my eyes off the encroaching horde. "Seriously? You're going to argue that *now?*"

"Caribbean monk seals. They're extinct." He hefted his lamp post. "The last confirmed sighting was in 1952. They really shouldn't be here."

Splorch. A tentacle sealed itself to the top of the bar.

Thwup-clunk. Trax's lamp smashed into the appendage and the bar.

"Huh. I expected more of a splat. And you know about seals how?" I swung at the two other arms that waved into sight. One wrapped around my post. I yanked. It yanked back.

He batted it away for me. "I paid attention in class, duh. There was a video about them in freshman biology. They look just like the pictures. And they're supposed to be extinct."

"Hey, Trax. They're *Lost.* I don't think they care." I managed to pin one to the bar with a particularly good swing, and then hammered it once more with a follow-up. The end sheared off and flapped messily back over the edge. I eyed the flopping monstrosity with distaste. "Lovely, that."

He snorted.

Another rubbery arm wrapped around my weapon and tried to pry it away. A sudden jerk pulled me forward a step—just in time for three more arms and beak to pop over the edge. "Oh, fu—" *Smack-splorch.* Octopus flesh sealed over my cheek.

"Kel!" Trax lunged forward and rammed the butt of his lamp into the beak. The Mad flew backwards.

"Ow." I staggered back, holding my face. The suckers had taken some of my skin with them. Really? Yes, really. I supposed my body was real enough to bleed after all.

"You okay?" He grabbed a can of soda from under the bar and chucked it. It bounced off something and flew back into the air before landing with a clatter and rolling across the room.

"Yeah. Fine. Just a little scrape." *I'm not about to get beaten by an octopus.* I wiped the blood off my cheek, and then bashed a newcomer off the counter baseball-style.

It landed on the edge of a coffee table. The arms thrashed violently, but it looked kind of dead. I squinted. "Did I get it?" Served it right.

On the other side of the bar, the soda can was rolling under a lunging seal. There was an indignant squawk after the can disappeared from view.

"Watch it!" Elizabeth shouted.

"Sorry!" Trax called back.

A metal post slammed across the seal's face. "No, it's good. You distracted it. Hang on, I'll be there in a sec."

"Behind you!" Trax shoved me out of the way and caught a wiggly arm on his pole. One of them had snuck through the regular entrance to get us from the back. He stabbed at it.

I jumped to cover the whack-a-mole that was the counter battle, before anything could creep up and get his back. One of the remaining two had pulled itself all of the way up. I helped it down again, right onto the other climber. *Splat-thunk.*

"Yeah, take that!" I shouted after them. Score!

Smack.

"Augh!"

One of them had caught itself on a chair. And gone after the same damn cheek. "Get your tentacles off her, you damned squid!" Trax hefted his lamp post and whaled on it.

It might have been more effective if he'd been hitting the arm attached to my face, but his angle wasn't right for that, and I couldn't seem to aim around the searing pain in my face. I think it was trying to pull itself up by my flesh, the dirty little bastard. That or by the three arms sealed to the plastic bar.

A hand wrapped around the rubbery arm and yanked, tearing it off the octopus. Derik dropped the twitching appendage and grabbed a heavy-looking dish from under the counter. Aiming at the body, he punched forward. *Splarshk.* The mass of jelly convulsed around the dish impaling it. "That's the last of them," he said.

He dropped the plate to help me detach the octopus arm from my face. The suckers moved *inside my skin.* The burning feeling grew worse.

"Owowowow," I whimpered.

I have to give him this much — the man didn't laugh.

Trax hovered a little too close, getting in Derik's light. Derik glared at my brother until he backed off, then leaned in to pull the suckers out of the spot where the blood gave enough moisture to form a good suction seal.

Wincing, I looked at Trax, trying to distract myself, because I was *not* about to be sick. "Octopus."

"What?"

"You called it a squid. It's an octopus. And those are arms, not tentacles. There's a difference. Didn't you study this stuff in that biology class of yours?"

He rolled his eyes. "We were talking about endangered animals. No, I didn't study squid."

"The mollusks of the world mock you." I smirked at the smartass, and gagged around a gasp of pain. A sucker in my cheek moved again, resisting the gentle tugs. Ugh.

"What?"

"Shush," Derik scolded. "I can't get this off if you keep moving."

I shut up.

My hands stopped shaking when I closed my fists and breathed slowly. Probably shock, but nothing felt real, not even the pain. It hurt, but—

I'd been fighting octopuses. In the Tides.

I wasn't here to fight; I wasn't here to be scared. I was here to stop the Tides.

I started counting backwards from ten, but stopped when I hit negative forty. If I was still scared then, I figured, counting wasn't going to help.

Trax bent down to pick something off the floor: the letter that had started it all. He skimmed through it, frowned, and shrugged. His fingers began to scratch at something on the paper.

"What?" Elizabeth asked, watching his face.

"It's just a bunch of gibberish. Looks like computer code or something. There's a key taped to it, though." He held it up, a glint of gold in the light.

Peering over his shoulder, she shrugged, and then snagged the key from his hand. "Probably somebody was studying programming. Don't worry about it. Go help Derik make sure nothing else is going to come through." Flipping the glint of gold over, she squinted at it. "Wonder what this goes to?"

I took it from her hand and stuck it in my pocket. "Can't hurt to hang on to it."

She nodded, watching me put it up, and then her eyes slipped to my cheek. "Wish I had a little whiskey," she muttered.

"I could use a drink, too," Trax admitted.

She grinned at him, an evil, taunting twist of her lips. "For disinfectant."

Trax coughed, his cheeks touched with pink. I choked. Dear goodness, no. My face was already throbbing. Pouring alcohol on it was the *last* thing I wanted to do.

The four octopi lay in disturbingly boneless, thrashing piles of death. The one that had fallen over the edge of the counter had a well-formed bootprint buried into its face; Trax's last opponent was quite thoroughly speared on a lamp. Overturned chairs and scattered debris on the other side of the bar told me that Derik and Elizabeth had gotten their fair share of a workout with the seals.

Derik prodded at the corpses, checking for response. Nothing made any coherent thrashes, so he ignored the twitching bodies and surveyed the room, closing one of the doors.

It disappeared.

I swallowed hard. "Please don't close any more."

He stared at the wall, and nodded.

My face and Elizabeth's left arm got makeshift bandages. Derik, damn him, sacrificed the clean back of his shirt for the job. There wasn't much else in here to use, and the front of his shirt was completely ruined anyway, but his well-cut six-pack didn't help my peace of mind in the least.

"Do you think we'll change?" Trax asked.

The three of us turned to stare at him.

"Into Lost. Like them." He pointed to the bodies.

I scratched at a spot where the shirt-bandage was rubbing on my ear. "We haven't yet. That's a good sign."

Elizabeth hefted her lamp. "We're in Wonderland, guys. Don't eat anything."

There was one door left. It didn't take a lot of discussion to decide to head that way.

Chapter Twenty-One

This new room had been a kitchen at some point. I didn't hear anything moving around, so it seemed safe to assume that there were no Lost in here. Derik dug out a set of kitchen knives and passed them around, and then grabbed four copper-bottomed heavy pans. Tracing the rim of one foot-wide piece shaped somewhat like his beloved De Buyer at home, he muttered under his breath. I was standing close enough to hear: "You poor thing."

I quirked a brow at him.

He blushed. "It's rusting." A sigh. "Good commercial set, but at this point, it's worth more as weaponry. Crime against cookware everywhere." Relinquishing the hefty frying pan to my hand, he adjusted my grip on the handle. "Use the pan first, and the knife only if you have no other choice."

"But—"

A finger tapped my lips. "You don't know how to knife fight. Trust me on this."

I scowled, but stuck the knife through my belt. He pulled it out and moved it to the back of my hip.

Did he think I was dumb enough to accidentally cut myself on it, or something?

There were no other doors in the room. I noticed this, doing a quick survey of the room, and tugged on Elizabeth's sleeve. "Do you know how to break through metal walls?"

She looked at me like she thought I was nuts. "Why would I break through a wall?"

I pointed at the door. "Because that's the only door in here."

She glanced at it. "There's also the door we came through."

The door I'd been looking at didn't lead to the common room we'd just fought in.

And it was still the only door.

"Um." The others looked at me. I pointed to the door. "That's the only door."

Derik spun himself in a slow circle. He apparently didn't see anything I hadn't. "Okay. I'm starting to freak out a little."

I nodded.

Trax grabbed his frying pan firmly in both hands. "So there's something wrong with the physics of this place. Big honkin' deal. I've played this video game before."

Derik did a double-take, and then burst into a deep, rumbling laugh. Clapping Trax on the back, his shoulders loosened. "You know what? I have too. I'd bet anything it's a classic one-way portal scenario. Let's go."

I rolled my eyes and quirked a brow at Elizabeth. "I don't play video games," I said to her.

She shrugged. "I do."

I gaped at her back as she followed them.

"Come on!" she called back. "And stay away from cake!"

I took back every snarky comment I'd ever made about Trax's games. If we ever got back to normal-land, I was going to take up a new hobby.

On the other side of the door, I found Elizabeth digging through an ancient oak desk that she and Derik had shoved in front of the other door. The dark scrollwork on the monstrosity depicted Poseidon, trident raised, and a sinking city I supposed must be Atlantis. Papers littered the top and stuck out of the drawers. "They all look like the same code as that first letter Trax found."

Derik prodded the covers on a four-poster bed sitting against the far wall. The mattress sat waist-high, coils spearing through the quilted top. "Looks comfortable," Trax drawled. He moved to investigate the closet, lamp held low and ready.

I dropped to the floor to look under the bed. Nothing could be seen in the gloomy light, so I slid closer. Wait. "I see something." There was a metal handle on the dark box, but it barely moved when I pulled at it. The weight of the bed had it well and trapped. "Someone give me a hand?"

Someone being Derik. He grabbed the creaky treasure chest and dragged it out, with me pretending to help push.

"I'm guessing the captain was a pirate?" Trax joked.

The lock resisted the firm tug I gave it. "No creepy parrots allowed. Anyone see a key?"

Elizabeth patted her hip and raised an eyebrow at me.

"What are the chances?" But I took out the key Trax had found and compared it to the lock. It matched, and then slid in perfectly, turning with a quiet *snick*. "Okay, that's odd."

Elizabeth leaned against one of the bedposts to poke a solid black spring sticking out of the mattress. "You found a key in room where there was a fight. Of course it fits the first lock you find." She flicked the coil and got the dull *thunk* of cold iron. Sucking on her fingernail with a grimace, she gave it a swift kick with the heel of her shoe. The spring didn't seem to notice.

Trax's gaze slid her way, and lingered. "Random keys and treasure chests, a staple of any game. Hurry up and open the chest. And don't forget to strike a pose."

I shot my brother a withering look before pulling off the lock and creaking open the lid. The box was full of folded papers and envelopes, all weighted down by a sleek leather flip case. Taking the flip case out and holding it over my head for the others to see, I opened it so I could read it by looking up.

Derik knelt behind me to study it closer. "You found a license."

1st class music Power, certified. A man with ice-blue eyes and white-blond hair posed for a photograph, the government stamp of approval half covering his license number. All Powered got a license when we officially passed our basic competence tests, but only the highest levels needed to carry it with them. Mine was in a drawer somewhere; as a sixth class it didn't do anything but tell people I was useless.

In the upper left corner was the silver star of a government employee. Aaron Leid was an investigator. Derik pulled a green sheet of paper out of the box. "Investigation of Lorren's Oil drilling rig, at request of Thomas J. Rogers. Subject: three missing persons; missing equipment including boat and company computers. Non-essential, non-priority. Report as needed."

Elizabeth slid to the floor beside me, a yellow paper in her hands. "Listen to this. 'I haven't found much unusual in the investigation yet as far as disappearing crew goes. There is a disagreement between Rogers and the captain of the rig. The drills are getting deeper. The captain told Rogers that they're right smack in the middle of the oil, and going deeper won't help, but he insists. So the captain put the second drill to work on Rogers' pet project...' He goes off topic from there, some stuff about safety codes and the crew complaining about needing a new game system in the rec room."

I caught glimpses of the letter. Something about the format... Leaning over, I took the paper from her hands. Weird. "He printed out his e-mails? That seems like a waste."

Derik took it from me. "This isn't a regular print-off. There's no e-mail server, no site address at the bottom. It's like he copy-pasted the message, e-mail addresses and all."

Trax took the letter back, finishing the circle. "I haven't seen a single piece of tech around here, not even a phone. You don't think that in today's world, there wouldn't be one lying around?"

We all looked at one another. Elizabeth returned to the desk and began shuffling through half-decayed sheets and envelopes.

"I don't want to say it," she said after a minute.

Derik joined her. "You think the computer's been reduced to a pile of papers. And the password-protected files are in the chest?"

"I told you, I didn't want to say it." Stepping back to the middle of the room, she pulled out another envelope. "Don't think everything in the chest is important, at least." She handed it to him.

He looked at the writing on the front. "No, thanks."

"What?" Trax intercepted it, pulling out the letter. "Increase the size of your — nice. Classy. Handwritten spam."

I snickered, raising an eyebrow at Derik. "Maybe you should give it a try?"

"It's already big enough," Derik muttered, turning red. "You wouldn't want it bigger."

My face felt suddenly hot. I fingered the three-inch wide, foot-long knife in my belt. "Who says I want it at all?"

Trax choked.

Derik squirmed. Victory.

Elizabeth dropped the junk mail and grabbed two handfuls of letters. "We should go through these."

Shoving the chest aside until there was a clear spot large enough for all of us, I pulled some letters into my own lap. "Grab a stack. Important in the middle, spam on the outside."

There wasn't much. Just a few references to Rogers, whose authority the captain grumbled about, and lots of letters to friends. The investigator may have also been flirting with someone named Suzanne. One of the letters had a picture of her. It flashed between a blonde model with pointed ears and a forty-something trucker. Did Leid know? I couldn't tell, but Suzanne admitted to being married to a lady in South Carolina, so I guessed so. Sounded like something I'd have to ask Trax about later.

"From what I'm gathering, Rogers was trying to dig below the oil to get at unfiltered Power." I flipped through the pile of relevant mail we'd compiled. The rest was spread out around us, confining us to a small circle of unlettered territory. The violent scratching coming from the back of the desk we ignored. Whatever was over there wasn't large enough to move it, so we weren't about to deal with it. "There's a substantial pocket in this area."

Elizabeth wrinkled her nose in disdain. "Idiot."

I nodded. Pockets of gas-like magic were often under or near reservoirs of oil and natural gas, and occasionally buried under mountains in sealed-off caves. Usually Power leaked up through all kinds of rock on its own, filtering out the chaos and reducing in potency on the way. "Why would he want unfiltered Power? It's too risky."

Risky didn't begin to cover it. Derik threw a sheaf of papers back onto the pile. "That explains the Tides. But how? The magic wouldn't even come out without an intelligent mind to interact with, and it would have to be someone with the genes to interact with magic. Without a will to direct it, it stays nascent except for the slow trickle upward." The cohesive nature of magic was responsible for that.

"I bet it's all that research of his," I said. "He wants to find something out about Power."

"But..." Trax dug out a letter from the bottom. "This is from the investigator again. 'He thinks he knows more about Power than any of us Powered do. Next time he tries to tell me what's what, I'm going to get the captain to keelhaul the bastard.' Rogers isn't Powered. What does studying it get him?"

Trax's bleached Mohawk was an unusual spot of brightness in the poorly lit room. I bit my lip, and stood up. "We should keep going," I said.

Derik pushed the desk away from the door as Elizabeth waited with her frying pan in one hand and her knife in the other. When the green head came jabbing through, biting at the air with a rabid single-mindedness, she gave it a good wallop. The dog-sized turtle snapped back, but she was quicker, delivering a well-aimed deathblow to the back of its neck. Had it retreated into its shell like a normal turtle, it would have probably been safe.

The Mad weren't much on self-defense. I'd noticed that.

We'd gone from a bedroom to a locker room. Helmets, coveralls, boots, all the things that men on the rig would need and probably didn't want to store in the limited space available in their rooms. There were two doors. "The one on the left," Derik ordered, and went through without checking the other. Trax followed, picking up a pair of boots on the way.

"What are those for?" I asked.

Hopping, he compared the boot to his foot. Looked like it could fit over his shoe. "I dunno. But in a game, there's usually a point to every room, either something you fight or something you find. Nothing to fight in here."

"Don't jinx us." I steadied him as he tripped.

Elizabeth came through behind Trax and me, the four of us ending up in what must have been a security room. Mountains of paper were stacked on the desks. "Anyone who suggests we go through *all* that gets shot," Derik muttered. Trax crammed his feet into his new-used rubber boots and eyed the piles warily.

I picked up a stack. "I'm not suggesting anything," I answered, and started sorting.

"I am," Elizabeth piped, "so go ahead and shoot *me*. I want to see how you manage it." She smirked at Trax, and his lips curved up. He hid the smile by reaching for a pile.

It wasn't as hard as Derik feared. The stacks were neatly organized—security feeds, processing files, programs. Only e-mails and text files were legible; the rest were in binary or code. So we only had to go through seven mid-sized stacks, and those could be quickly and easily sorted.

Trax, of course, managed to get the pile of saved messaging sessions. I noticed him going through them a little too slowly. "Something important in those?"

He blushed, and tossed them into the 'worthless' pile. "Is anyone else getting thirsty?" he asked.

I nodded absently. "Yeah. Not much to drink around here, though."

Elizabeth made a strangled squeak.

She was staring at us like we'd turned into the Mad.

"What?" I asked.

"You're thirsty?" she whispered.

Trax nodded.

Derik cursed. When I looked at him, he explained. "I wasn't hungry, or thirsty, or tired the whole time I was a Hunter, except when I was too far from the magic, and recovering from the trip."

"But..." Wasn't that a good thing?

Elizabeth shoved the papers off her lap. "Take whatever looks important. We need to get moving."

He grabbed three letters and my left hand, pulling me up. "There's nothing I'd trust to drink here," he said.

"Okay, but is that really freak-worthy?" I asked. I opened the letters as we began to move back to the door. It still led to the locker room, wonder of wonders.

Trax tossed a paper onto the floor after quickly scanning it. "It occurs to me," he said, "that if we can get thirsty, we can also dehydrate and die."

Okay, that was freak-worthy. I collected everyone's papers, tucking my frying pan under my arm. "You lead; I'll read and catch you guys up on the summary."

I stepped over a stack of boots and helmets. On a whim, I paused, turning back to pick up a helmet and cram my feet into a too-large pair of boots. Elizabeth watched. After a moment, she did the same. We followed the boys through the hatch.

They weren't there.

Or we weren't.

I looked at Elizabeth. We both turned around. "Same door?" I asked.

She nodded, helmet visor flopping over her eyes. "Same door. Hon, you've got to stop breaking the world."

I sighed. "Trying," I answered, and ripped open a letter, one of the two we'd tagged as being the most important.

"Look out!" *CLANG*.

I stumbled back into the wall, crumpling the papers in my hands to keep from dropping them—losing most of them anyway, and my pan, too—agony radiating from my middle where I thought her handprint might be emblazoned on my flesh. Gulping at air I couldn't quite pull in, I saw the seal rearing back for another lunge, teeth bared.

Slamming the attacking seal again with her pan, Elizabeth waved me toward the door. I tried. Not my fault oxygen is required for certain things like movement.

Darkness fell across my face—a shadow. Maybe I didn't so much 'dodge' as 'flail out of the way,' but I didn't get hit by the second seal. However, I did fall back through the hatch. It slammed shut behind me, Elizabeth's foot kicking it closed, and disappeared.

And then I was on my own.

Chapter Twenty-Two

The knife had bit into my hip.

Not badly, but I was bleeding, and my bloody rear was peeking through the slash in my jeans. "Graceful," I croaked to myself between gasps of air that left my breastbone throbbing, and pressed down on the stinging cut.

I was alone.

The realization prickled the skin across the back of my neck, and I lay still and silent, listening.

In the distance, I heard the *thrummmm, thrummmm* of the drills. The walls pinged and creaked, and the steady *crash, splash* of the ocean promised me that the Gulf was out there somewhere.

But the only heartbeat I could hear was my own, and the only breathing, too. Pushing myself up, keeping pressure on the bleeding cut at my hip and trying to ignore the burning from the wound on my face, I looked around.

I'd landed in a deserted-looking room that appeared to be a maintenance closet. Brooms, wrenches, oils, and other odds and ends cluttered the shelves, sticking off every which way. Nothing that looked like a first-aid kit, though. The light bulb overhead had the half-burned look of the long-dead kind, but bluish light permeated the room from no apparent source, almost the exact intensity of a cloudy day's daylight through clear water in the first ten feet of a dive.

Should I head out to find the others? *Shhhfff.* My knee brushed one of the two papers I'd managed to hang onto.

This place really *was* a puzzle. I didn't know why. I didn't know how. But I could understand the Lost, and I was capable of hearing things no one else could. Even if there was someone else out there who had the ability I did, I was here, and they were not.

I *would* figure this out. I would drop the Tides.

And this was as good a place as any to read through my cache. Somewhat safe, and hidden enough that I should notice anything coming before it noticed me.

"Deal with what you have at hand," I told myself, "before you go looking for trouble." Taking a deep breath and trying to force my hand to stop shaking, I picked up the papers.

They were both updates sent from Leid to his boss. In the first, amid reports of interviews with crewmen, whom he'd noted had so far all seemed to be telling the truth of their own ignorance about the missing computers, he mentioned Rogers had a private research lab on board. By the second, dated two weeks before the Tides struck, the investigator still hadn't seen the lab, but Rogers had promised to show it to him the next day, talking about filters designed to draw magic out and drills and pipes and hybridized Power refinement. Leid theorized Rogers was planning on using a new kind of pipe for unfiltered Power based on a series of receipts and shipping confirmations, but he hadn't found out much about the filters, only that Rogers was proprietarily paranoid about sharing the research. Leid's latest supposition was that the disappearing crewmen might have snuck into the lab and taken something valuable before running, although Rogers denied the possibility. The computers missing, he'd insisted, hadn't contained anything sensitive.

By the time I'd gotten through reading, the papers were half-covered in smears of red, but my newest wound had slowed down to a sluggish ooze.

I rolled my waistband down and re-secured my belt, the best I could do in lieu of a bandage. It hurt, but then, everything hurt, including a growing ache behind my eyes and in my throat. "Water, water, everywhere," I quoted to the empty room, which did not deign to answer me.

Time to move on. There was no guarantee anyone else would be able to find me, no matter how long I waited. Sucking in a deep breath, I forced myself to stand and took a quick inventory of what I had left. Papers and a knife, rubber boots and a helmet. Everything a girl needed to survive fighting monsters aboard an ocean rig, right? I left the papers on the floor.

My frying pan was gone, leaving me with a free hand. The grimy handle of a metal broom just promised infection, so I passed on it. But the shiny silver wrenches and tools in the corner looked well-kept. I grabbed a hefty-looking wrench and tucked it into my waistband. The knife stayed in my hand; it had already done enough damage.

Writing on the far wall caught my eye. The letters were thick, ugly blocks of reddish-brown. I didn't pretend not to know what they'd been written in.

"Rogers is going to show me the filters," they said. And scrawled in another handwriting below, a neat and precise cursive slowly slanting up the wall, "Power is as much mind as body."

I'd heard someone else quoting that recently, saying it aloud. Who?

A momentary flashback, Sandra and Trax and Derik and me, in a cheap hotel room. *Trax stretched out on the bed he and I had crashed on. "I can say something to the public," he suggested.*

Derik dropped the remote in my lap. I turned on the TV.

"Good point," I admitted a few minutes later.

An interview with Rogers was progressing in the foreground. "Power is as much mind as body," he said, as the news ticker rolled.

Rogers. I was damn near sick of that name. And where did Leid fit into all this?

Shouldn't there be a way out of this room?

I tapped the handle of the knife against the wall where the writing was scrawled. *Tong-tong.* Hmm. A few spaces to the left: *thunk-thunk.* To the right: *Thunk-thunk.* Something was back here. I kicked, and the thin metal under the words tore free.

Stairs headed up. Lacking anywhere else to go, I took them.

Cold, fresh air blasted across my face. I was at the top of an observation deck, and it was dark as a night with a half-moon. Something *squawked*. I ducked, and talons scraped against my helmet. The seagull dove again. I swung the knife. *Crack*. I'd hit it with the flat of the blade into the window. It fell, a limp bundle landing at my feet, and I rubbed my wrist. "If the ASPCA comes after me," I told it, "you started it."

The feathers ruffled in the sea breeze, and eyes stared back at me, unblinking, and no one was here to make me look away. My stomach twisted. Trying to impale me through the head or not, the Mad had still been alive a moment ago. Somehow, it was much worse when I was the one who'd killed it, when there was no one else around who would have been hurt. Pressing the back of my hand against my lips, I stepped over the body. *No choice.*

I was a hundred feet in the air up a rigging, and almost in the dark sector. Below, I thought I could make out two upright figures moving among a bunch of flopping bodies—the guys? I squinted, and the air seemed to sharpen, bringing them into focus. Yes, it was them. I shouted, but the sound seemed muffled, even here.

One of the seals snapped at the slimmer figure. My heart jumped through my throat. But Derik had Trax by the back of the shirt and out of the way, slamming a heel into the side of the seal's face. And then he was dragging Trax aside again, an attack from behind dropped with the back of a frying pan. Trax, both hands wrapped around the handle of the kitchen knife, braced himself and thrust forward. Red splattered. A large body collapsed between the men, and Trax took a step back and wiped at his face a little too hard. Derik yanked the knife out and gave him a slap on the back, only to grab him out of the way once more, out of the reach of an octopus that had crept up behind them.

Pain flared in my knuckles, where I'd bit until my teeth broke through my skin. I couldn't watch this.

There was a plastic door behind me. Something—some kind of movement—caught my eye as I was turning to go into it. I paused and looked up toward the top of the main rigging. *It* stared down at me, head cocked, claws curled over the rail.

A Hunter.

It grinned, and disappeared.

The Hunters protected the Tides. That was where I had to go.

I went through the plastic door and found a lab, and froze just inside the door. The scientist was still hard at work.

At least, I assumed it was the scientist. The octopus compared beakers held by two of its arms, staring into the murky liquids. It swiveled its seat with a third arm, looked at me, and then swiveled back, unconcerned. A fourth arm picked up a glass rod and stirred one beaker.

"Hi," I said, because it wasn't attacking.

A fifth arm raised, tip waving at me, and then settled back down.

It would have been a witness. "Mind telling me what happened?" I asked.

It didn't bother to give me an answer.

"If you touch my hand, I should be able to understand you." Although, that would mean I'd have to inch closer. First one foot slid forward, and then the other.

The beakers set down, and the octopus swiveled around again. I held out a hand.

The suckers were gentle against my flesh when they settled into my hand. *You better not be wasting my time.*

"I'm not," I answered. "I want to know what happened."

An earthquake? Something. A gas leak, maybe. And then the lights went out, but it didn't get dark. Five of the octopus's other arms flapped. *Don't remember much.*

"Yeah, I guess not. Do you know what Rogers was doing?"

Who?

"Rogers. Head of Lorren's Oil research division, the Rogers' Research Institute. Your boss, probably." I glanced around. Beakers lined the room, and pencils were scattered around the room at random. A row of test tubes dried beside the sink, dripping onto a torn t-shirt, and jars along one wall held the long-pickled creatures of any science classroom. Seeing the last three in the row, I swallowed hard. A bird's beak and some octopus arms.

Just because it wasn't Mad, didn't mean it was sane.

Sounds familiar. Don't remember now. Captain told me to find a way to change us back. Back to what?

I looked at the arm in my hand. "Human, probably."

Oh. No, sorry. Too few arms.

"I bet the captain wants to be human again, though."

The flesh was changing color to match my skin tone, streaks of red mimicking the blood still smeared on my palm. *Always knew the captain was impractical. Whatever; never argue with the landlord or the moneybags.*

"Impractical?"

Much more effective with the fangs.

My mind cast back to the Hunter. "When did everyone start changing?"

Are you thirsty?

"Yes."

Do you want to change?

"No."

Don't drink the water.

It took its arm back and spun back around. I had the feeling I'd been summarily dismissed.

At least not everything here was Mad.

There was a notebook off to the side, papers neatly organized by yellow-labeled tabs. Some of the sections were unreadable coding, but the header "Lab notes from previous scientist, decrypted" caught my eye. I flipped to it. There was one entry. *Attempts to instill Power into unPowered test subjects failed. Power cohesion prevents unfiltered magic extraction from source. Condensed filtered magic, drawn and collected with copper wiring, run through subjects. Does nothing, as expected. Conclusion: unfiltered Power cannot be obtained without a mental extraction factor and a physical separation factor. Key is determining separation factor. Will attempt to find proper filter in future experiments.*

Sloppy handwriting scrawled across the bottom: *Probably why I got the job: last scientist was an idiot who liked to play with fire. #whatcouldgowrong #thanksdarwin*

Going back out the door took me to a platform. Open air tossed my hair into my face, but most of the sky was cut off from view by the thick scaffolding and the pipes that ran along it. Walls of gears partitioned the platform into sections, herding me toward the center, where the floor fell away. Pumps rose and fell in that gap; steam hissed out of tubes. *Clank, clunk, hiss, clank, splash.*

I couldn't tell if I was alone or not, but I assumed not. Anything living could probably trace my path by listening to the splashes of my footsteps in the pools covering the rough rubber matting. Water beaded on the top of my rubber boots. I licked my dry lips, trying not to think about how delicious a glass of water sounded; my temple throbbed, and my legs felt heavy. Maybe I should skip the water and just take a nap?

The screeching bark warned me. I wheeled, grabbing the wrench out of my waistband and jumping to the left. *Thud.* Three hundred pounds of seal landed where I'd just been standing, my calf inches from bared teeth, teeth that snapped as the seal squirmed closer. I swung with the wrench. The pathetic *klunk* told me that I'd not made much of an impression.

Nix that. I'd made it mad. Well, madder.

It reared up, mouth gaping open, and lurched at me. I dropped the wrench and wrapped both hands around the knife, slashing at the snout that had just barely missed me. This time, the blade sunk into flesh, blood dripping down its nose. It reared up again, and in slow motion lunged at me. Surely I could move faster than this, my feet mid-air in my leap backwards, but gravity was moving too slowly and it was going to crush me —

It sprawled at my feet, snapping, just short of my boots. Instead of slashing, I dropped myself onto it, twisting so I fell knife-first — straight at its skull.

The blade *crunched* into bone, which caved in. The teeth, so close to my calf, stopped moving.

I couldn't get the knife out. It was stuck.

Something else barked from behind me. I turned.

Shit. Another one.

The wrench was under the body of the first seal. I jerked desperately on the knife, but to no avail. The second one leapt at me. I hopped sideways, but my boot caught on a flipper of the downed one, and I tripped, sprawling over its back.

Claaaang. "Over here, dumbass." The seal aborted its attack and turned to face the more annoying threat.

Elizabeth. Thank god.

She jumped out of the way of its lunge and sliced down with her pan at the neck. Something *snapped*. It sprawled over the floor, and didn't move again.

She offered me her hand, and helped me up. "Try not to hit bones," she drawled, a hint of Mississippi in her voice. "It's really hard to get your weapon back when you do."

"Yeah. Noticed that." I pushed against the first seal, my feet slipping and sliding. "Don't drink the water."

She eyed the grimy, damp puddles. "Not that thirsty yet, thanks." Kneeling in a dry spot, she helped push until the body shifted enough for me to wiggle the wrench free.

The words sunk in while I brushed my knees off. Straightening, I stared at her. "You're getting thirsty?"

Her gaze fell away from mine. Answer enough.

The room was in constant motion, gears churning and whirring. Elizabeth started toward the door. "Like the décor, at least," she muttered, admiring a set of small bronze gears tucked into a scrollwork frame.

"Wait," I said.

The wrench might be useless in a fight, but there were nuts and bolts here. A butterfly memory flapped through my brain, fluttering through my headache. "Stop the drills," I muttered to myself, and fixed the wrench on a large moving nut. The gears lifted me off my feet, putting my whole weight on the wrench before the nut turned.

When my feet touched back down, I spun the wrench around, managing two twists before it pulled me back in the air. This time, as the nut rotated down, the wrench slid off. Elizabeth caught me and pushed us to the side.

The metal of the joint shifted just slightly. The angle was wrong for the pressure. With the scream of twisting metal, the joint bent, and the nut exploded off, ricocheting against the far wall. We ducked. And then Elizabeth was yanking me back toward the door and through it, as metal screeched and twisted and tore.

A classroom, fifty feet in the sky, with three window-walls that opened onto darkness and one long blackboard, received us. Below us, a racket of agonized metal told me that my antics were wreaking some kind of havoc.

"What is this?" Elizabeth picked up a textbook from one of the desks, and dropped it again as the entire room shook. Something groaned near the center of the room, the cry of metal.

198

Before the room stilled, I was stumbling my way forward, catching one of the books as it began to slide off the edge of a seat. Every desk had one. *Remedial Powers: Your Basic Guide to Using Your Magic.* Tucking the wrench back into my belt, I flipped a book open to the page I knew too well, not bothering to look down. "'Power is as much body as it is mind, but also as much mind as body.' Look at the chalkboard."

She followed my gaze. "Powers. It's a chart of the types of Powers." On the left, the list began with strength, heat, flight. On the right, illusion, dream.

In the middle, there was only music.

Thud. Thud-thud.

The center of the room sagged, furniture tilting off-kilter, books sliding off desks.

Boots on linoleum stomped toward the door. "This room isn't stable. We should go."

"Physical Powers and mental Powers. They've listed the types of Power." I shook my head in confusion, moving closer to the blackboard with the book in my hands, searching for another clue. What did *type* of Power have to do with anything?

"How do Hunters move in Tides?" Elizabeth asked. And then, "Really. Floor sinking. That's a bad sign."

We'd traveled. We'd flown. "You're a heat Power," I said, and traced a finger under the first rule. *You cannot change or remove yours.* "In order to fly, you had to lose your body, because a body decides how your Power manifests. But what happens when you get a new one?" Music Powers who went deaf were still classified as music Powers, even though they couldn't use their magic anymore; blinded illusion Powers were still illusion Powers when forced into retirement. But a tone-deaf child had learned to hear rhythms, and there'd been a blind illusion Power at Mechany's — she'd been able to change the things people tasted.

Wood under the floor cracked, and not far from my feet a meter-wide section of linoleum sank inward, drooping as if nothing supported it.

Something ripped, clattered against metal, again and again, and then, seconds later, was quiet.

Elizabeth was right; we had to leave. I turned to join her, leaving the puzzle behind me, and bounced off a desk.

Screeeech. It slid past me, hit the sagging point, and tore through, dangling. And then with a *rip* it was gone completely, and I could see nothing but air and sparse metal scaffolding below.

Clatter. Clank. Crack.

Another piece of metal underneath the room swung free, a beam glistening through the hole in the bright white lights of the classroom. The whole room lurched.

Furniture inched across linoleum with the unholy choir of squealing metal on bare classroom flooring. I jumped across a hole that appeared at my feet and spared a final glance over my shoulder at the chart.

"Going. *Now.*" Elizabeth dodged a desk and grabbed the doorframe, swinging her legs up and into the next room. The floor was slippery, my boots barely giving me any traction. Falling to my knees, I crawled toward her outstretched hand. "Hurry!"

"Trying!" Dropping the book, I kicked hard, and grabbed her wrist.

The floor buckled and caved.

Our gazes met. Her eyes were wide, her lips thin, but her grip firm. "Climb," she ordered, voice hoarse from her face-down position with her stomach over the edge.

"You'll fall."

"I've got a good grip on the frame with my legs. Climb, dammit; I can't hold on to you for long."

I kicked around for footing. A pipe dangled at an angle, enough purchase to push up with my feet. She pulled as I jumped. "Sorry," I muttered, grabbing her belt and hauling.

"Oof. 'Sokay." Her voice came out as a squeak, though.

With the help of the doorframe I made it the rest of the way. I hauled her up to her feet, and her off-balance stagger dropped her into me, sending us both tumbling into the next room.

Chapter Twenty-Three

We fell into the arms of Derik and Trax.

Sixteen limbs, three frying pans, and two steak knives tumbled into a single knot at the foot of an abandoned bed. Gingerly, we sorted ourselves out. "Are you guys all right?"

Trax laughed, a bitter sound. "Still alive. You?"

I nodded, wrapping an arm around his neck to reassure myself he was.

Derik had picked up a bloody cut on his chest. He dabbed at it with a ruined rag, his pan set on the floor by his feet. My brain screeched to a halt at the damp sheen of sweat across his muscles, even with the streaks of red. Now that just wasn't fair.

And those cuts had to hurt. I saw again two small figures on the deck, far below me.

"How'd that happen?" I asked, unable to help myself.

His gaze met mine. He glanced at Trax, who was prodding Elizabeth's ribs at her directions as she breathed deeply in and out, and then he pulled his eyes back to me, pasting on a self-deprecating grin. "Got clumsy, that's all. Trax is safe, which is what counts."

I bit my lip, and moved to help him. As I took the rag from his hand and wiped gently, I noticed a line of red trickling down the back of his neck from a cut on the back of his scalp. His fingers touched the tear at my hip. Concern flashed across his face. I laid a hand over his. "Not bad," I assured him. And then, to distract him, I gave them an update on the things I'd learned.

"And I'll wager this is the room Rogers stayed in while he was trying to get things set up," Elizabeth said, picking up a moleskin journal after I finished. "Bastard has a diary right here. A real one, even, not an ex-computer: there's no code in it."

"I wonder what he was planning on using as a filter?" Trax asked.

She flipped through. Her lips pursed. The journal *whacked* down on the bedside table.

We looked.

Trax read the section aloud. "'Subject seven is a music Power. Most successful so far. The connection may be the processing mechanism, the passive magic being physical and the active magic being mental.' Physical is affecting the world around us or sensing how things really are, and mental's emotions and how the brain interprets things, right?" He waited until I nodded. "But what about active and passive?"

I spun the book for a closer look. "Active magic is the kind you have to pull to you, like when I'm trying affect someone's emotions. I sense for the magic, which is this fizzy feeling, and pull it in with an idea in my head of what I want it to do. Passive is the kind that doesn't require a draw on Power, like when I listen. It's just a part of me, and even if I have to concentrate, it's not really work, just focus."

Derik's chest was hot on my back, the lump of his makeshift bandage pressing against my spine. "Like when I exercise with someone else, I have to pull on my Power to make it apply to them, but when I'm recovering, it just heals faster on its own." He touched my hip, hesitant.

I ignored the hand, looking at Elizabeth. The arm migrated around my waist.

"Heat," she said. "I use effort to warm things up, but I just don't get cold if I don't want to."

My brain turned over, trying to sort through the puzzle. "How does someone filter magic, though?"

Elizabeth was looking at me. "How didn't you die or go Mad when you…" And she looked Trax.

"He's my brother," I defended. "I wasn't exactly thinking about it. I just knew I wanted him to be more like me, so he wouldn't be gone."

They all looked at me.

"Trax," Elizabeth said, "have you tried *listening* to anything lately?"

His nose wrinkled in confusion.

I negated the ridiculous thought with a slash of my hand. "That's not possible. Either you're born with a Power, or you're not."

Her fingers brushed the page in front of her, and my stomach lurched as it took in her meaning. Rogers was trying to find a way to change that rule, to change *all* the rules. He'd unleashed the Tides in his search, tortured people and destroyed millions of lives.

And here in the Tides, where everyone should be like ghosts, we had bodies real enough to kill. Even Trax, whom I'd made like me. Remade.

Had I found the answer Rogers had been looking for? Was I…?

"That chart you saw. Mental-based Powers are rarer than the others," Derik said. "Music, dream, illusion Powers. And illusion and dream Powers are mental in both stages of their use— illusionists see through other peoples' eyes and create hallucinations; dreamers see other people's dreams and change what other people dream. But music Powers hear what's really *there*, in the world, not just how people interpret it."

This whole place was illusion, damn it. I stepped out of his arm. "We need to keep going and see what lies at the heart of this maze before we ask ourselves about the theoreticals."

Elizabeth turned toward the door, Trax following. Derik grabbed my shoulder after they'd walked out and disappeared, before we could step through.

"I know you hate me for letting him come," he said, "but the choice *was* his, and I won't belittle him by taking it away. Just like I wouldn't stop you from following him."

I turned, stopping his words by a hand over his mouth. His blood streaked across the back of my hand, a remnant of my poking at the cut across his chest. "Just..." His eyes were so damn green. I remembered the agony of Valdez holding me back from climbing into the horse trailer with a screaming Hunter. What if we hadn't gotten him to the Edge in time? "Just don't, okay? I don't hate you." Maybe I should have. But I didn't.

His eyes closed, hiding a soul-deep pain. His lips moved against my palm, his voice muffled but understandable. "If you had been following him, I'd have followed you." He had. He had followed me into the Tides, and kept Trax safe for me, as safe as he could.

"Why?" I rasped.

A smirk curled under my hand, and his eyebrows waggled. "Don't you ever look in the mirror, Kel?"

Irked, I stepped back. "Of course I do!" His eyes went wide, the joke he probably thought I'd laugh at falling flat on our feet. Too bad. I was serious. Sweeping my arms down and out, I invited his eyes to see what I saw, not that I thought he would. "But every time I do, all I see is me."

He sighed and stepped forward, reaching to grab my waist. "Kelly—"

I dodged, shaking my head. "I'm not a catch. You? Smart, handsome, brave, amazing cook. You could have *anyone*. I'm– Irritable. Cold. Angry. A broken music Power."

Twisting lips, clenching hands, flaring nostrils—I'd never seen that expression on his face, that fire lighting his eyes. He didn't miss this time. Yanking me close, the brim of my helmet bouncing against his chest, his arms entangling mine, his voice vibrated into my soul. "You are not *broken*." His chest heaved, bare skin hot under my hand. "Doesn't it occur to you that I'm lost too? From the moment I walked in to your apartment—"

It took me a second to realize he'd stopped, it was so abrupt. "What?"

His hands started to withdraw. I grabbed them. Tried to pry the answers out with my eyes. We stood too close for him to avoid my gaze for long. I widened my eyes and raised my shoulders, and he crumbled.

"It's just—" A shift, and I was crushed against him, feeling his hands run up and down my shoulders. "God, Kel, you're *tough*. You'll tackle anything that dares threaten what you love, and if something's impossible, you still try, even when most people would give up. When *I* would give up." There was something suspiciously like a nuzzle to my helmet. "You work to keep people safe, and you care about the world. And you don't hesitate to do something hard, if it's the right thing to do. Yeah, you push people away—but it's because when you love, you love so hard, you'd probably break if you loved wrong. You think I don't see how you grieve for your parents?" His chest heaved. "And I want that. I want *you* in my life, even if it's only as neighbors. As long as I can see you happy. Do you know, it's the first time I've ever known I wanted something?"

I couldn't breathe. When had he punched me in the stomach? But he hadn't; he'd only… good as told me he loved me.

Yeah. Punched in the gut.

I tried to make my lips work, to say something. To tell him the truth burning inside me, that I was addicted to him, that I couldn't imagine life without him.

And yet he hadn't told me about Trax following me into the Tides. It caught my tongue, and twisted the words into a knot in my throat.

The moment passed into two, and then he slowly released me. Still I couldn't speak. Fear seized me to my bones, shattering my soul—I was going to lose him, lose him because I *couldn't* say I understood why he'd done it, couldn't say I forgave him, couldn't return his words. His eyes turned away, hollow and sad, and his mouth opened.

I didn't want to hear his words, so I threw out my own, spun away from him and turned my own doubt into a shield around me. "You didn't even tell me he was following us. You never gave me the chance to change my mind."

Silence. The journal sat on the bedside table, the words of a man who cared nothing for anyone. I slammed it closed.

A choking from behind me. He'd gone pale, white and wide-eyed.

"What?" It came out of me angry, a snarl that ripped through the air. Because I couldn't forgive him until he gave me something to forgive him with.

"I'm sorry." His hand was over his face, the other at his throat. "I—you're right."

"Right about *what*?" I threw my hands up into the air.

"I took away your choice. I—" The words broke off.

I waited. When nothing came, I hurled the journal to the ground. *Bastard,* I accused that journal; *all of this is* your *fault. I hate you!* The room began to blur, and a sob tore through my chest, and I was turning to run away, because I just couldn't bear for Derik to see me fall apart.

But then Derik was pulling me into him. "I'm sorry." His breath was hot on the back of my neck, his arm supporting my weight, my helmet flopping over my face. "I was *wrong*. And I was so damn blind by my own obsession with *choices*—" The arm spun me around and held me tighter. "So blinded I forgot that arguing against a choice is a choice too. I wouldn't stop you from following him—but I'd argue for you not to."

The angle of my head under his made it hard to cry, made me breath more slowly, made me think. I pushed the hat out of my eyes. "You didn't ask me to stay on the other side."

"All the Hunters—they said you might be able to do it. There's something about you, Kelly, that gives them hope, in the way you give me hope that life's worth living, worth holding on to. You said you might be able to drop the Tides. I thought—I still think you can."

When I pressed against his chest, he loosened his arms enough for me to lean back and meet his eyes. "What will you do? If Trax puts himself in danger again?" *Give* me *hope,* I begged him silently.

"I'll give you the choice." He pushed a strand of hair behind the strap of my helmet, brushed my chin with his knuckles. "I'll tell you and let you make up your own mind. But..."

"But?"

Shifting his weight, he bit his lip and looked to the side. "I won't stop him if he makes up his mind. Not even if you ask him, ask me. He's still an adult and it's *still* his life to choose."

Derik would never force a choice on someone else. It wasn't a part of who he was. And I —

I respected that.

"Okay," I said. "I won't ask you to." Because keeping Trax safe from himself was *my* responsibility. I tried at more, tried to tell him I loved him and it was going to be okay.

But what if I died here, and he didn't? What if we never made it out, either of us?

The words stayed buried in my throat.

He opened his mouth. I had no idea what else was left to talk about, and I didn't think I could handle more in any case.

Because I *did* love him. But promises? This wasn't the place to risk them.

So I stopped whatever he was going to say with my lips.

His hands fisted in my shirt; his skin was hot and sticky beneath my hands. I pressed into him, leading his lips with mine, telling him — without the words I couldn't say — what I felt.

And then he was taking over, answering me. *I'm sorry; I love you; don't leave me*, his lips said. It made my head spin, the promises he was giving me, the feel of his hands in my hair and on my body, the hard press of his tight stomach against my shirt. Heat ran through me, from him, from inside me, everywhere; skin was hot under my hands and every inch of him was firm, strong, and *mine*.

The taste of salt and copper and a sweet mustiness washed over me, leaving me drifting in his arms on a current I couldn't summon the will to fight.

He broke away, the rush of oxygen bringing the awareness that he was the only thing holding me up. I gasped against his collarbone, trying to pull together my scattered thoughts. He was shuddering, too, palm still cradling the back of my head.

"We have to keep going," he rumbled.

"Uhn." It was the best I could do at the moment. He steadied me on my feet, holding me away from him until I was able to stand on my own. I rubbed at my eyes, and ran my hands through my hair, and straightened my shirt.

But there was a smile on his face, and I had hopes I hadn't lost him for good. Because, in that moment, I was certain I'd die if I ever did.

Chapter Twenty-Four

We came out through the door to find them waiting for us. Trax raised an eyebrow. Derik met his eyes. They stared at one another. My face burned under my brother's blue-eyed scrutiny. I think my lips twitched into a nervous smile, but it might have been more of an embarrassed grimace.

Still, Trax looked away first.

With a knowing thumbs-up of a smile, Elizabeth motioned to something behind her. "If you're done," she said, "I think we've found something."

It was a set of chimes, all alone on a table beside a notebook. "Why do he and the scientist get notebooks, when others get letters?" I asked to no one in particular.

Derik flipped through the headers, setting his pan down on the table beside Elizabeth's. "Organized mind; better computer skills; who knows. Complaining?"

"Hell no," Trax said for me. "What's the gist?"

"Nothing," Derik answered, sounding irritated. "It's blank."

Elizabeth picked up a wooden hammer and tapped the chimes. They must have been broken, because all I heard was a dull *tunk*.

"Do that again," Derik ordered.

She did, to the same effect. Derik shoved the notebook in front of me. "Again," he ordered, taking the hammer from her. When he tapped, words lit up across the page.

"I bet it was encrypted somehow," Trax suggested. "Can't read without a key. Even a madman wouldn't keep files like that where anyone could access them."

Elizabeth gestured for Derik to keep going.

Subject responds, a fourth class earth Power. I was right. Living filters are the key. But I lost this one, too, like the others. When the unfiltered magic goes beyond their capacity, subjects change into animals, and excess unfiltered Power extends beyond them in a bubble that seems to warp reality based on the filter's life experiences, subconscious connections becoming reality. Baseball fan, for example, causes everything to be touched with baseball paraphernalia.

Filters maintain filtering abilities when capacity has exceeded, but overflow surrounds them until disconnection, and they descend into shock when disconnected from the magic. Others exposed to overflow Power, if Powered themselves, also change into animals; unPowered disappear. All changed subjects reverted to human or reappeared in the absence of magic; exposed subjects more likely to survive if main filter dies.

Trax had his hands over his ears, trying to read over our shoulders.

"He was already accessing the unfiltered Power," I said, over the *thunk--tunk-clunk--tunk*.

My poor twin winced, shooting a disgruntled look at Derik.

Elizabeth nodded, a line forming in her brow. "I was assuming the Tides happened when he began extracting the magic. What happened?"

Trax snatched the hammer from Derik. "Give me that before you break my head," he snapped. "You're worse than Kelly."

Startled, Derik stepped back and let my brother take over beating the chimes.

Trax finally noticed we were all staring at him half a song of rhythmic *tunk*s later. "What?"

"What do you hear?" I asked.

He looked down at the hammer in his hand. "Um, chimes?" Derik looked at me.

I shrugged a denial. "Random thwacking." We looked at Elizabeth.

She shook her head. "Nothing at all. They're silent, like the Hunters." Derik nodded in agreement, lines appearing on his forehead.

Trax slowly placed the hammer down on table, like that would make us forget he'd been playing.

What had I done to my brother?

The words began to fade on the paper. "Keep playing," I ordered him, and turned back to the notebook.

Tunk-ta-tunk-ta-tunk-ta-tunk...

Professional rock star. If there was one thing he could do, it was keep time.

"Who was the victim?" I flipped through, hoping they were seeing something I wasn't.

"It doesn't say a name." Elizabeth spoke with a voice deep and slow, carrying in it a hint of tears despite her dry cheeks. "I think he didn't care."

No, it looked like he didn't. All the notes were about various subjects of his trials, different abilities listed and their eventual demises noted in the side margins as an afterthought. I bit my lip, and tried not to think about the excruciating pain Derik had suffered in the trip down. A control set included people without Power, none of whom Rogers had been able to pull Power from. They were listed as "disposed of."

There was only one hint, three pages from the end. *Need a stronger Power. Possible obtainment through government. Low-priority investigations often get assigned to music Powers instead of illusion. Will ask for an investigator for missing workmen. Use the subject obtainment transport crew as overflow subjects; wouldn't do to leave evidence around. Also need to sink the collection boat, chloroform, extra restraints, and a few computers. Can't forget the researching agent in N.O. Cut brakes or bribe? Harder to replace than transport crew; connections with N.O. gangs too hard to re-establish. Bribe.*

I couldn't take it anymore. "Let's go," I said, slamming the notebook closed. No one argued.

Trax crammed the hammer into his belt beside his knife before retrieving his cookware shield. I didn't comment. After all, I had a wrench.

We were outside again, even higher up than I had been before. I thought I recognized the platform, the metal grate beneath our feet and the grimy, white-painted railing with a bold red stripe running under the banister. Below and to the left, I could see two seagulls perched on poles, and farther down were a pair of blobs on the deck. One was moving, the other was flopped in a pool of red. Yes, this is where the Hunter had been standing. "It was darker, last time I was out here." And it had been. The twilight gloom was more late-day haze now.

Trax leaned over the rail, worrying at his lip. Derik, I noticed, edged closer, eyeing my brother's belt with his fingers twitching. Trax most definitely did not notice. "The center of the darkness has moved. No, it's... it's smaller."

He was right. I traced the edge of my wrench and grinned. "Stop the drills," I said, and ignored the odd looks the others were giving me.

Squawk.

"Shit!" Elizabeth spat, grabbing my arm.

Derik grabbed Trax's belt and hauled back, pulling him out the way of a dive-bombing seagull. Then another zoomed past, and another, and talons cracked against my helmet, sending me reeling.

Elizabeth had me up and moving before I had my balance back, shoving me through the door, the boys right on our heels. Derik slammed it closed, and we stood, gasping, in a room that now had no door at all. It looked like a command room, only the consoles were dotted with a multitude of old-fashioned wooden steering wheels. The floor was wet, puddles of water everywhere. My boot splashed down in one.

Trax rubbed his temple and licked his lips. "This place is giving me a headache," he muttered. His lips were dry and cracked, the stage at which I'd usually shove a tube of cherry-flavored lip balm at him and tell him to suck it up and smell like a girl for a while. Of course, normally his chapped lips were from wearing makeup and fancy stage clothes and dancing under hot stage lights.

211

We needed to get something to drink, or to end this.

Elizabeth faced away from me, one hand up in the air at an angle, the other trying to hide her weapon behind her back. "Hey." It wasn't aimed at us.

I followed her gaze. He was folded along the command console, a baseball cap somehow balanced at a jaunty angle on his head. I sort of expected a pipe to be sticking out of his lips, but the salty seadog of a Hunter was too busy using his teeth to smirk.

Derik stepped in front of me, moving carefully to avoid stepping in the water. "We don't want any trouble," he lied. Or maybe he didn't know he was lying.

Sliding around him, trying not to splash anyone as I waded through the puddles, I grinned back at the Hunter. "Mind showing us how to get to the lab?" My fingers touched my wrench.

A big hand settled on my shoulder. Derik was trying to stop me before I made trouble. I ignored him. As long as he stayed dry, he wasn't a problem. We needed another pair of boots.

Elizabeth stepped forward. She, too, was smiling. The Hunter met her eyes and rolled to his feet, then leapt down off the command console, Hunter silence marking his footsteps. They stared one another down, each baring teeth in a grin that spoke of death and terror.

I put my mental money on Elizabeth.

And then she looked away.

Well, I guess he did have more experience. He wove over to me, and I motioned the boys back before they could drag me behind them. "It's okay," I said. "I need to talk to him." I held a hand out. "Just a touch, and I'll know what you're saying."

The second the fist-sized paw touched my palm, I knew my mistake.

You didn't think a man could keep himself from going Mad for this long, did you?

I laughed. "Sorry, ma'am."

The seadog Huntress cocked her head at me, and I got the mental image of a grizzled woman in her mid-fifties commanding a bunch of rugged sailors with sharp barks. *I'll give you my part of the riddle, but you'll have to give me something in return.*

"What?"

212

You have to tell me what you're going to do with it.

"Ah." Not sure that was a good idea. She might be herself, but Derik hadn't been Derik, and Elizabeth wasn't Huntress Elizabeth by a long shot. I stalled. "Is it really a riddle?"

She nodded, the brim of her baseball cap dipping. *Warren says it represents some science-type psycho-babble shit. Rogers left things running when he was called away. Done it a couple of times before, but never that long; Leid couldn't handle the magic, and it broke loose when he lost his grip on reality. Without Rogers to cut it off manually, it just kept pulling more and more of itself through — cohesive and all. All of it got dragged through Leid's head, and then mixed with how other people saw stuff as it spread and absorbed them, too. Apparently magic and video games go together in enough heads to really screw with reality.*

"It can't make you play by its rules. The decision is yours."

I'm made of magic now. Wistfulness, pride. She'd been a strong woman to begin with. Under my hand, her fur twitched and pulled — she wasn't used to waiting. *Ask carefully, two-legs,* she warned when I opened my mouth. Her red eyes were steady and remorseless, her fangs peeking out in her grin.

"We get to ask a question," I said to the others. "Any ideas?"

Elizabeth piped up. "How do we stop the Tides?"

Stop the drills. Sadism flashed in her eyes, a delight that wasn't born of her human side. *You already knew that. Wrong question. But she's already experienced; how nice for me.* A warning. Elizabeth dodged, but not fast enough.

The Huntress could have breathed, and done it that way. But instead she slammed into Elizabeth, knocking her down into a puddle.

It was faster, here, than when Derik had turned, and maybe that was a mercy. Snaps and pops and shriveling skin, a neck that grew long, her face bulging like something inside was trying to claw its way out through her nose, and clothes melting into skin with dark fur prickling out of smooth flesh. Fear screamed in her eyes until she squeezed them shut tight, long eyelashes against cheeks that were changing shape, and fists tight with pain turning into round paws with sharp claws. Her mouth opened, but only a strangled gasp came out, square teeth extending into fangs.

And then it was over, and she lay still, and there were two Huntresses.

The captain grinned at me around a mouth full of red mist, a blood-colored version of the transparent mist Derik had used outside the Tides, and then nudged the Huntress sprawled at her feet. Elizabeth rolled up, froze from snout to rear, flexed a paw, and tossed her head in panic.

"Elizabeth?"

My voice startled her into motion. Claws scrambled over the floor, and she lunged in my direction, but before she could reach me, she crossed one paw over the other and rammed face-first into the floor. Rolling onto her side, she dug long furrows into the floor with her claws, her gaze meeting mine. Large dark eyes were wide with panic, and she was panting, too-wide jaws opening with red mist between them—and then snapping shut, swallowing the magic. In a heartbeat she was on her feet, and she leapt into the shadows and disappeared, her head bobbing and thrashing as if she were fighting some beast within it.

The young ones still fight. The Hunters had said that. She was fighting the compulsion of the Tides.

"Elizabeth!" I cried after her. What could I do to help? I could—

I couldn't do anything.

A brush against my leg, fleeting, as the captain dashed by me. *The price is high, sweetheart.* She bounced off a wall and up through a half-hidden trapdoor in the ceiling, ignoring the trellis of cables leading up to it.

And then we three were alone, staring at a metal pan and a baseball cap in puddle of water.

Clang. The rubber bottom of my boot echoed against the metal flooring. "No, dammit!" I'd lost Elizabeth all over again; I'd lost *another* person!

Trax grabbed my arm. "It wasn't your fault," he choked, the tightness of his voice an accusation against himself. His voice cracked, his throat too dry. "God, no."

I sighed, letting myself fall back into Derik's arms. Had I known he was right behind me?

I thought I had. He caught me, anyway, and his hands rubbed along my ribs, squeezing me close.

"I should have…" I stopped, shook my head. They were

guys; they'd claim responsibility, even though it was my damn fault. I should have stopped her—

Like I should have stopped Sandra, or Valdez, or Trax.

Here, here I could cry. I wiped the tear away and bit the back of my hand until the pain outdid the burning of my eyes.

Taking a deep breath, I focused on what we needed to know, tucked Elizabeth's face into a corner of my head to scream over later. *Again.* "We need to ask a question, and that was the wrong one," I said instead, and it came out almost steady.

"How can you . . .? She's Lost, Kel." Trax's hand sat against his chest, fingers curled tight and knuckles white. "Really lost."

"We haven't got time to scream at empty buildings, or argue with fate," I said, and added under my breath, "Not this time." *Twice. She paid my price twice. Damn it, why?* But I took his hand and held it between mine, stilled the shaking, reminded him I was still there. We'd lost so much, but I still had my brother. I could be strong for both of us, if I had to be. Yes, I would.

Derik yanked at his hair, and scratched at a cut on his own back until the scab peeled off and a slim line of red seeped up, and stomped the floor. But then, with a tight voice, he said, "She's right. Forward. We can only go forward from here. We'll do it, right, Kelly? Bring everyone back. Rogers' journal implied we could."

I had to try. I owed it to her. To her, and Sandra, and Valdez, and Mom and Dad.

"Yes. Yes, we will." I took a deep breath, slow and steady, and let Trax's hand slip from between mine so I could pace. "We need a question."

Rogers wanted to control Power, maybe even make himself Powered. The Tides hadn't begun until after the drilling had reached success. Someone—several someones—had been killed as living filters. Who was the filter? No, that wasn't it. *Who* wasn't important; we already had a name and if we couldn't figure the rest out from the world around us, we just weren't trying.

"How do we filter the Power?" Then my mind went back to Trax, to a floating and transparent wraith. "No," I answered myself. "That's not it."

"Will anyone really come back if we end the Tides?" he asked.

I shrugged. "Doesn't matter. We're going to try to end them anyway. We've got to stop the drills."

Oh. The drills. Drill-s. I'd stopped one; there was another. But in a place where everything was symbolic and mutable...

I'd bet every Italian dish Derik had ever made that the second drill couldn't be stopped with a wrench.

"Okay," I said. "Let's keep going."

"What's the question?" Derik asked my back.

I twisted to look at him over my shoulder, and then turned back around and climbed the ladder. The price was too high, and I couldn't lose either of them.

No one suggested I try to take her frying pan out of the water.

The trapdoor in the ceiling opened out into a short, wide room decorated in crumbling wallpaper and worn red velvet, the floor a barren sheet of age-stained metal. The captain was waiting in front of an elevator at the other side, ornate copper scrolling of the old-fashioned elevator greened by age and magic. Breathing deeply, I closed my eyes. The room smelled like dust and forgotten memories.

Cold speared through my hand, and I jumped, eyes flying open. Of course; I'd forgotten that silence cloaked their movements.

She smirked up at me. *Ready?*

I nodded. The others were behind me. Maybe I should have tuned them in to my plan? No, they'd try to do it for me. I couldn't let them do that. Derik had shuffled Trax to the back; he'd take care of him. The rest—well, I didn't think her heart was in killing us. There was a scientist, insane but not Mad, who had told me the captain didn't like being a monster.

What are you going to do with what you learn?

"I'm going to stop the drills."

I can't let you do that. Baring her teeth, she began to suck air in.

"I know. My turn."

She stopped, and let the mist trickle out of her jaws. There was time to attack me in a minute; a bargain was a bargain. And it gave Derik time to get into place. There were no puddles here. This was a better battleground for us.

I really should have told them my plan. But no, this was my battle. I'd not risk them. I opened my mouth to ask—

216

Trax's voice cut through the beginning of mine. "How do we get to the center of this maze?"

Keep going. All roads lead to the center. Fire shimmered in her jaws.

I didn't have to wait for her to know that Trax's was also the wrong question.

"No," I growled, and grabbed Derik's knife from his belt.

She was faster, but Derik was already pushing me out the way, shouting at me. Trax screeched, and any other time I'd have mocked him about that shrill sound, but I was too busy hitting the floor to bother.

The knife hit with a clatter two feet from my outstretched hand.

Something flew over my head, a large shadow crossing the floor, flying toward —

"No!" My feet scrambled against the floor, slipping with the ridiculous *squeak-squeak-shriek* of rubber on metal.

There was a thwack of metal on flesh; a clang of metal on metal, and a thunk of flesh on flesh.

Plain boots stopped by my nose. "Get on the elevator," Derik ordered, yanking me up by my shirt. The ground flew by under me.

Trax's choked cry.

With a *thud* I landed in the elevator. Bouncing off its back wall, I caught myself against the door. Trax staggered into the wall to my left, weaponless, a hand over his chest. He coughed and sucked for air, the breath knocked out of him.

Derik had thrown him out of the way to fight her himself. He swung his commercial-grade steel frying pan with all his Power.

Strength was nothing against a Hunter. Time flickered; she was already behind him, light pouring from her mouth. He screamed.

Clang-clong-clong. The frying pan hit the floor, bounced, bounced again.

Then it was still, and Derik —

Derik was a Hunter once more.

He shook himself, then rolled to his feet, already too graceful.

"No," I whispered again, and fell to my knees.

Chapter Twenty-Five

Derik didn't run like Elizabeth had. Instead he looked up at me and grinned, his teeth on proud display. *This is what you asked me for*, he seemed to be saying. *Happy now?* I'd just gotten him back; what fool I was to think I'd get to keep him.

Oh, sweet life. What had I done?

The Huntress nudged him with her nose. He snapped at her. Baring her fangs, she swatted at him.

He snarled and hit back.

She backed away with stunned wide eyes until she tripped and fell in a flop that defied the grace of Hunters everywhere. Derik rose to stalk her, violence flashing in his eyes, and she snapped herself out of her daze. I was certain they would meet one another in a clash of blood and fang, but she ran instead, flashing through the door.

Leaving Trax and me alone with Derik, the rogue Hunter.

Naturally, it was toward me that Derik turned.

Trax grabbed my wrist, having sometime wobbled over to me. I think he might have tried to push me back, but this was

Derik; it was *Derik*, damn it! Shoving aside my twin, I thrust my hands into wiry fur.

Ice shot up my arm at the touch of a cold nose. *Are you all right?*

"Derik..." My eyes burned fiercely. "You're still—" *you.*

He suffered the arms I threw around his neck. I could deal with this. I had to. Because he was still my Derik, Hunter or not.

I told you I would keep him safe.

Speaking of him—

The relief in me snapped into anger. I turned on my brother. "What the hell were you thinking, Trax?"

He twitched, surprised. But then his eyes narrowed. "Me? What were *you* thinking?"

"I had a plan, dammit! If you had just—"

"Just what?" His question bit through my words, stopping me with the bitterness entrenched in his voice. "Just sat back and let you risk your life? Did it ever occur to you to let us in on this plan? To tell us you *had* one?"

I stepped back. "I was trying to keep you safe, idiot."

"Bull. Shit." He stepped into the space I'd vacated, finger stabbing me in the chest. "You were trying to get yourself killed, is what you were doing."

"I was not!" Had I turned five again? "If you'd bothered to ask—"

He did ask. Cold bit through my hip as I nearly tripped over Derik. He'd moved behind me without me noticing, patiently waiting to add his argument. *You just chose not to answer. Why not, Kelly?*

Trax couldn't hear Derik. Trax didn't need to hear Derik to keep up his end of the harangue. "I'm sick of this! Sick of you trying to put me in a pretty little box and keep me safe. Don't you get it? I'm here too. I need to help."

He may be your brother, but he's not helpless.

My hands tried to cover my ears, but they were blocked by the helmet. I fumbled for the catch. "The world needs you, Trax," I pleaded. "I'm just a broken music Power. I can be spared, and you can't."

He grabbed my wrists. "And maybe I need *you*. Did that ever occur to you?"

I pushed at him, and got nowhere. "People need you. You're their hope, their hero."

"And *you're* mine!"

What a lark. "Then you're fucked," I shot, and it was a verbal smack, staggering him back a step when my pushes could do nothing. "What am I? I make rent as a grammar- and spellchecker. I've got Power I can't use, and I can't fight worth shit; I got Elizabeth and Derik turned—Ow!"

Pain lanced through my left calf, shooting through the numbness straight into my spine and completely disrupting my thought chain. *I got myself turned, thank you,* Derik snarled in my head. *And so did she. He's right, whether or not you like it — we're here of our own will, and if we risk ourselves, it's our own right to do so. You don't get to make that choice.*

"Risk yourselves? Okay, fine. But you don't get to risk yourselves for me!" If I hadn't been pinned between them, I would have run ahead, kept going to stop the argument I didn't want to face, but they weren't about to let me go. The cold had begun to creep up my thigh into my body, making my balance waver.

Trax steadied me with a hand on my arm. "Yeah, we do. I'll do it even if you tell me not to. Because you're my sister and maybe *I* want to keep *you* out of trouble. But unlike you, I'll give you the choice to help." His voice turned coaxing, crooning, melodic. "Let us help, Kel. Tell us your plans."

It was a drug, the soft plea that swept in and wrapped around the corners of my anger, dulling them, dulling me. A gentle weight sensation began behind my eyes, where my Power called to me just before I used it. I wanted to melt into his voice, and let him keep me safe; I wanted to be the princess in a tower and let them—

"Stop it!" I kicked him in the shin before he could actually *pull* and call the Tides down on us. I'd put money on it, that he didn't know what he was doing. How could he? What he was doing wasn't possible in the first place. He yelped and dropped my arm, hopping away with a curse. Letting my weight fall against Derik, I shook my head clear. If his voice was that strong without using Power... "Maybe you're right," I muttered. He was too far into this, too far to go back.

"You think?" he snapped, still rubbing the bruise.

It was easier to bury my face in my hands than to face them, so I did. But I sighed, too. "Derik. Elizabeth is a tool of the Tides now. Why aren't you?"

His muscles shifted against the back of my thigh. *I feel something calling*, he admitted. *But it feels foreign. Captain told me to move, and I thought for a moment that I would, that I had to. But I didn't want to, and it was like it crumbled when I pushed back. I think — I think she can't control me, because I wasn't born in* these *Tides.*

Madison. Lake Mendota. We'd been saved by Jorgen and his minions, and they'd probably never know it.

I placed a hand between his ears. "I've asked you to keep him safe, and that wasn't fair to you, because that's not why you're here. I'm sorry. But will you fight for both of us?"

He grinned a Hunter's grin. *About time you asked. But I don't think she'll attack again until we're in the final room. She wasn't expecting to have to deal with me.*

I lifted my head. "Okay," I said again, and then, "Here's the plan. Or what I have of one, anyway."

Chapter Twenty-Six

The scrollwork copper gate clanked open the next floor up. I leaned out, getting a look of what we were facing. Hands pushed me the rest of the way. "Better onward than backward," Trax said, and I couldn't really argue with that.

The hallway dripped and sizzled with perspiration, pipes of all sizes weaving together to form walls and ceiling around metal plate floors. She sat waiting for us in the center, her body loose and relaxed. The surprise the captain had suffered below made no appearance here; she could have been off-duty and lounging over a beer and a ballgame. She rose onto her haunches we approached.

"I get a question," I said.

Her head bobbed once, and she glided within reach. *You do. Don't get it wrong; lover-boy is the only one not born in my Tides. Can you afford to lose another?* She smirked at me. *My new Huntress won't be able to resist me for much longer, not here, where the magic is strongest. Your brother? He has no practice resisting the demands of the magic. He wouldn't last even this long.*

Trax stood by my left shoulder, while Derik pressed against my hip. I swallowed and shifted my weight onto my left foot. "How do I stop the other drills?"

The nod of her head told me I'd asked the correct question. *There are only two drills,* she answered. *Rest one, run both, rest one, run both. The filter can't run both all the time. When the pain becomes too much for him to feel it all, he loses consciousness and one drill stops pumping. Warren thinks it's his body trying to save itself; I think his mind just can't handle it. One way or another, gives us time for repairs.*

"He can run the other in his sleep?"

I wouldn't really call it sleep. He hurts too much to ever sleep. But I bet, if you took away the pain, he'd be able to rest completely. She crouched.

Derik bared a fang.

The captain nodded, and turned. The door's paneling disappeared as she approached it, and I knew the battle waited for us in there.

Steam hissed as a drop of water hit a pipe by my face.

"Ready?" I asked.

They nodded. Together, we followed her.

Derik's head swung back and forth as he looked around the room, taking in the oversized gears and butterfly-shaped blue-burning oil lamps flickering along the walls. Pools of black water glistened with an oily sheen. Condensation dripped into a pool, and water danced, shattering the reflections of the patina-covered copper interwoven with darkened steel.

Something small fluttered into the air from the center of the pool where the drop had fallen, fading so quickly I wondered if it was real, but then another drop fell, and another flutter of blue and silver wings made me swallow.

"I haven't got a clue what this is supposed to be," I admitted.

"Hell," Trax said, pointing, and I wasn't sure if it was a curse or an answer.

Chains twisted down from the ceiling to wrap around the man's wrists, locked to churning gears that made the boney figure rise up and down like a marionette. The flickering blue light slashed across his razor-sharp cheekbones; blond eyelashes rested against his too-white, hollow cheeks. Pale pink lips were chapped and broken, a trickle of dark wetness glistening faintly on his chin.

I thought he was dead. The back of my throat burned, the faint taste of bile hitting my tongue. Someone had a ghastly sense of humor.

"Help me..."

I jumped.

Pale blue eyes fluttered open. Endless eyes. Deep eyes.

I pulled the wrench out of my belt. "He's locked into the second drill." The realization danced through my gut. I had to free him. But how? Chained on his altar against the wall, surrounded on three sides by a murky puddle, the sacrifice watched my every step with glazed eyes. The water sloshed against Trax's and my rubber boots, tiny wings of blue rising with every splash, eerily silent in a world of speaking Lost, and then I was through and on the tiny dry island in front of him. I knelt. "You must be Aaron Leid," I whispered.

"Help me," he groaned again.

"Yeah," I agreed, and touched the chain.

His scream echoed through the room. Light twisted down the chain and into his body, showing me for one painful instant every bone in his arm. His eyes rolled back in his head, and he sagged, an unresisting puppet to the machine.

No wonder the Huntress had let us get this far.

Wiggling between Leid and me, Derik nudged me back and away. Like sandpaper on my ears, I heard the soft retching of Trax dry-heaving. My own stomach roiled in sympathy.

The light flickered and twisted, lace wings shadowed on the walls. A scent of spice and oil filled the air, magic so thick it clogged my lungs and muddied the thoughts in my head, twisting my mental voice to say words I didn't want.

Intruders. Protect the source. Pressing a palm to my forehead to dull the throbbing, I tried to drive the stray thought out. So thirsty. Maybe a sip of water would help. *No, can't drink the water.*

I should kill them. Chase them off? Yes, they don't belong here. Don't let them close.

Numbness invaded my calf, Derik nudging me, concern in his eyes. I took a deep breath and rubbed my temples, and the thoughts evaporated.

I had to save this man; I had to stop the drill; I had to do it without killing us all. But a wrench wasn't the answer this time.

What was?

"Hey, look at this." Trax had gone around Leid and was looking at the wall. There, behind Leid, a crevice held round wooden table with an assortment of musical instruments on it. Trax picked up a beautiful violin and ran his hands over the smooth wood, then selected a bronze-cast flute to admire. These had to be the key somehow.

My brother, the music Power. Leid, a music Power. A world based off perception. The captain's advice: *I bet, if you took away the pain, he'd be able to rest completely.* An idea began to form in my mind.

The *srch* of claws on metal distracted me. I opened my ears. *Sa-sa, sa-sa, sa-sa.*

The memory of a bloody handprint on an elevator wall smeared across my inner eyes. I bit my lower lip. The captain would fight us; the Hunters didn't make noise by accident.

Turning toward the source of the noise, I stared up into the hissing, steaming mess above us, and saw my own death written in a pair of red eyes gleaming through the darkness. "Not going to fly that way," I told the captain, tightening my fingers around the handle of my wrench. Another whiff of oil and spice, and shadows twirled and spun in the steam, hundreds of them, bringing the not-me back. *Chase the intruders out.* Dizziness.

Derik slid forward to crouch in front of me, growling upwards. His fangs flashed in the blue firelight, half-promise and entirely threat; the gleam seemed solid, and the ground steadied beneath my feet.

"I don't want you hurt," I whispered, dropping my hand to his neck. She'd been at this since the beginning; he was still new. How could he hope to stop her?

Kelp-forest eyes turned toward me. *What goes for Trax, goes for me too,* he said. *You know she'll fight me first, if we let her. Don't attract her attention; this is my job.*

The captain would fight because she had to; she'd fight Derik because I was her only chance to be free. And she'd drag it out as long as she could, because I needed the time. But she'd fight, and when he fell, we'd be hers.

His choice. Not mine. No matter how much I wanted to protect him.

My eyes burned, raw and hot, and the tears that had come last time failed me now. Useful, though, because I wouldn't be able to see if tears were in my way; the pounding in my head didn't need blurred vision to make it worse. Derik gave the smallest and gentlest of sighs, and rested his head against my thigh. I placed my hand on his head, and wondered how terrible it would be to join him, in a form in which I could feel no cold.

It wasn't an unpleasant smell, magic.

Fly-so-free, spin-and-swirl.

No. I wouldn't run.

Eyes flashed in the distance. I turned my back on Derik and left him to do what I couldn't.

Trax started to follow him, pulling the knife out his belt, but my hand on his shoulder stopped him. "I need your help," I said, and nodded back to the man in chains behind us.

Trax hesitated, his gaze following Derik. His lips thinned and the knuckles of the hand holding the knife turned white. "Really?"

"Yes, really," I said. "I think I know how to stop it. But I think it will take us both."

Water dripped from the ceiling, flashing downward between us, filling my nostrils with thick air, and the shapes fluttered again, the reflections of the lights rippling.

Protect. Defend. Destroy the intruder. Guard the source.

Something was wrong with Trax's eyes—a twitch, a vague stare, empty blue. What intruder? There was only my brother. "I can't do it alone."

His shoulder jerked under my hand, and he was back. "What do I—What do I need to do?"

An old-fashioned mandolin begged to be used, but I settled for the guitar instead; the wood was as worn as the one that parked on the wall of Trax's room until he needed to think.

"Do you remember Dad's working songs?" I asked, and held it out.

Trax took the guitar from my hands and nodded, strumming a few bars. "It's in tune," he said, surprised. His voice cracked again. "Are you going to play that mandolin? You suck at strings."

"A point to every room, right?" I pointed to the hammer in his belt. He plucked it out and handed it to me, lips twisted in a wry smile that said *told-ya-so*.

Splash.

Snarling, ethereal screeches echoed. But I couldn't go help. This was Derik's fight.

Splash-thud.

Flump. A snarl, and something clanged into a wall, followed by a whimper. I spared a look, and my heart caught painfully at the base of my throat, my limbs locked in panic.

Derik was dashing by the captain, splashing her in the face, but she was already moving despite the blinding water, locked on. Before I could scream warning, she caught his leg in her teeth and yanked, and he went down, rolled, and buried a hind leg in her chest, claws digging deeply and thrusting her off.

But her flight cast her into a wall, and with a lithe twist she bounced off to crash him into the ground, nipping at his ribs. The force of the attack had rolled them into the water. He caught the side of her head with the back of a knee, and she flew. *Clang.*

He was already on his feet. But he didn't seem to be putting much weight on his left foreleg, and I *knew* that the wet sheen to his coat wasn't all water. A double-looped reflection of a blue light swooped across his shoulder, moisture floating up and filling my lungs.

Intruder. Invader. Remove, kill, defend the center.

Derik's gaze met mine, and his teeth bared.

When had I moved to the edge of the water? Trax wavered on his feet beside me, guitar drooping in his hands, but even as I watched he blinked rapidly and cradled it correctly. We had to focus. I pulled him back, positioning him in front of Leid.

Splash.

The captain landed in the puddle around us, sending up a spray of butterflies. For a moment I flashed back to the diner again, a flock descending on me—but no, while I expected the cold, tinny excitement of butterflies behind my ears, in my own head, instead I got the world on *mute*. Her gaze meeting mine, the captain cracked a crocodile grin.

Reflexively I put an arm in front of Trax and stepped back, but he was stepping forward, into her reach. Not alone, he wasn't;

I prepared to charge, but she was now looking over her shoulder at Derik, across the room from where he'd thrown her, wearing a smirk of triumph. Fear coiled through me, a piercing knife in the heart. Snarling, Derik hunched his haunches and launched. "Move!" I shouted, shoving Trax, ducking.

Derik seemed to fly in slow motion, that leap made with a power and trajectory that would bring him to us... too late, because the captain was already opening her jaws, red mist glowing. We couldn't scramble for cover fast enough.

A shadow passed over me.

Heavy clawed feet slammed into the captain's chest, knocking her into the shallow water, pressing her head into blue-black water and sending more blue butterflies dancing into the air.

Derik's paws hit the empty ground in front of us, collapsed under him, and sent him rolling. He used the momentum to get back on three feet and spun to see a light-furred Huntress with long eyelashes rip a set of furrows in the captain's shoulder.

"Elizabeth!" I gasped.

What was it the Hunters had said? The young ones strove to be more than a memory of who they had been—to still *be* themselves. But... *"My new Huntress won't be able to resist me for much longer."*

How long could she last?

The captain slid out from Elizabeth's pin and dashed around Derik's reach, and with an explosive jump leaped higher than my head to rebound off a wall. Landing with knife-like claws slashing into Elizabeth's back for grip, the captain launched off again, sending our Huntress sprawling in the water with a spray of butterflies and a whiff of oil and spice.

Come to me.

The command pulled on my limbs, my body leaning forward and my foot beginning to move. "No," I said aloud, and leaned backward until gravity asserted itself. With the thump of flesh on metal I crashed into the blue-black plates, landing with Leid's screaming skull filling my vision. Ow. A bruise throbbed on my rear, the cut on my hip pulled with a sharp flare, and a dampness told me it was bleeding again—but the pain made me roll reflexively, onto my stomach, where I saw Trax still moving. I grabbed his legs, and he stumbled, falling to his knees, clutching the guitar to his chest with one hand and catching himself with the other.

"Thanks," he said, clinging to me, breath coming too fast.

Derik snarled, the sound raising in volume as if he were moving very fast, and we looked up.

The captain had landed five feet away, her paw raised above the water, Derik hurtling towards her, but Elizabeth still sat in the water, head low, her eyes gone glassy.

With a snicker the captain raked her forelimb through the shallow moat, and droplets of water flew our way. The spray flashed and danced in the low light, twinkled and shimmied and fluttered—

And then it wasn't water flying, but a million minute butterflies, a flock descending upon us to ask us to dance and play, their thoughts rushing ahead of them in a tidal wave pressing at the edges of my mind, oil and spice drowning me—

My brothers and sisters, all of us, throwing ourselves at the threat, stopping the two-legged bodies that want to destroy us; we're already destroyed. Come play?

Another voice. A whisper that was half scream, voiceless and pleading and torn with agony, wrenching me out of my skin. *I was chained and there was nothing but pain, so much pain; HELP ME; FREE ME; STOP THE DRILL—*

Fangs flashed. Crimson fog swirled between Derik's jaws and poured over the oncoming tide of splash-made butterflies.

And every butterfly charging through that mist liquefied. The voice melted and I was back in my own skin, wet splattering over my face and drenching my shirt, at once icy and fiery hot, burning. Soaked with water touched by distant magic and a rainbow sheen, my brother a writhing weight across my back where he'd collapsed, I struggled to move, and my lips parted.

Water. I tasted it on my tongue: gingerbread, cloves, allspice overlaying a coppery, sharp, bitter flavor. It was cold; it bit into my skin and my lips and through my throat to my soul, and the pain in my head flared until I couldn't see.

A knock interrupted my vegetable chopping, the smell of potato juice soaking into my skin. Trax, sitting on the counter with his guitar in his hands, strummed the strings and smiled lazily at me. Wasn't he supposed to be in New York? No; he was my twin. A part of me. We were safe in here, warm and safe.

"Are you ready to see Mom and Dad tomorrow?" Trax asked.

That's right. They were coming to see us. As long as we stayed here, where they could find us, we'd be with them again. "Stay here, and don't go out." Who had said that? A woman's voice. For some reason I couldn't remember what her voice had sounded like. It must have been Mom.

There was a knock on the door. No, it was too early, too soon. Trax and I couldn't be interrupted yet. We'd miss our parents' visit.

I went to the door, made of blue stained glass butterflies in copper framework, kitchen knife in my hand. Blond hair and kelp-forest green eyes stared back at me through the translucent glass. Derik's hand reached through the butterflies and cupped my cheek. "Are you there, Kelly?"

Fool. I wrapped my hands around his and tried to pull him in. He should be in here, too. "Of course I am. I don't want to be anywhere else."

A McDonald's cup frozen in ice in a faraway lake flashed in my mind.

Derik didn't move — couldn't, I saw, stuck in the door. That's right. He didn't live here. "You have to come with me, Kel. They're trying to trap you here, in the depths of your own mind, out of your mind, since I won't let them have it."

Go out? Out the door? Past his shoulder, rain flew, snowflakes whirling and dancing between the drops.

"Mom and Dad are coming. I can't go." And it was so cold out there, and so safe and warm in here.

"Think, Kelly." Derik's eyes were so green. "You know that's a lie."

Memories: a drysuit sat abandoned behind me; a cheesesteak pita dripped onto a pudgy hand.

"No," Trax said. "No, I want to see them again."

"Am I lying?" Derik asked. "You can tell, I promise. Listen when I say it: Your parents are not coming. The captain put that in your head, so you wouldn't try to escape."

A writhing body in the mud. Gunfire — the blood of a friend. Pizza and a liar on the television.

Trax groaned and crossed his arms over his chest. "You're mistaken. Just because you're not lying doesn't mean you're right."

Mom. No, that was all a lie? Dad. They were dead, gone for three years. I couldn't – I couldn't give them up. I yanked at my hair, trying to stop the knowledge, to block out the memories of the too-quiet nights and a failed, restless vacation. Was it so wrong to want to see my parents again? Why did I have to lose them? Why couldn't I just pretend?

But a middle-aged woman with blonde hair and painted nails rolled through my head, and a meaningless date with an otter-man who died a hero. "Owen," I whispered, "Sandra."

Tears rolled down Trax's cheeks as he repeated her name. "I... She died for me," he said. "I didn't deserve it; she didn't deserve it. I can't just leave her... Kel, I have to go. I have to." He pushed himself off the counter and stumbled, sliding to his knees, his eyes shadowed with indecision. "But I can't go through that. I'll disappear."

"No, you won't." Grabbing my wrist and pulling it to his lips, Derik breathed, and warmth tickled my skin. From the corner of my eye, I saw Trax rubbing his arm. "Not anymore."

Derik's chin was rough. Was he getting a five o'clock shadow? He was so blond, it was hard to tell, but the prickly scratch on the skin of my palm said yes. "If you let me go, I'll be lost."

"I won't let go. Trust me, Kelly. That's all I ask."

Did I? Did I trust him to keep Trax safe? To help me find the strength to face everything I'd lost, to stand by me as I faced all the disasters I was responsible for – did I trust him not to leave me?

Was his love worth risking my heart?

A streak of red appeared across Derik's bare chest, rips and tears appearing in his jeans, a ripe bruise forming on his shoulder. I saw an underwater dome, and a rippling bubble of magic, and heard Trax yelp as Derik shoved him aside. And I saw the Hunter who'd lost everything venture into the Tides with me, despite it all.

I could choose to be safe, to keep myself and Trax safe in a place magic would leave us forever alone, where we could forget everything and everyone and believe the lie that our parents would be here soon. We could stay here, where nothing hurt and we'd never have to face worry or fear again.

Or I take us back to a world where death and madness reigned, where Derik lived in a different skin, and where maybe I had a chance to fix things.

My responsibility.

Another memory, of wiry fur against the back of my legs, tripping me, keeping me from running from myself. Hands on my wrists, and Trax close to tears, but still so, so eloquent, demanding the right to help.

"What do we do?" Trax asked now. He'd made his choice to come into the Tides. My responsibility, but his choice to follow or stay behind, and he'd not chosen to be safe. I looked at him again, at the guilt haunting his eyes. Knew what he chose.

Not just my decision. Our responsibility.

Reaching back, I took my brother's hand, and followed Derik through a door made of wings.

Memories scampered on otter paws through the back of my head, and two Huntresses howled, and Derik snickered, and Leid screamed.

My head cleared. I was laying on the ground, and Trax was by my side, forehead cradled in his palm, pale but clutching the handle of a worn wooden guitar in his right hand. Still human. Not Mad. And we were—

Fighting.

Derik's paw sat on my ankle, his dark blood trickling onto my skin from a wound just under his knee baring raw muscle. The captain had abandoned her attack on us to breathe red mist into Elizabeth's face, and the Huntress reared back, thrashing her head. When her head came back up, she bared her teeth—at us.

I heard Derik's voice in my head: *Do it now!* He jumped past us, landing clumsily on his injured leg.

Whirling to face Trax, I held the hammer at the ready over the metal plating. "Play Dad's song," I urged, my voice cracking, nodding towards the skeletal figure hanging limply in the chains. Leid—his eyes were glazed, no longer registering movement, hoarse whimpers edging through a scream-ruined throat. I doubted he was fully conscious anymore, dragged back into the haze of his torture. But my head *was* clear, and the lights weren't shimmering in quite the same way. "Take away the pain."

Trax, face white, looked back over at Leid. "Kel..."

"Do it."

My twin lifted the guitar, hesitated. "I'm not— I can't—" The sound of a body slamming into a wall of gears and chains interrupted him. I couldn't look. Derik's only hope was for us to stop this, *now.*

"Do it," I said again. "Since we lost our bodies, it only makes sense that we're made of Power. I'm almost music, but you're not tone deaf, so you're fully musical, and in these Tides you're made of Power. Living Power." And probably Powered.

He plucked a note from a string, and bit his knuckle. "Tell me what you're thinking. Please, Kel. I don't understand what's going on. Not like you do."

Not telling him my reasoning last time had stolen Derik from me, and Trax was all I had left. I'd been wrong—I couldn't solve this on my own, and if he didn't know what I planned, he couldn't play his part correctly.

So I put it together for him. "Music Powers hear sounds, and change how people respond to those sounds. This place is governed by perception: how Leid's subconscious interprets the magic flowing through him, mixed with how other people perceive wild magic. So I think if you change the perception, how he interprets the magic, you can change the reality itself. And if he doesn't interpret it as pain, as being helpless, I think he might be able to stop. I'm not musical enough to do it; my Power can change a rhythm, but it's the music that changes how people feel."

He plucked the first three notes of the thinking song, and stopped. "I don't know how."

"I'll walk you through it." And I began to beat a familiar rhythm, with fingers that trembled at first but steadied as I fell into the pattern. "You'll feel something in your head when you sing, something that feels warm and fizzy. When I tell you, reach for it."

Tapping his foot to my beat, he started to play.

The notes *thrummed* through the hall, louder than the acoustics should have allowed, a blade that sliced through the noise of the Hunters' fight. Leid gasped and pulled on his chains, his back arching.

The room sounded too quiet under Trax's tune. The three Hunters reeled with each purposeful strum, struggling to stay on their feet instead of fighting.

Then Trax began to sing, his sweet, sweet voice broken and torn.

"Now," I said.

And for the first time in his life, my brother *pulled* Power.

233

Inside the Tides.

Tap. Tap. Tap. I beat his hammer against the bench, pulling Power into me, joining him. "Don't hold it," I advised. "Just let it pass through you. Think about the song, but don't tell it what to do."

It filled me, and still I felt it gathering, a titanic volcano building within. The Huntresses shrieked, their voices slicing into the fabric of reality, two beings made of unreality. Twin *splashes* marked their falls into the murky water, and the oily liquid took flight, kaleidoscopic wings dashing and whirling through the air. Derik's snarl collapsed into a howl, claws scrambling over metal, faltering, sliding. Voiceless butterflies swirled on silent wings through the room, cavorting everywhere, more and more and more, faster and faster, growing darker and darker, until the world was lost in a cyclone except for Trax and me and a broken man.

Music Powers were the filters. And we were born to music.

I *listened*, too, because there was more to it than pulling. I listened for the *sa-sa – sa-sa – sa-sa* of Derik's heart, and *tha-tah, tha-tah* of the broken man's heartbeat, and I listened for the tides, the ocean tides that belonged to the Gulf of Mexico. I'd never heard these tides before, but an ocean was an ocean, and I'd spent years diving off the Carolina coast.

"Listen to the sounds of the waters, Trax," I instructed softly. Power and chaos swirled around me, in me—to him, from him, as if we were a single entity, and this time it didn't burn or freeze, or else I was numb to the pain. But I felt the strings of the guitar biting into my fingers. No, his fingers. The chords he played were deep, round, each distinct and wholly unique—music as I'd never heard it before. But his tune wasn't what we needed. "What notes do you hear?"

"None," he muttered, fingers still playing, eyes half-closed.

"What does the ocean sound like?" I asked instead, slowing my taps to almost nothing, blending them into the waves far below.

"It sounds like…" His fingers slowed, picking out a new tune, and he cocked his head to listen to a song I couldn't hear. "Like this."

"Listen for that. We're in the ocean, so you should hear that."

234

The sound of an incoming tide whispered under my feet. *Saaaaaaaaaaaaa* – it said.

The filter moaned.

"I hear it," Trax murmured. "I hear the waves against the rig."

I listened for the *slosh* of the water. *Listened*, then, for the song of the ocean. Dives were so loud, and yet so quiet; water amplified the million tiny sounds of ocean life until everything was drowned out in mutual chaos, yet the rush of the ocean itself always roared over it all, the constant by which I'd measured my undersea world.

The vessel beneath our feet trembled slightly. Another moan from Leid, and then a sigh.

"Play Dad's song," I said again, "and listen for the ocean. Remember how it felt, to be small, by the ocean, in the ocean. Remember how it felt, Mom and Dad teaching us to float in it."

"The waves went up and down," he muttered. "Like a roller coaster. Fun."

In my head I pictured a dive, the ocean around me. Beautiful. Wild. Peaceful.

Fun, not drowning, not painful. Just floating.

"Play Dad's song now. Think about how nice the water feels." *Ta. Ta. Ta.* I beat the rhythm. Trax played it.

Tha-tah. Tha-tah. Tha –

Tah.

With a final sigh, the blue-eyed man slipped away from his pain.

With the shrill cry of metal on metal, the gears stopped moving.

And then there was only the sound of the ocean.

Chapter Twenty-Seven

Last time I'd stopped a drill, it had torn itself apart. This time, it tore apart reality.

The vortex of darkness split into thirds, bands of light streaking through to illuminate wings once more, and growing wider and wider as the butterflies faded into nothing. There was no more Power to create them, and so they vanished, scores and scores at a time, until I could see a dark, dank room, blue-burning lamps flickering on the walls, bronze pipes steaming and vibrating above.

I kept tapping my hammer because I didn't know what else to do. Trax's chords, though, faltered, and in the spaces between sound the world shattered. Chains tying a skeletal man to a machine melted and twisted into handcuffs on a stained hospital bed. Walls covered in tire-sized gears shrunk into the plain, cramped quarters of a small lab, with links and bolts raining from the sky to become old needles and chipped glass jars. And on the damp floor—

Derik, sporting a bruise the size of my fist across his jaw and a roadmap of shallow cuts over his legs, a horrific cut across his shoulder and an elbow the color of a ripe peach, inched his body up by his good arm until he was—more or less—on his feet. My heart stuttered but my hand didn't falter, and then another wisp of Power danced away to show me the others.

Writhing, mewling, gasping and choking, two women were pulling themselves out of filthy water from a dripping sink pipe, an overturned bucket close at hand. A silver-edged battleaxe plowed her way upright, wrenching Elizabeth up by the back of her shirt. Elizabeth stumbled and clung to her, still disoriented, a cut dripping blood into her eyes, one of her tiny clock earrings gone. A lesser woman than the captain might have fallen under the sudden weight. The captain just set her back on her feet with a steady hand and a gruff pat on the shoulder.

Derik moved to check the pale man on the bed. "Dead," I heard over my *ta, ta, ta*.

My hand stopped, and the rhythm with it.

The last of the Power swirled away, spinning off harmlessly and dissipating into the air.

Trax's gaze met mine. It was a single thought, one neither of us spoke, but both of us heard—*we killed a man*.

Never mind that he was glad to go, that it was necessary. Dead was dead. We were, as of now, murderers.

Trax touched my elbow. "It had—"

"To be done," I finished for him. "Doesn't make it—"

"Matter any less." His eyes were the dark Carolina sea, murky and deep. I took the hand he held out to me, and let him pull me into standing.

My feet had me tottering toward Derik before my head knew what was going on. He opened his arm, and I fell into him. Was I shaking? All I could think for that instant was that my arms were around *him*, and he was flesh and skin, not ice and fur. "I found you," I whispered into his chest; "you were lost, but now you're mine."

"What?" he asked my hair, pulling a now too-large helmet off my head. It clattered to the floor beside the bed, and I forced myself to see what I didn't want to.

The captain closed Leid's staring, ice-pale eyes. "He was a skinny thing, even when he came onboard. I wish I'd known. Rogers said he'd gone back to the mainland to finish his investigation."

It was too much, and my gaze slipped up, away, to the wall beside the bed, to a chart naming different kinds of butterflies.

Something above us *screeched*.

"Hey guys," Elizabeth interrupted us, "I've played this video game before. And I'm pretty sure that means we need to leave. Now." She was staring up at the ceiling, holding Trax's forearm and poised to run.

Derik scooped something off the floor — my helmet — and crammed it onto his head. It fit him perfectly. "Hold on and keep your head down."

"What? Oomph — "

Derik's shoulder was not made for riding. The strangled whimpers coming out of my mouth to the beat of his footsteps apparently didn't bother him, however, because he didn't put me down. But from the sounds of everyone else's boots scrambling around, that was probably for the best.

I braced myself against the solid muscle of his back and looked up.

Clang. Screech. Klunk. Metal had begun to wrench apart, dropping bolts and shards in a deadly rain. *Klack.* Something bounced off Derik's helmet and clattered to the floor.

I dropped my head down and covered it with my hands.

We burst out the door of the building to find ourselves at the base of the drills, no longer hundreds of feet in the air. The rigging was tearing apart, components already hanging on by threads. "Into the housing complex!" the captain shouted, and we followed her away from the collapsing structure as it dropped into the sea.

The backs of my heels slammed into Trax's back. Derik barked a protest and pushed him forward, making room, and then stopped himself at what he saw. I wiggled off his shoulder and down onto my feet. He let me, too distracted by what he saw.

The Lost —

Were no longer lost.

Five men, mountains of muscle and grizzle and hair, sat shell-shocked on a pair of puke-green sofas. Thick red blood streaked the ground. I would have followed the trail, but I was distracted by a gutted laptop on the counter, its memory chips laid bare to see, and then Derik's hand was over my eyes and I could see nothing but dark. "Hey!" I protested.

"Just sit tight," his voice rumbled, tight and tense.

"God, no," Trax moaned. "Don't look, Kel. Just don't."

I tried to squirm away, but the hands on my face were tight, and I couldn't see what was bothering my brother, my twin, couldn't take it away from him. I should have —

An unfamiliar voice spoke up. "Captain? The rigs?"

"Wait until it settles, Mack. We'll deal with it then. See who's still with us."

"What happened to…"

"I'll tell you later. Let them have their peace, for now."

And that was answer enough. I cried, then, into the palm, and when Derik turned me around to face him, I hid from the sight.

Eventually, the awful noises outside stopped, and the captain hustled us out of the lobby and back into the warm, salty air. Derik helped me sit down beside Trax and Elizabeth. Men and women wandered by in various states of shock and disrepair, calling out names. A bottle of water was placed in my hands, accompanied by a "don't worry; it's safe to drink," and so I sipped on it, tiny little swallows that soothed pains I'd almost forgotten.

The captain piled the living lost beside us. A motley assortment of those who had once been Powered, their eyes stared into nothing and their voices whined or raged. The Mad really were mad. Of the thirty-four Powered who had survived, six had kept their minds.

One was the captain. Another was a scientist, a young man in a labcoat. He knelt to stare into my eyes. "I thought it was you," he said, and then walked away, muttering about missing arms under his breath. I suspected he pushed the definition of "sane."

The captain didn't pay us much mind, except to drop by and tell us that help should be on the way. I wondered aloud why the oil hadn't erupted, or a fire started when the rig collapsed.

"Safety mechanisms," she answered. "Multiple shunts and good disengaging gears. There will be a little spillage, but not much. And everything considered, I don't think it's top priority."

Then she left us alone. I wanted to help, thought several times about standing up and bandaging people, or guiding them around, or doing something besides sit in a heap on the deck.

I would probably have to go inside at some point if I did that.

I stayed where I was, and shared my body heat with Derik and Trax and Elizabeth.

The helicopters came at nightfall.

Chapter Twenty-Eight

Most of the helicopter ride I spent in a daze, with a vague sense of nagging guilt keeping my eyes on the ground. When would I ever get the chance to fly in another helicopter? It was probably criminal not to stare at the lights twinkling below. Between the howl of the wind and the small puppy-pile of drowsing civilians, it wasn't like a conversation was going to happen.

The copter stopped three different times, each time adding fuel and dispensing people. The sharp-eyed man in charge would point—"that one, those two, the one in the red"—and his three or four chosen were rolled out into the waiting jaws of blue- and white-clad people, armed with gurneys and clipboards and too-gentle voices. Maybe there was a method to his cherry-picking, perhaps from the short conversation he'd had with the captain and Elizabeth on the deck of the rig. Or maybe he just got tired of so many staring eyes, and felt the need to ditch the worst-off.

Elizabeth was pulled from us on the third stop. She gave Trax a single backward glance and then slid away, ignoring the hands extended to help her down in favor of almost knocking over a nurse. Someone had the sense to offer her a wheelchair instead of a gurney, not a privilege given to any of the others. When she was spun around to be loaded on the elevator, she lifted her fingers at us. I saluted her back, and then she was gone.

We were the last ones left, Trax and Derik and I. It was still dark, hours after I expected dawn. When we settled down the fourth time, the sky was just edging orange over an island of asphalt in a sea of barren dirt, the acrid air biting through my dry lips.

A gentle nudge into a wheelchair here, a soft "not long now, ma'am" there, and I was inside a building that was mostly sterile walls and streamlined efficiency. There weren't many windows; those that dared peek outside only offered glimpses of carefully manicured desert flora. Tan and bronze paintings made an effort at creating warmth, but the white fluorescent lights turned them shallow and tawdry.

They took us into a room with a line of six hospital beds and assorted machinery, pale yellow curtains promising a facsimile of privacy for each bed. I suffered myself to be strapped down with an IV, the dark-haired woman in scrubs efficiently checking my vitals with a steady hand and a professional smile. "Dr. Lou," she called herself, and I didn't bother to argue for a full name. The people in uniforms got out of her way when she walked, though.

After my first trip to the bathroom, she unhooked me from the IV, and a man with a pair of silver bars on his collar sent me off to a small room in the middle of somewhere probably quite important. By coincidence or design, the same people who'd questioned me about my interlude with the Hunters were assigned to interview me again.

I wasn't going to put my money on coincidence.

But I did give them my story, the whole of it, even the things they already knew, because somewhere out there Rogers was setting up another drill zone under Lake Mendota. He was probably murdering people to satisfy his experiments, too. And I wasn't about to try taking him down on my own. Hadn't I already done enough?

Well before I was finished, my words became a mish-mash of syllables that sent my story sprawling over simple phrases. My lead interrogator, a harsh-looking man with a kind voice, called the others off as soon as I'd brought them more or less up to date. "That's enough for today, Kelly," he ordered with a pat to my hand. "We'll let you rest and pick up tomorrow where we left off." Offering me his arm like a gentleman, he took me back to the infirmary, and sat me down on a white cot beside Trax's.

I pretended not to notice when he locked the door as he took Dr. Lou out of the room for a discussion. If he was polite enough to pretend civility, I wasn't rude enough to end the charade. It made us all feel a little better, after all, and I had no intention of being uncooperative anyway.

She came back in and shooed Derik and me off Trax's cot, where we'd migrated, and then pulled out an assortment of machines. "I know you're all exhausted. We'll be hooking you up to monitor you for the evening. Just making sure there's no lasting effects, and no sudden surprises." While she set things up, we were chivied to a decontamination room for showers, thankfully private, and offered reasonably modest hospital gowns for sleep.

"I like the flap in the back," I commented, stepping out to let Trax get in.

The young private — excuse me, aide — who had escorted us nodded sagely. "If you're going to be stuck in a dress for a month or two recovering, might as well have something that preserves your dignity."

Derik pretended to pout, eyeing my rear pointedly. "I think I prefer the old design."

I 'accidentally' stomped on his foot as I walked past. Probably would have had more of an effect if I'd been wearing real shoes instead of disposable slippers. Whatever. It was the thought that counted.

Since our little infirmary didn't have any windows, I assumed it would be dark enough for a restful sleep. My hopes were dashed by the blinking, bleeping machines set up by three of the beds. A good dose of cold gel and small metal sensors later, Dr. Lou had us tucked into bed. "There's a call button here if you need something," she told us, and left us to sleep.

I gave her five minutes before beginning the havoc. Tossing off my blankets, I ripped off the sensors and stood up. To the orchestra of a hundred whining, wailing machines, I pulled the covers off Derik, slid in beside his befuddled expression, and tucked myself back in.

"Cold?" he asked, one of his arms already winding around me.

"Experimenting," I answered, and cuddled closer, enjoying the solid heat of his body.

The door burst open, Dr. Lou flying in. Her shoes *screeched* at her sudden halt. She glared at me, shot a look at the empty nest of wires back on my bed, and raised an eyebrow.

I raised one back. "They can't all be necessary," I said, and cushioned my head on Derik's chest.

The edges of her lips twitched. Going over the pile, she grabbed two and pulled them over, dragging behind her the rolling tower of computerized recording devices. She hooked these up to the nodes on my temples. "These are," she said to my grimace. "Don't take them off."

Flipping the kill-switch on the heart-rate monitor, she walked out, and left us to our sleep.

Derik's other hand brushed my hair out of my face. "Experiment over?" he asked, only a little reluctance in his voice.

"Experiment's over," I agreed, and laid my head on his shoulder to get comfortable. "Safe to say, they don't follow standard hospital operating procedure." He grinned, and looked so happy I had to lean over for a quick kiss. Only his hand somehow got into my hair and quick became not-so-quick—

"Hey-hey-hey!" Trax yelped. "I'm right here!"

Blushing, I broke away. "Sorry," I muttered, and settled against Derik. I could feel his hands combing through my hair, though, and heard the steady *sa-sa, sa-sa* of his heart, and it lured me into sleep.

#

"It looks like about half the Powered are unaccounted for," Dr. Lou said, placing a plate of eggs in front of me. "We're estimating about sixty percent of those have simply migrated, and will reappear when things get sorted out."

I poked at the from-a-powder scramble with my plastic fork. "That many are truly lost?" My gaze met Trax's. *Dad.*

He broke away to dunk a once-frozen biscuit into the catsup he'd asked for, ignoring my gag. "What about the unPowered?"

Plopping down at the fourth spot of the fold-away table, she propped her head on one hand. "Better. They didn't have the same option to move around, so we know that those who are missing are really missing. We're estimating around ninety percent returned."

We'd woken up without complications, and Dr. Lou had apparently gotten enough data from our sleeping brains to disconnect us for a 'real' meal. It had been Derik's idea to ask her about the fallout, and whatever the official regulations were, she'd decided to update us.

I'd wanted to ask about our parents. I hadn't yet.

I should. It was something Trax needed to know—no, something *I* needed to know.

Derik sipped the glass of water in his hand, not even looking at the heaping plate by his left hand. With a sideways glance at him, I stirred my eggs. When he showed no interest, I brushed his shoulder with two fingers. "It doesn't do you any good if you don't eat it."

Trying not to wince, I stuck a bite into my mouth and swallowed quickly. Trax nodded approval and showed solidarity by heaping a second serving onto his own plate.

Derik shuddered. But, after a moment, he stuck his own fork into his food and shoveled three bites down. I flattened my palm against the table beside him and managed to twist at least half my mouth into a smile. His spare hand settled over mine, and he kept eating.

Twirling my juice glass in my hand, I stared at the fluorescent orange liquid. If I could just bring myself to ask, I could get it over with quickly, I could find out. "Will they be able to sort everyone out? I mean, everything's in ruins, there's no fresh food and much of what's left has spoiled..."

Dr. Lou pushed the pile of salt packets toward Trax, who grabbed one and ripped it open. "The armed forces are stepping in and rounding everyone up," she said. "I won't pretend that it isn't chaos, but we've sent in most of our first-class music Powers to keep people calm, so there hasn't been much in the way of riots. The Internet is still down, of course, with the power being out almost everywhere, and working phones are far and few between, but I think things will be sorted out within a couple of months."

At the mention of *armed forces*, Derik's fingers tightened over mine, and his fork stopped long enough for him to start a question. "I don't suppose you've…"

I glanced at him, but his face was pointed down.

Funny to think a bunch of cowards like us managed such a crazy thing as collapsing the Tides.

"Military rolls are still coming in," she answered the question he hadn't fully asked. "We haven't located all of your family, given the migration of the restored Powered, but your mother has joined a unit in northern Mississippi, and your brothers are setting up emergency relief camps near Wilmington. We're looking for your sister and father, but getting everyone fed and sheltered comes first. I doubt we'll have even the armed forces pinned down in the next couple of weeks."

Trax tugged on the limp Mohawk dripping over one of his eyes. "And?"

Raising a hand, palm out, she shook her head. "We're barely managing military rosters. But I promise, there are people looking."

Derik said nothing, reaching for the protein shake Dr. Lou had set beside his plate. Popping the top, he chugged it in a manner suggesting a desperation to avoid any unnecessary tastebud contact. I took his hand back when he finished, and pretended his grip was gentle enough not to hurt. Somehow, I didn't think he was paying too much attention to his strength.

We got another checkup after lunch, and a promise of real food for dinner if we made our interrogators happy. From Dr. Lou, that probably meant take-out from the facility's main kitchen regardless of what we said, but it would be a welcome change from the breakroom-inspired menu.

When I finished up with my interviews, I was permitted to head back on my own. That my soft-spoken agent had declared me officially "harmless" probably had something to do with this, although I wouldn't be surprised if most of the reasoning came from the fact that all the doors leading to interesting places were locked with key-cards. There were plenty of doors that weren't locked, to be sure: a broom closet, a linen closet, a few unoccupied bedrooms with crisp white sheets on the rolling beds and bedpans tucked between the wheels. Hiding for a few hours wouldn't have been difficult, if I had wanted to do so. But I wasn't interested in causing trouble, nor even in trying to escape from the cold-walled desert building. Doors stayed put when I closed them.

It was funny, the things I never realized I had once taken for granted.

I was trailing my fingers along the wall, trying not to think about anything beyond the slippery-smooth white paint, when I walked into him. He caught me on the bounce, large hands steadying me by my upper arms. "Missed me that much?" Derik asked, one thumb stroking my skin.

My head hurt, my throat was sore from talking, and I hadn't heard any promises of home, freedom, or normality. I leaned forward and collapsed into him, letting his arms catch me fully and hold me close.

He smelled like hospital soap. Sharp, bitter, functional, and uncompromising—the least fitting cologne I could imagine for him. But under the sterile soap-scent I could make out his musky warmth, and it melted over my frayed nerves, shielding them from all the things I was trying so hard not to think.

Maybe hiding for a couple of hours wasn't such a bad idea, after all.

#

Dr. Lou's voice reached us through the door. "Yes, *both* of them are missing. Just wait until I call before bringing dinner up… Don't be silly; there's no need for a search." Sounded like she was on a phone. I wondered if it could dial out, and then decided that even if it could, the only people I really wanted to call probably wouldn't have service yet, or wouldn't be allowed near a phone if they did. "If you can't figure it out, Kip, then I can't help you. Like I said, I'll call when they show up."

Derik reached around me to push open the door. Dr. Lou turned around, took in my rumpled hair, and nodded once.

"Never mind. They're here; send it up." She smiled at us in an off-hand manner, and pointed toward the folding table.

Trax glared at Derik as we walked over. "Dude," he grunted, "that's my sister."

Moving past, I poked his shoulder. "Get over it," I advised, and ruffled his Mohawk before sitting down.

My brother rolled his eyes and sighed as loudly as he could. But instead of commenting, he just turned to Doctor Lou and asked in a casual tone, "Any news about the others? How's Elizabeth?"

Our good doctor, hand still on the phone she'd just hung up, gave him a tight smile. "Still human. No worse off than you lot, I hear. Ready for some real food?"

The cafeteria steak was edible, even if Derik did make faces at it. Dr. Lou made him eat three.

Chapter Twenty-nine

We spent two weeks in the government facility, completely inside the first and somewhat freed the second. The rock garden in the courtyard was sprinkled with cacti and hardy plants; our interviewers were gradually traded out for psychologists, and mine was happy enough to talk in the garden. "Rogers?" I asked at one point. Because, for some reason that day, I sort of wanted to know about the outside world.

"There's a warrant out for his arrest," he assured me.

"Warrant?"

He shrugged. "Went into hiding as soon as the Tides dropped. Made the international most-wanted list, though, and even the rest of the sweethearts on there probably wouldn't hesitate to turn him in. A true rogue has no allies."

It was as much as I could hope for, I supposed, and let it pass. But it brought something else to mind.

"What about the charges against Trax?"

He looked up into the sky, at a bird flying far overhead. "The warrants out for you and your brother have been dropped, as I don't think we can reasonably claim Derik has been murdered," he answered, a trace of a smile on his lips.

The bird was making long, curved loops over something in the desert. "And… the people on the rig… the Mad?"

He sat up. "I was wondering when you'd ask that. Long story short, Kelly, and I'm sure we'll need to talk more about this—but self-defense isn't a crime. And on a battlefield, a soldier isn't reprimanded for defending his fellows. Life isn't something taken lightly, but you did what you had to do."

The stone bench wasn't all that comfortable, even though soft cotton pajamas had long since replaced the hospital gown. Just one of the disadvantages of sitting outside. I drew my knees up to my chest and watched the bird fly in a too-blue sky.

#

One morning, as my therapist was grilling me about Trax's feelings toward our parents, another helicopter landed. A few minutes later, Valdez, Elizabeth, and Sandra stepped out into the dry heat of the rock garden.

"Kelly!" Sandra cried, and then I was smothered in long blonde hair and too-tight hugs. "Look at you—your face!" Her fingers gently prodded the scar my cheek, sympathy in her eyes.

I shrugged. "Not too bad, considering," I said with a half-smile. "And Derik calls it 'dashing.' His are worse, so he doesn't get to call it anything else."

She crooned a note of sympathy, and let me move on to grasp Elizabeth's arm. Valdez pounded me on the back, a hearty knock that wobbled my knees. Sandra's shriek told me that Derik and Trax had decided to come figure out the commotion.

I let him suffer for a few seconds. His fault for following me, after all.

But when I turned around, expecting a blue-faced Trax buried in blonde arms, I saw instead a motherly woman scolding my not-so-old twin for his recklessness. Long gel nails glinted emerald green in the sun as her hands slashed through the air; I was happy to note that she'd at some point managed to get them redone. And by Trax's smile, he was too.

I was an oblivious fool. This never had been a war of romance to him; at some point the fangirl had become a fan-mom, and I'd completely missed it. Where had I been?

Dr. Lou sidled up to me. I hadn't even noticed she'd come outside. "Kelly," she said, "you'll all be leaving in the morning. I've packed up a few bags for the lot of you, clothes and things, and I want you to keep taking the vitamins set out. Plus the journals. Fill those out."

"You're releasing us? So soon?"

A half-smile. "You'll be leaving in the morning," she advised again.

"But why?" Not that I was arguing, but it was quiet here.

She waved at Sandra. "Ask her," she said, and went back inside.

#

Sandra had been busy. When the Tides has receded and then disappeared, everybody had been brought back. In the chaos, Sandra had snuck the others out and gotten her hands on a computer. And like the true reporter she was—

"It was the exclusive of the century," she said from her seat on Trax's bed, knee-to-knee with Elizabeth. "Spread like wildfire and half the country had it before anyone thought about squashing it, and by that point there *wasn't* a point. They've started clamoring for their hero."

Hero meaning Trax, who at the moment sat beside me and kept pretending not to stare at Elizabeth. At some point, the rest of us had become sidekicks to the famous rock star who'd braved the Tides to rescue his family. Me? Oh, Sandra had made a to-do about my contribution, but for all her efforts, I was no rock star. I wasn't the one who would have disappeared into nothing by stepping into the Tides, wasn't the one who'd snuck past half a dozen Hunters to follow my sister into certain doom.

And bless her soul, but Sandra knew me well enough not to press the point.

So now people were looking for Trax. Where was he? Two weeks later, and rumors were flying, and Sandra had chased them down enough to discover that a sailor rescued from an oil rig had seen a too-pretty boy with a Mohawk and a girl with almost the same face, out in the middle of the Gulf where no strangers should have been.

I opened the hang-up bag Dr. Lou had packed for me. Pajamas, toiletries, high heels. A suit and pantyhose. I winced. "Really?" I asked.

Sandra pulled out the black pencil skirt and jacket. "Those will look great on you," she decided with a satisfied nod. "And the blue blouse is a nice contrast. Bring out your eyes."

It was a powder-blue, of course, because heaven forbid they allow bright colors in here. Trax's button-down in his bag was as black as my jacket, but his suit—because it was Trax—was a faded-jeans blue. *He* didn't have to wear heels, the bastard. *Or* pantyhose.

"Just wait until you see the vitamins," Elizabeth said, drawing her knees up to her chest. She'd been getting much the same treatment we had, but elsewhere; the Feds had spent more than a little time prying out her life as a Hunter. She'd not met my gaze when she'd said there was a lot to tell, and I didn't press.

I crammed the ridiculous skirt back on the hanger where it belonged, and plunged my hands into the zippered pockets of the bag for the pills I was supposed to shove down my throat. I came up with them, plus a journal and a box of cheap pens.

The pills either really were vitamins, or a pretty good imitation thereof. In a days-of-the-week container, they weren't labeled, but a sticker on the bottom of the plastic ordered me to take them with breakfast each day. Some of them were more appropriately sized for a horse. I made a face.

"What's with the diary?" Derik asked, pulling the journal from my hands.

"You've probably got your own," Elizabeth grumped. "We're supposed to fill it out—you know, mention any strange side effects, dizziness, murderous urges. The whole shebang."

He *huffed* a laugh. "Mmm. Murderous urges?"

I glared at the shoes some joker had stuffed into the bottom zipper of my bag. "Hang on. I'm feeling one come on now."

Trax snorted. Heartless cretin. Digging through his own bag, he pulled out a small leather sleeve. "We need passports?"

I glanced at the plain black leather in his hand, and looked again. "Huh. Why do you have one of those?" Poaching it from his hand, I flipped it open and frowned. It was a basic magic license — the sort that all Powered got — with a *certified* provision.

You didn't need a certification provision if you were below second class.

"Baxter Davidson, first-class music Power," I read aloud.

Derik snickered. "Baxter?"

Trax stared. "First-class music — ?" He snatched the certificate from my hands to look at it himself.

A throat clearing drew my attention to Elizabeth. "You killed a man with music," she said calmly. "That's a first-class level."

Derik's chuckling stopped, leaving the room in a blanket of silence. Rubbing the back of his neck, he paced over to his own stuff. "They said I'm a higher class now, too. Too much to expect, to get that deep in and not change at all. Sarge's made me do a few exercises, not that different from what I used to do, just more. Like working my way to a larger set of weights, without the work." He placed his hands on his cot and flexed his fingers, watching the mattress spring back. "You always have to be careful with weights, even small ones. But big ones, more so."

An imitation of a grin slid across Elizabeth's face. "Trade you playing with fire."

She and Derik shared a look, and the silent exchange spoke so much I wanted to cover my ears.

Then Trax *snapped* the leather closed, and tucked it back into his bag. "I guess, since I'm licensed, I'm going to have to start taking classes."

I patted his shoulder. "They're not as bad as you think," I lied to him. "You'll have it mastered in no time at all."

"Just shoot me now," he groaned. "That bad?"

"What?" I objected. "I just said — "

The wry expression on his face stopped me short. "You're my sister. I always know when you're lying to me."

I shrugged. "Eh. Tried."

We actually got real rooms for sleeping in that night. Nobody commented when I joined Derik in his, although someone had gone to the liberty of placing a spare set of sheets on the otherwise clear counter.

In the morning, Derik laughed to see me comparing the pajama pants to the skirt.

"No, you can't," he answered the question I hadn't asked: could I get away with meeting the public in PJs? "But there's a pair of pants for traveling in. They don't want us really dressing up before we get there."

I sighed in relief. I would take whatever reprieve I could get.

We flew in another helicopter to the old capital, D.C. I guess it was a statement, a sign that things would be returning to normal. It was the Vice President who shook our hands and introduced herself, though, so I suppose there was only so much 'normal' the government was willing to risk. "We'll be giving the speech on the Washington Mall," she said, "but not until the crowd has settled."

Then we were left to cool our heels in the historic White House, just like people had done before Tides. Funny to think that it was still the symbol of our government. I wondered if the President might one day move back in.

Valdez clasped my shoulder. I looked back at him, at the slightly annoyed expression on his face, and patted his hand. "Don't worry," I promised. "I'm sure they'll let you be useful again one day."

He snorted. "Somebody's gotta take the blame, girl. At least it's for stoppin' the Tides, and not startin' them. I hate being symbolic."

The aide who'd briefed us on what to say came back to split us into groups. Elizabeth got to wear her Recovery team uniform. Lucky. Sandra and I shrugged into suits, Sandra with considerably less sulking. I discovered my own magic certificate when I was pulling the pantyhose out of the bag.

"Um," I said.

"What?" Sandra asked, smoothing down her skirt. The expensive pen in her breast pocket, the strategically placed pocket at her hip with a convenient notepad—she was the picture of a reporter.

"It's wrong." I opened it to show her. *1st class rhythm Power, certified.* "What the heck is this?"

Elizabeth took it from me and held it up, squinting at it as if that would change the words. "Huh. Never heard of a rhythm Power."

"It's a new designation," the Vice President's voice came from the doorway. She tapped her wrist. "We've got twenty minutes. There's just enough time for makeup, and then we're on our way. Do you all know what's going on?"

Yes, we'd been through the drill, on the way over and twice since arriving. I let Sandra give the affirmative for me.

We arrived in sleek black cars, all of them indistinguishable from one another, and were ushered to a stage set at the base of the Washington Monument. To my surprise, the Mall was packed and overflowing. Sandra looked a little too smug. "Good press," she said with a smirk, "means good publicity."

We stood in a half-circle on the stage, let the Vice President drape award medals around our necks for exceptional service to the States, and tried not to look bored as Trax gave a speech. They'd shaved his fuzz and spiked his Mohawk to perfection, bleaching the roots and touching them up with blond dye. I thought his blue suit was just rocker-like enough to remind the audience who he was if the hair wasn't enough, but the speakers insisted on saying his name every thirty seconds or so until they finally got around to handing him the microphone.

Somewhere in the middle of his 'Thank you, doing my duty to my country, nothing I treasure more than my fans and my people' speech, a chant took over the back of the crowd. "*Sing, sing, sing,*" the people said.

We'd been ordered not to deviate. We weren't supposed to be taking questions. But the crowd was talking, and people in uniform were starting to pop up around the edges. So my brother made an announcement. "I'm sorry," he said, interrupting himself and facing that part of the crowd. "I would sing you the song that dropped the Tides, if I could. I would give you a new song, one that I've never recorded before—if I could. But going into the Tides is not without cost." He ducked his head, modest, grieved.

"I am retiring from concerts," he said, "for now, because exposure to raw magic on the level as I have endured has changed me. I am now a first-class music Power, and as such, will no longer be performing for live audiences except in service to the country."

Silence.

Pure silence.

And an explosion of noise.

After that, there was no quieting the crowds. Either you were born with Power, or you weren't—except for Trax. We were hustled out in two groups, Trax and me and Derik together, before the crowd could grow uncontrollable. Trax tried to grab for Elizabeth, too, but there were too many suits swarming between them, shuffling them in opposite directions.

The Vice President was laughing when we met her in the Green Room. "I told him you'd admit it," she said, and held up a cell phone. "The President sends his best wishes. And by that, I mean a few choice words."

Trax slumped into a sofa. "They're my fans," he said. "I had to tell them something."

She smiled wryly. "You were going to retire *quietly*, to spend time with your family."

He took my hand. "Like Kelly isn't getting dragged into this, too."

The Vice President sighed. "Of course, you're both employed by us now," she said. "But it would have been easier if we had kept it quiet."

"And Derik, too," I demanded.

A hand waved. "That's a given." There was a knowing smile on her face as she met his eye; a grimace in his. I wondered exactly what level was on *his* new license. "You all will be having a well-deserved vacation for a couple of months before your official government training. I told them you needed that, so you'll get plenty of time to spend together. There's a nice estate in Southern California you'll enjoy. I've been there. Gorgeous view, great area. Little rough on the décor, but it grows on you, and in the meantime you can take a few surfing lessons, go scuba diving, the works."

A hand on my lower back announced Derik's presence there. "So we're not getting pressed into immediate servitude?" There was a smile in his voice, lightening the implications into a joke.

"Believe it or not," she said, "we're on the same side here." A wistful expression crossed her face. "I'm from Florida, you know. Now that it's back... they found my sister. I'll get to see her again."

Trax and I exchanged a look. There was so much confusion down there right now —

There was a rap on the door.

She stood up and went to the window. "Mine isn't the only family they found," she said. Trax was the first to join her.

"Mom! Dad!" he shouted, face against the window, and Derik and I ran to join him.

Mom's dark hair was half-pulled free from a rough ponytail, her blouse wrinkled, the green of her eyes hidden by sunglasses as she stepped out of the sleek black car. Dad had more lines than I remembered around the edges of his blue eyes, his shoulders more bowed than I remembered. But they were alive, and here, and whole.

Elizabeth held the hands of an elderly woman by a second car, Valdez and Sandra and a couple of suits watching. From a third car behind them, another three people emerged, a middle-aged couple and a young woman, golden-haired and tall, all in fatigues.

Derik's gaze met mine, his hands splayed on the glass and trembling. "My parents and sister."

I rubbed an escaping tear from his cheek and smiled. "Can't wait to introduce you to my folks."

"Yeah." All the words he might have said, that were hiding in his eyes, and that was all that made it out.

Trax tugged on my hair until I met his eyes. "I guess it's official. He's one of us now."

"Yeah, well, remember that when he's helping you learn to use your magic." I poked my brother's shin with a toe and misquoted my old textbook. "Family's as much body as mind, but as much mind as body. You're born with it, but it grows with you, and changes as you do."

Trax made a face. "What the heck are you talking about?"

Rolling my eyes, I yanked him by his sleeve close enough to wrap an arm around his shoulders. "Welcome to magic," I said over his protest. "You're about to learn a whole bunch of rules, but remember, they're useless. We already broke them all."

####

About the Author

Rebekkah Niles is a North Carolina author. Always a lover of books, she's particularly drawn to fantasy, and couldn't help but fall into writing a fantasy world of her own. When she's not reading or writing, she can be found blogging, playing Dungeons and Dragons, chasing her cats around, being chased around by her roommate's foster pets, or studying the publishing industry. Ever since she began watching the now-mercurial world of publishing, she's been fascinated by the industry. Each day is an adventure, and that's just what she loves best!

If you'd like to learn more about the world in which *Into the Tides* is set, and discover web-exclusive extras such as maps, author commentary, and short stories related to the world, you can visit her author website at rebekkahniles.net.

Want to tell the world you're Powered, or think your pet might secretly be a Lost? Check out Tides-related artwork and merchandise at her CafePress site, and take home a little piece of the Tides for yourself!

The e-version of this book may be found at Amazon.com, Barnes and Noble, Smashwords, iTunes, Kobo, and many other retailers.

www.ingramcontent.com/pod-product-compliance
Lightning Source LLC
Chambersburg PA
CBHW060311260626
47160CB00007B/2564